SKENDLEBY
A CHRISTMAS HAUNTING

BY NICK BROWN

Published by New Generation Publishing in 2013

Copyright © Nick Brown 2013

First Edition

The author asserts the moral right under the Copyright, Designs and Patents Act 1988 to be identified as the author of this work.

All Rights reserved. No part of this publication may be reproduced, stored in a retrieval system or transmitted, in any form or by any means without the prior consent of the author, nor be otherwise circulated in any form of binding or cover other than that which it is published and without a similar condition being imposed on the subsequent purchaser.
This book is a work of fiction. Any resemblance to actual living persons is entirely coincidental

ISBN: 978-1-910053-20-1

www.newgeneration-publishing.com

New Generation **Publishing**

"The distinction between past, present and future is only a stubbornly held illusion."

Albert Einstein

About the author

Nick Brown is a writer, archaeologist and ancient historian He is also the author of The Luck Bringer series, the first of which "Luck Bringer" was published in 2013.

For Jill
With love and thanks

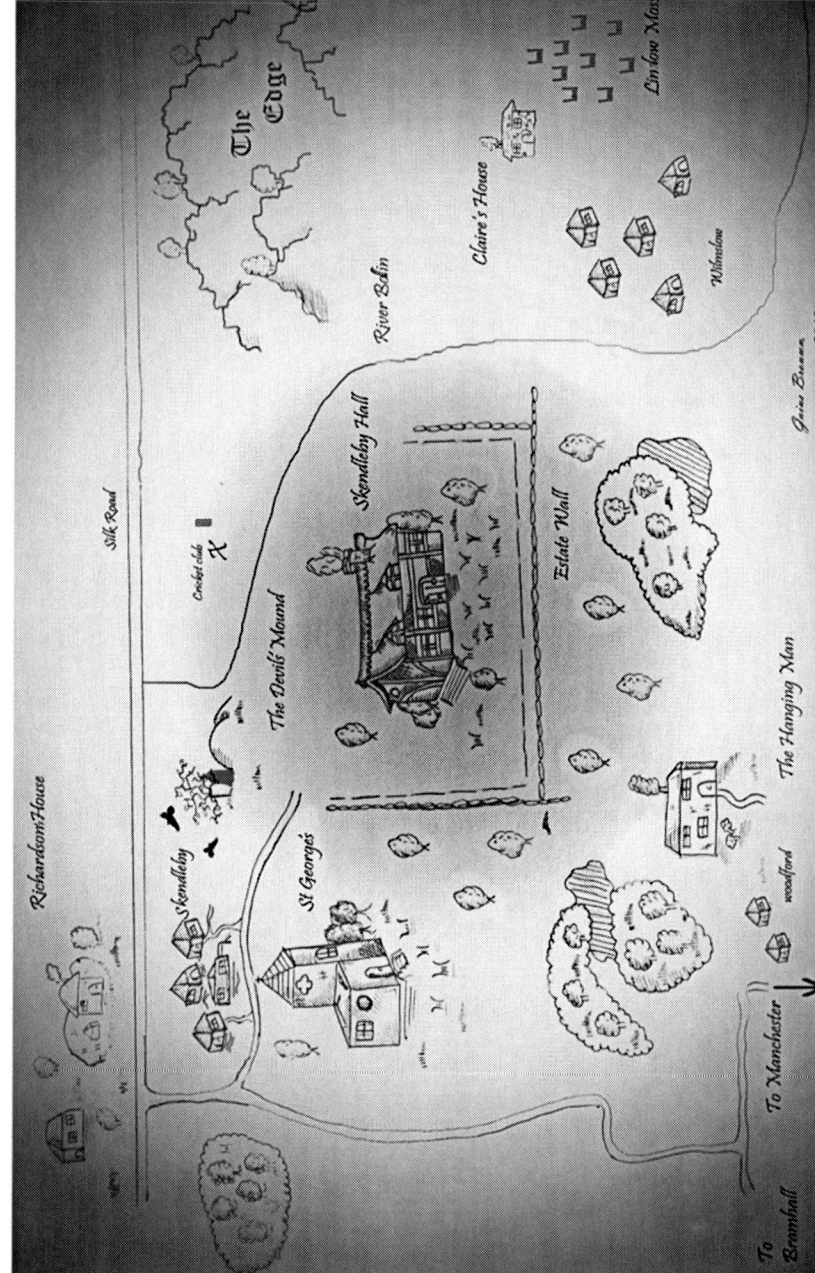

The Cheshire Plain 2500BC

She regained consciousness: they were dragging her towards the burial chamber, her legs and arms leaking blood from the cutting. In front of the tomb Beautiful Hunter was tied and crouched over a small pit, his shin bones had been broken and he was whimpering. For a moment the part of her mind still her own felt pity. He had been her bed partner at the celebration of her first show of blood and this had pleased her, now he was being sacrificed. In death he'd guard her tomb so she could never escape.

The people of her tribe huddled under the bare trees watching from a distance. The nearest they dare come to this cursed place. The shaman had to threaten them with eternal darkness beyond the stars to force them to make the long journey. Now they wanted to go home and begin the rites of purification.

The effect of the drugged drink the shaman tricked her into taking was beginning to wear off and the demonic entity inside her mind was waking. It was agitated; it knew this place and feared it. She tried to think back to the time when this parasite had entered her: she thought it must have been when the blonde strangers visited her village for the midsummer sacrifice. Their wise woman had spoken to her and taught her magic: magic that made the women of her own tribe jealous. Perhaps she had put this thing in her.

But there was no more time: they'd reached the dark entrance. She felt fear in the men who carried her. For a moment they hesitated but the shaman cursed them and they moved on.

Inside the mound it was cramped and cold; the thing inside her screamed words of hate and fear. Words that her own lips formed but she couldn't understand. She looked back at the entrance and saw they'd killed Beautiful Hunter and were burying him in the pit.

Then there was nothing but pain as the shaman began the ancient ritual, cutting the special bones from her arms and legs. They did this so the demon, now trapped in her body forever, couldn't pursue them in the afterlife. Finally when the cutting was over they laid her, barely conscious, on the icy stone floor and placed the terrible stones over her. She felt her ribs cracking under the weight.

But there was worse: the shaman had carved the watcher's eyes into the stone. The all seeing eyes that would confine her in this dark tomb, hidden in this desolate place for eternity. Then they began sealing the tomb behind them. The eyes tormented the thing inside her and it began a strange chanted curse in its terrible language. Her lips made sounds she couldn't recognise but she knew it was angry and wanted vengeance.

She watched as a hand beyond the entrance pushed the final stone into place killing the light and locking in the dark. In the darkness she screamed and the thing inside screamed with her.

Lindow Moss: The Present Day

Her own scream shattered the silence: Claire Vanarvi jerked awake with a heart jolting start in the darkness of the tomb. She forced open her eyes and to her relief found she was out of bed and standing by the window, drenched in sweat but shivering: the central heating had long since gone off and the room was cold. She stood taking deep gulps of air as she tried to re-orientate herself. Eventually things came into focus and she recognised the familiar features of her bedroom. Feeling her way back to bed she turned on the bedside light and looked at the alarm clock; it was just past four in the morning. She sat on the bed trying to breathe deeply and evenly but however hard she tried her heart wouldn't stop pounding.

So it was back after ten years' remission: night sensations of the restless dead. This time was different. There was something familiar about the dream; not the ancient ritual and living burial; but the place. She recognised the place. This made it personal like a warning aimed at her. She re-crossed the room to the window, pulled back the curtain and looked out. It was still and dark and beyond the orange glow of the streetlamp the shapes of the trees that fringed the Moss cast moving shadows even though there was no breeze.

She went back to bed but sleep was no longer possible and anyway she daren't drift back into the nightmare waiting in the darkness of the tomb. The dream had been too clear, too detailed and the woman frighteningly familiar. She didn't want to even think about it so got out of bed and padded in bare feet to the bathroom, the soft pile of the carpet feeling strangely comforting. In the bathroom mirror she caught sight of her pale face framed by long dark hair. Her eyes looked startled as they stared back at her. This took her back to the dream; she didn't want to look through dead people's eyes again.

Downstairs she sat at the kitchen table drinking tea and trying not to think. Gradually she recovered her nerve sufficiently to understand it wasn't a dream, it was real; a fragment of experience so intense that it never faded but lingered on over the centuries corrupting and disturbed; a psychic impression still reverberating and her unconscious was its wavelength.

By the time she'd poured the last dregs from the teapot into her 'Occupy the City' mug, the element that troubled her most had begun to make some sense: the place. It was the archaeological dig she drove past every week, in the grounds of Skendleby Hall. It had received some coverage in the local paper and caused protest from the parishioners of the local church.

What could have been so powerful to break through the defences she'd built up over ten years living a normal life? Or, and it was this that froze her blood as she sat amongst the domestic debris of her kitchen, what was it that was coming for her?

She sat on at the table but the violence and horror of the dream wouldn't recede. It stayed with her because while she'd dreamt she'd felt the girl's terror; in fact during the dream she was the girl. Now she was calm enough to think, she knew something was summoning her, the dream found her for a purpose, and there would be a reckoning.

By nine thirty she was emotionally drained but as the morning was in full swing and the sounds from the streets were drifting into the house she felt safe enough to return to bed. When she awoke she'd decide what to do.

CHAPTER 1
THE TRENCH: NOVEMBER

Giles was grinning madly, angular face upturned towards the sun, squinting at Steve and Rose standing on Devil's Mound. His dishevelled lanky frame animated as he raked nail bitten fingers through his hair in excitement.

"You're sure? It's definitely man made and older than the village? Then it must be some weird type of burial mound, maybe a Cist inhumation. Jeez that's brilliant; there aren't meant to be any round here; we've got something of interest at last."

He'd driven to the Skendleby site to close down this boring, money eating dig. But Rose suggested that as the strangely brilliant weather continued, there was time to carry out a brief exploration of Devil's Mound, which lay at the eastern boundary of the village. This had always been considered a natural geological feature formed as the ice sheets receded 10,000 years ago. But her exploratory trench and geophysical survey indicated that the mound might conceal a small stone built chamber. This was the first find of any real interest the excavation had revealed.

She'd been nagging at Giles and his deputy Steve for weeks to give her a chance to at least dig a trial trench. Behind her back they'd laughed at what they thought was her unhealthy obsession, but as always she persisted, wheedling first one then the other. She knew all the fault lines in their long relationship; all the jealousies and insecurities; and as she constantly assured both of them of her loyalty and friendship in the end she got her way.

But it was climate change that made it possible. Summer that year had started on time and then it seemed the calendar had stuck on August. So Rose was in luck, as without the extraordinary weather of that late summer, the dig would have long since ended and the mound bulldozed to make way for the pipeline that British Water were going to cut across this stretch of the countryside. There were rumours of a bid for planning permission for some shady commercial development in this part of the green belt.

The county Archaeological Unit, directed by Giles, and based at the university, had secured enough funding to conduct a rescue dig to investigate the suspected presence of an Iron Age village at a location that the pipeline would cut right through and obliterate. The site lay in a large field between the boundary wall of the Skendleby estate and a curve of the River Bollin, between the villages of Skendleby and Woodford on a patch of ground that, due to local superstition, had not been occupied since records began.

This was strange as it lay in a belt of rich farmland where any available plots were snapped up by developers for select executive enclaves, several of which scarred the countryside interspersed with footballer's electric gated mansions. To the south west lay the Edge: a ridge of wooded sandstone cliffs riddled with ancient Bronze Age and nineteenth century copper mines. Air photographs taken during the previous dry summer revealed crop marks suggesting the remains of a small prehistoric village lay beneath the surface of the field. The county Unit had one summer to excavate the feature before the construction work started the following spring.

The weather had been peculiar, even in a time of global warming, providing perfect conditions as the hot dry weather of July, August and September drifted into a late autumn Indian summer. Then into the warmest November on record, described on MSN as 'the end of the seasons as we know them'. The skies a deep cerulean blue as one glorious day followed the next. So the dig could continue beyond its anticipated span and the team complete a detailed examination of the early, if unremarkable, Iron Age village of Skendleby. From the excavated evidence their village appeared to have been suddenly abandoned during the fifth century BC, over four hundred years before the Roman invasion of Britain.

It was the freak weather that gave Rose the opportunity to investigate the mound with which she had become increasingly fascinated since the dig had commenced. At first she hardly noticed it but as summer wore on she came to think of it as her own; some nights it was there in her dreams and gradually it came to obsess her.

By August she'd made a habit of sitting alone on it to eat her lunch each day and one day as she was peeling an apple the certainty of what it was hit her; it must be a type of barrow burial from a much earlier period. A feature that only she had been talented enough to recognise and which she'd conceal as the credit for this discovery should be hers.

She wasn't going to make the mistake of sharing it like she'd shared the best years of her life with that weak pitiful man. So slyly and carefully she'd been badgering Giles to let her conduct the digging of a trial trench to confirm her suspicions. Giles had consistently refused on the grounds that the size of the village and resources available meant there was insufficient time to finish their excavation of the village. She dismissed this; somehow she knew that the good weather would continue as long as she needed because the mound wanted her to find it and would wait for her.

Eventually she got her way with the trench and began nagging Steve about a full scale excavation. She confided that she knew that he, as the better and more published excavator, must be as frustrated with Giles's pedestrian supervision of the dig as she was. She told him that as he was intuitive and brilliant he could understand her need to excavate the mound. She reminded him that if there had been any justice in the world he, not Giles, would be Director of the Unit with full time tenure rather than working short term contracts. Rose said Steve could easily persuade Giles to let her have a go at the mound, and if it was a significant feature it might help him advance his chances of a contract extension. She would make sure he was credited with the results. She favoured him with her most sympathetic smile as she said this.

Rose prided herself on the sympathy she extended to all the diggers, from the trainee undergraduates through to Giles, whom she often reassured by saying that she, unlike the others, appreciated the burdens that came with responsibility. She told him that she often defended him behind his back against the others. She never had an unkind word for anyone on site, rather she encouraged them to confide in her their problems and secrets and as she always said,

"I'm like your older sister, love, there's nothing that won't feel better after a good old bit of goss with Rose."

But Steve had been no more willing to indulge her than Giles, he was bored with the site and wanted to be off, which confirmed Rose in her judgment of him as a feckless and selfish waster.

But eventually her efforts paid off: she was working on the mound end of the trench on what was to have been her last day when Steve suddenly loomed above her brushing his long black hair back over his forehead with a grimy hand.

"Me and Gi have decided to give you a bit of help so I'm going to put Jan and Leonie on this with you, Rose, the students can tidy up the odds and ends on the village. The forecast's good for a bit longer so you've got a few more days to finish. If the mound's a natural feature you'll have at least provided some more data on the village boundary."

Jan and Leonie slouched across to join her; they were experienced professional archaeologists who, along with Steve and Rose, provided the core of the excavation team.

"Here you go, Rose, this can be like a girls' outing, anything to get away from investigating the village middens."

They joined Rose in the trench; despite it being November, like most of the archaeologists, all wore shorts and T shirts. The three of them squatted in the shade of the trench. Jan and Rose lit up.

"Are you on or off with Steve at the moment, Leonie, because if it's on we'll have to alter the way we refer to him."

Rose exhaled smoke and winked at Jan.

"It's hard to tell with Steve if you're on or off with him, it depends on who else is on or off with him at the same time, but I think that there's a strong probability that I'm at the point where on becomes off so call him what you like."

Rose produced her special sympathetic smile and placed a supportive hand on Leonie's shoulder.

"Oh, I'm so sorry, love, and you seemed so happy; but that's Steve all over isn't it?"

"Doesn't matter, I saw it coming, but you'd better watch what you say in front of Jan, she's got a higher opinion of him than I have, probably because she sees less of him."

"Oh, bless, but she'd like to see more given the chance, isn't that right Jan, love?" Rose replied, smiling to herself as she got to her feet having finished her smoke.

"OK back to work, girls."

For the next few days the sun continued to shine and the trench progressed during bright but shortening daylight and Rose's certainty that her mound contained something exceptional grew until she was able to confirm what she had suspected and called Steve over from the main dig.

"Steve, Steve, I think we've found it, come and see."

Steve hurried across to the trench where the three women were crouching at the far end nearest to the mound. They were covered in dirt and sweat but clearly exhilarated.

"There, at the village end of the trench, we've got the remains of some type of wall obviously built by the villagers, probably just before it was abandoned. But then look just halfway along, see that patch of darker earth that crosses the trench, it's the remains of a much earlier ditch. We don't think it's connected with the village at all; we think it's to do with the mound. But here's what's really interesting. Inside the mound there are traces of a crude stone wall. If I am right, and I know I am, then the mound is covering a small stone structure that's much older than the village. We need to investigate further to see if there's an entrance. You'd better get Giles to come down now because we're going to unearth the biggest find round here since the body in the peat bog at Lindow."

She watched as Steve rang the Archaeology Unit's headquarters at the university. Within the hour in the fading light Giles arrived at the site.

With a sparse social life and money problems from a messy and bitter divorce Giles was, for a change, in high spirits and, unusually, offered to buy drinks at the local pub. So at 6pm the early doors regulars at the Hanging Man were surprised to be joined by a group of about thirty scruffy and noisy archaeologists.

After the Unit's minibus had driven the students and volunteers back to the city Rose stayed on with Giles and Steve to plan the new phase of the dig. Lingering over a final drink at a dimly lit table in the corner by the fire she stretched her legs towards the hearth and sat back watching the flames' reflection in her glass.

"Just think, boys, if this is a Neolithic burial it will be the biggest prehistoric find in this region since Lindow Man, then you'll really have something to show your media friends."

Giles nodded but seemed pensive.

"Yeah, Jim Gibson from the *Journal* is bringing a photographer on site tomorrow but he thinks we may have problems."

"Such as?"

Rose asked suddenly anxious.

"According to Jim the guy who's bought Skendleby Manor has plans for it."

"What plans?" She snapped back, becoming angry: no one was going to stop her mound from getting the recognition it deserved.

"Rumour is he's plans to develop it as housing with a multipurpose leisure complex and one of the big supermarkets as anchor tenant."

Steve, who had just returned from the bar with a rum chaser for himself, snorted in disbelief.

"No chance with the planning laws round here, Gi; a petty bureaucrat like you should know that better than anyone."

Normally Rose would have loved this dig at Giles to lead to a heated argument but now she wanted reassuring about the dig so looked at Giles with her most admiring gaze and asked,

"But surely with all your expertise in planning matters, Giles, nothing could come of it."

"Yeah, normally, but, according to Jim, who gets most things right, this guy Carver in the hall is a nasty piece of work and used to getting his own way. He made his money on short selling and generally screwing up other people. He has contacts and he's put together the usual seductive proposal, you know how it goes, promises loads of local benefits and jobs; total con of course, he just wants the money, but they got away with something similar on the bypass remember."

"But even so he could never get it through any planning committee: this is designated land."

"If he had the bent councillor who chairs the committee in his pocket he might. Our finding a monument of national interest on there is the last thing he needs. Remember the trouble we had getting access in the first place?"

They were interrupted by the barmaid, a formidable lady who ruled the pub with a rod of iron. She stared at Giles and said with some asperity,

"I don't normally interrupt but I couldn't help overhearing; nothing will ever be built on that land, nothing that will come to any good anyhow, and if it was built there's no one from round here who'd be daft enough to go to it. It's surprised us you've not had any problems over there. They're running a book behind the bar on what's going to happen to you first. Still plenty of time for that: not that it's any of my business."

She cleared the glasses from the table and moved off without waiting for a reply. Steve threw back his head and laughed.

"Well, you've made a good impression on her, Gi."

But Rose didn't feel like laughing when Giles continued,

"Listen; better not mention what I just said because the photographer Jim's bringing tomorrow is the bent councillor's daughter."

They finished their drinks and got up to leave, as they passed the bar heading towards the door Rose overheard a snatch of conversation.

"And when I went downstairs the back doors was wide open and both the dogs was dead. I hadn't heard anything; it scared the life out of us and now the wife won't be left in the house alone."

Outside it was dark and turning chilly, a gibbous moon was rising over the woods on the estate behind the dig.

"Strange isn't it," Steve said as they walked across the car park, "the locals reckon that the site is a place to be avoided. Legend says it brings bad luck yet we've had this incredible weather and now we might have uncovered something mega. If that's bad luck, bring it on!"

Rose, walking just behind the two men, suddenly experienced an intuition of what might be in her mound. She hurried to catch them up trying to put the thought out of her mind.

***

Next day the excavation of Devil's Mound started promisingly under Rose's direction. The perimeter of the stone structure was quickly established. The weather that week was even more perfect. The early morning mist quickly burnt off as the sun rose in a deep blue sky. The stubble in the field still a parched faded yellow contrasting with the leaves of the trees of the estate boundary turning to copper and gold as the year grew old. The days were warm but not hot, the sunsets deep red and the nights crisp with the promise of frost. The team worked quickly and in harmony, relishing this rare extension of the heat of late summer, keen to finish the dig but reluctant somehow that it should all end and they go their separate ways. For the core team of archaeologists, Giles, Steve and the three women, the beginning of this final phase of the excavation was enhanced by the rare potential of the mound.

Rose and Leonie were marking out the estimated entrance to the chamber when Jan pointed to Giles striding towards them leading a heavily built man with greying hair, wearing a smart suit, totally out of place on the site. Behind him was a nondescript, young woman with dirty blond scraped back hair. She was festooned with camera bags and wearing a camouflage anorak and beige combat pants.

"Rose, this is my mate Jim Gibson, the editor of the *Journal*, and his photographer, Lisa."

Rose looked carefully at Lisa, who avoided her gaze and didn't reply to her greeting. There was something sullen and closed off about the photographer, something impossible to engage with, it was like talking to someone who wasn't really there. But Rose noted that the girl was strangely attracted to the mound. She climbed onto it and after taking a few shots was running her hands over its grassy surface and gazing at it with a strange, sly smile when she thought no one was looking.

Rose didn't want her on the mound touching it like that and was about to tell her she shouldn't be climbing on part of an excavation. But she didn't need to, Lisa scrambled down smiling to herself. Then, as she walked past Rose she turned and looked her in the eyes with an expression Rose couldn't interpret and whispered just loud enough for her to hear,

"Feeling jealous? You should be."

Lisa walked off following Giles and Jim. Rose watched them go; she was feeling jealous but she was also trying to work out why she found the presence of the girl so threatening: she was shaken out of this by Leonie calling out from the trench.

"Look over there: months of no interest at all and we've suddenly become the centre of attention."

"If you think that two visitors making a prearranged visit makes you the centre of attention you're easily satisfied love," Rose sneered, trying to recover self confidence.

"Doesn't say much for Steve, eh Jan?"

As she and Jan were laughing at this Leonie said more urgently,

"Not just them, whoever it is over in the woods near the estate wall. He's been watching us ever since we started working on this mound. He turned up the day we started the trench. I'd never seen anyone over there before. He's started to creep me out."

Rose snapped back,

"No one's going to be in there, its estate land, owned by some spiv who fiddled a fortune in the city. You can bet he's no interest in us or lets anyone onto his land."

However, she and Jan turned to look at the dense clump of trees over by the shoulder high stone wall that girdled the estate, but before they were able to see anyone, they were disturbed by Giles.

"You've got until next Thursday evening to finish this exploration and come up with something good. I'm meeting Jim next Friday to report on our progress and I've told him we're onto something newsworthy. We've got extension funding for two maybe three more weeks then that's it. He's coming back the week after next to take some more footage and the *Journal*'s going to devote four pages to us, so try and make it good."

With that he was off back to his car and the Unit's offices at the university.

That afternoon Steve worked with them on the mound. Although a much better and more experienced archaeologist than Giles he hated the business of sponsorship funding and administration. In fact he hated responsibility of any kind but he and Giles had been students together and whenever Steve returned from his excavations abroad Giles always found him work. He was an excellent excavator but his passion was for the archaeology of the Early Neolithic and to him a dig like this was a way of making a living until something more exciting came along, or his private life made it necessary to move on rapidly. Devil's Mound, however, was beginning to intrigue him and he was almost as determined as Rose to open it. He and Jan were fine towelling round a feature they suspected might be some type of pit connected with the mound when a student from the site shouted him over. Getting to his feet and dusting himself off irritably he noticed a florid shiny faced man with longish hair, spectacles and a clerical collar striding towards him hand outstretched.

"Excuse me for disturbing you, Dr Watkins, but your colleague informed me that as the director of this site it's you to whom I need to talk. I'm the Reverend Edmund Joyce, call me Ed. I'm the priest of the parish; in fact I'm the priest of the parishes on either side of your excavation. Some of my parishioners thought it might be a good idea, not to mention neighbourly, if I were to conduct a little service of blessing for your site and I was wondering if tomorrow would do."

"Why, have we been cursed?"

"No, not at all. Ah, I see you're being humorous. No, it is a little unusual, but since you have been digging here some of the older, and I might say more set in their ways, parishioners have become quite anxious that I offer a blessing."

"Why?"

"Well, you're probably aware of the local superstition concerning this spot, not that I attach any credibility to such foolishness of course, but I did feel compelled."

He paused nervously.

"That is, rather I agreed to make the offer."

"Wel,l that's really kind of them but we don't really have the time, the dig finishes in two weeks. Anyway, we've been here all summer, why wait so long to be neighbourly?"

"Yes, quite so, however, it's only been this last week you've turned your attention to what the elderly members of the congregation refer to as Devil's Mound. Yes, I am afraid that we haven't quite modernised sufficiently to have got across to many believers that the devil is merely a metaphor for social injustice."

"Well, we agree about superstitious mumbo jumbo at least."

Steve noticed the look of hurt or rejection flicker across the vicar's face and modified his tone but couldn't disguise the mockery.

"Thanks for the kind offer, Vicar. Please tell your congregation that we appreciate it, but it will interrupt the work. However, if any of my digging community feel the need of a personal blessing or exorcism I'll contact you."

The Reverend Joyce knew that beneath the thin veneer of politeness he was being mocked; he felt the familiar flush of humiliation begin to colour his face so said goodbye and turned to go. He felt angry and hurt by the dismissive treatment but also relieved not to have to conduct the blessing. Well, relieved and ashamed, his lack of moral courage confirmed; still he had done as he had promised.

Steve watched him go, gingerly picking his way across the trenches and piles of rubble. He noticed that despite his long hair the Reverend Ed was balding at the crown and wearing supermarket jeans. He returned to Rose, laughing at the experience, and spent ten minutes working up the exchange into a comedy routine. Rose and Leonie laughed with him but Jan told him it had been a kind offer and even if it was, as Steve had said, pompous mumbo jumbo, there had been no need to be rude and hurtful.

The heavy sun was beginning to sink red below the Edge to the west; it was time to pack up. They cleared up the excavated area round the mound and piled the tools into the wheelbarrow while the shadows gathered and lengthened.

"Come on, time to get cleaned up, and then off to the pub."

Leonie picked up her coat and prepared to follow Rose, who was pushing the wheelbarrow back towards the site hut. She stood for a moment watching the last of the sunlight turning the woods by the estate boundary a golden brown. Then she saw movement and something seemed to jerk out of the tree line, something that she was sure wanted to be seen. She shouted to Rose,

"Look, Rose, look, he's there again in the woods, like a spidery black figure: see there, a white face between the trees."

There was no reply; Rose was out of earshot halfway to the huts. Leonie decided it was best to catch up with her.

***

Woken by her own scream Claire Vanarvi sat up in bed fumbling for the light switch. The dream again, she looked at the clock – early morning, always the same. This time no sacrifice, just the mound covering the burial. But it wasn't the grass covered surface of the mound that concerned her; something inside it was awake and shifting around looking for something it could invade and corrupt.

CHAPTER 2
THE RECTORY

The Reverend Edmund Joyce returned to the Rectory feeling pathetic and empty as usual. He was relieved not to have had to perform the blessing, which he regarded as a superstitious hang-over from less enlightened times, but humiliated that he'd been ridiculed by the facetious archaeologist. He walked morosely through the crumbling graveyard of the ancient church towards the huge but sparsely furnished Rectory. This massive Georgian edifice, always empty and cold, seemed to cry out for the children he'd never been able to father.

He hated it here. He wanted an urban parish, a modern house and a young, diverse and cosmopolitan congregation; instead he was stuck in a rural hamlet with an aging flock whose mindset hadn't changed since the Middle Ages. These attitudes were best exemplified by Sir Nigel Davenport, who chaired the parish council and over-ruled any modernisation that Ed proposed.

The Davenports had been the leading family in the village since the fourteenth century. Although they no longer inhabited the Hall, too expensive to maintain and recently sold to a money man in the City, their influence hadn't diminished. Davenport, usually the most balanced of men, had become quite agitated about the archaeologists interfering with the mound in the field and both he and the parish council had insisted that Ed offer the blessing. This in fact was the only thing they'd insisted on since he'd assumed his incumbency and, for that matter, the nearest the committee had come to discussing matters of a spiritual nature.

But they approved of the inexplicable mistake he had made in last Sunday's service when, instead of reading Matt. 18:12-14, the parable of the lost sheep, he'd read Matt.12:43-5, the parable of the demon returning to his former home. This had forced him to abandon his prepared sermon and to extemporise on a theme of care for the mentally ill with the demon as a metaphor for cuts in public spending. But of course the congregation knew that this was not what the parable intended to say and so, in his heart of hearts, did he. The mistake perturbed him; it was not a parable he ever used or was comfortable with, demons, exorcism and all that other medieval stuff had no place in the modern church; so why had he read it?

He was still trying to puzzle this out as he opened the front door and entered the large and gloomy stone flagged hall. The small threadbare tapestry rug in the centre of the floor emphasised the vast area of uncovered stone as he walked across it into his study. He had a deadline for the parish newsletter to meet and Sunday's sermon to complete.

Apart from when he was asleep or in the church, the study was where he spent most of his time. Here he'd made the strongest efforts to modernise the house. He'd had the large draughty open fireplace covered over and replaced with a flame effect gas fire, installed bright spot lighting and covered the walls with posters and prints from his university days. The effects, he had to admit to himself, had not been quite what he'd hoped for and, in fact, the makeover lent the room a dispiriting ambience. At his desk he turned his attention to neither the newsletter nor the sermon, but to the project that he felt kept him sane in this parish, his editing, for publication, of the letters and notebooks of the Reverend Montague Heatly Smythe.

Heatly Smythe had been the priest of this parish in the 1770s until his mysterious departure in 1776 and subsequent disappearance from the written record. During his incumbency of Skendleby Heatly Smythe maintained a correspondence with Gilbert White, the vicar of Farringdon on the borders of Hampshire and Sussex, whose letters and notes were published and celebrated as the *Natural History and Antiquities of Selborne*. Heatly Smythe had been a fellow student and friend of White's at Oriel College, Oxford, where a collection of his writings between 1772 and 1776 had been lodged on the death of his last surviving relative at the beginning of the nineteenth century.

As an antidote to boredom and frustration during his early days in Skendleby, Ed had researched the history of his predecessor. The fact that he was himself an Oriel man seemed fortuitous as it gave him access to the Heatly Smythe collection. From the manuscripts it seemed that Heatly Smythe was no more enamoured of the parish than he was, and his letters, rather than possessing the freshness and directness of White's, conveyed an accusatory and self pitying tone. It seemed the parish had tried to exclude Heatly Smythe the way it seemed to exclude him; his request to be called Ed had been ignored and he was beginning to suspect that they called him Vicar at every opportunity deliberately to annoy him.

However, Ed was nothing if not persevering and had decided to add his own modern perspective to Heatly Smythe and produce a volume that recorded the changes in the parish environment over two centuries. One of Heatly Smythe's most irritating literary habits was to load his narrative with long classical quotes and by six thirty Ed was getting particularly fed up with translating a passage from Virgil's Eclogues where 'Willow blossom was being rifled by Hyblaean Bees', when his wife Mary entered the room.

"Ed, dear, you haven't forgotten that Councillor Richardson and his daughter are coming to see you this evening; I'm going out so you'll have to listen for the doorbell. Oh, and I forgot to tell you; when I was clearing junk out of the cellar I found a packet of old documents wrapped up in some horrible stained greaseproof paper. I've put them to one side in a box for you. Don't wait up I'll be late."

"Ok Mary, I'm just finishing now, I'll listen out."

Pleased to be able to take a break from Heatly Smythe, Virgil and Hyblaean Bees, Ed closed up his manuscript and made his way to the kitchen to put on the kettle and set a tray for his visitors. Councillor Richardson, a highly successful business man who chaired the local planning committee, lived in a modern mansion on a small exclusive estate where neighbours included footballers, celebrities and, Ed thought uncharitably, probably fraudsters, speculators and other criminals. He was not surprised that this estate was entirely unrepresented in his congregation except for Richardson, who he suspected was there as part of his political activities. Still, Richardson was conspicuously generous to the church's various appeals and donations to the collection plate. The purpose of his visit tonight was not, however, charitable.

His daughter had suffered a severe mental breakdown some years before. Though she was now capable of living on her own in a nearby flat and holding down a part time job as a photographer with a friend of Richardson's, she'd never fully recovered. Ed found her unlikeable and unsettling. Having tried every other resource in order to accelerate her recovery the Richardsons had turned to that avenue of last resort, the Church. Ed was chiding himself for such unchristian cynicism when he heard the doorbell chime.

The contrast between the Councillor and his daughter was striking. Richardson was tall with fashionably cut, short hair, chiselled features and a perma-tan; he radiated confidence and energy. His daughter radiated nothing, eyes downcast, pale features, mousey straw hair and neutral baggy clothes. Ed felt it was like encountering a vacuum.

"Find a room where Lisa can sit, Vicar, while we have a quick chat?"

Ed took Lisa to the study where he received all his parish visitors then led the Councillor through to the kitchen to make some tea realising as he did so that perhaps Richardson might not respond well to such a domestic task. He seemed not to notice.

"Vicar, I want you to spend some time with Lisa; she used to be a bubbly youngster, now there's nothing there. We've tried everything, the best private doctors, even alternative healers and other quacks, you know holistic mumbo jumbo, got nowhere, so I thought that you could give God a try, couldn't hurt now could it?"

Ed was fairly used to people regarding God as a last chance option but was thinking that this was the second time in the day that someone had dismissed the spiritual dimension as mumbo jumbo.

"Give God a try?"

"Well can't hurt can it? Nothing else seems to work. If you could sell it to her, even if only as some type of social work, it would at least give her an interest. Perhaps get her involved in some church group; you know the type of thing better than I do."

Richardson hesitated for a moment and now he'd stopped talking about his daughter his face became harder looking.

"Here's another thing: now listen, I hear you went to offer some type of blessing to those archaeologists today, that right?"

"Yes the congregation and Sir Nigel seemed to…"

Richardson cut him off.

"Well don't do it again, we want them off that land and now they think they've found something they'll be harder to shift. You know about our plans for that land."

Ed was flustered: he was uncomfortable with this topic and felt that Richardson wanted him to behave improperly.

"Yes, and I've thought long and hard about it but I'm not sure if I should be seen to be…"

Again he was cut off and he could see Richardson becoming angry.

"Well then, ask yourself this. Do you want to be the one blamed for losing all the new jobs the development is going to bring to this area of high rural unemployment? Blamed for losing the affordable starter homes? Go on, do you? Believe me you certainly won't enjoy losing Si Carver his profits. So it's time you sent that letter we wrote for you in support of the development to the planning committee pretty bloody quickly."

Richardson paused again and Ed felt he was trying to control himself and in the space Ed said,

"Well Sir Nigel…"

Again he was cut off

"What he and people like him think don't matter now, it's money that talks. He's the past and the past is dead, get it?"

He tried to smile and continued in a softer style.

"Ed, mate, we thought you wanted to modernise, you know change things. Well that's what we're doing in Business and Regeneration just like you're doing in trying to get rid of all the fairy tales and God stuff from the church."

Ed felt shocked and suddenly ashamed that it was perceived he was getting rid of the God stuff from church because deep in his heart he wanted more than anything to believe in the God stuff. Richardson looked at his watch.

"Look, I've got to drop in at a meeting of the local group opposing the third runway. Just to make an appearance, you know how it is. Then I need to make a quick visit to a farmers' meeting; silly buggers have got themselves worked up: there's been an outbreak of animals being savaged and killed in the fields round here these last few days. Some of them are daft enough to think that the archaeologists have let something loose. Who'd be a local politician these days? Still shouldn't take too long. I'll be back by about eight thirty so no tea for me, but try to get Lisa to have some and maybe a few biscuits. Hope you make progress and thanks a lot, Vicar. I'll let myself out."

With that he was gone leaving Ed slightly dazed and with the prospect of a rather different evening than the one he'd envisaged. The next two hours seemed to be the slowest passing Ed could remember. Lisa was not awkward or difficult, just empty. At times Ed felt he was talking to an automaton. His attempts to connect with her in conversation, interest her in church activity and, as a final attempt, join him in prayer all evoked no response except a polite, yet withdrawn lack of interest.

Eventually he took her into the kitchen for the tea and biscuits. She showed no interest in either, just sat upright on the chair, hands on her knees, avoiding any eye contact and on the rare occasions that he saw her eyes there was nothing there; just a blank soul. The silence seemed to echo round the walls of the vast kitchen and the ticking of the clock sounded louder and louder. Ed made one last despairing effort to get through to her.

"Lisa, tell me about your job."

"S'allright."

"And you work for Jim Gibson don't you?"

"Suppose."

"I believe he's a friend of your father's?"

"He doesn't have any."

"Your father tells me you have moved into a flat?"

"Yeah."

"And do you like it?"

"S'allright innit."

Ed had no idea what to say next. In a peculiar way he was beginning to find the girl rather frightening. He was distinctly uncomfortable being alone with her in the large silent kitchen in the empty house. He even wished one of his parishioners would ring as they usually did to disturb his evening with some complaint. Finally in desperation he blurted out,

"You went to take photographs of the dig today I hear?"

For a moment she didn't answer and in the silence Ed listened to the faint regular tick of the second hand of the electric clock as it made its painfully slow way around the minutes. Then he noticed that there was a change in Lisa: she seemed to be listening to somebody else in the room and smiling at what they were telling her. Then, for the first time, she turned her full gaze on Ed and he flinched.

"Yeah, I was meant to be there."

"Yes, to take photographs, Lisa."

She sniggered.

"If that's what you wanna think."

Ed wondered where this was going, he could feel sweat trickling down his spine as it used to during one of his 'episodes'. The sly smile that occasionally crossed her face changed it, but not in a good way. It transformed her bland expressionless features into something rather chilling. Now, with her eyes still locked onto his, she asked him a question.

"Don't you want to talk any more? Don't you want to know about Devil's Mound? I could tell you things, I know more than that silly bitch who thinks she found it does: she's got a nasty surprise coming. I know more than they think."

She sniggered horribly, disturbing Ed, who stuttered,

"What, what do you think Lisa?"

"That'd be telling wouldn't it? But I'll tell you one thing: I know they tried to hide it from me today: but it knew me and called to me."

"Lisa, you can't think that."

She turned her malevolent smile on him.

"How would you know? Do you think you matter to them, priest? Do you think they'd bother with you?"

Then shattering the unnatural atmosphere the doorbell rang and it was as if a spell had been broken: he rushed to the front door and his expression must have been obvious as Councillor Richardson greeted him with:

"So, no luck then? Still I suppose it was worth a try. Thanks anyway, oh, and don't forget to put our 'opener to the festive season' party in your diary, it's the week after next, everyone who matters will be there."

Ed noticed Lisa had silently materialised behind him and her father escorted her into the night. In the dark above him there was a faint sound of rustling. He looked up. Roosting high in the trees that circled the churchyard he saw the night black shapes of crows staring down at him. He couldn't remember seeing them before: but now, alarming and grotesque, packed onto the branches, they sat and watched the Rectory exuding silent malice. He closed the door quickly and stood by it for a moment feeling exhausted, panicked and in a strange way unclean.

That night he took double his normal dose of tablets and went to bed early. In the bedroom he tried and failed to pray as usual, then, leaving Mary's bedside lamp on, turned over to sleep.

But sleep wouldn't come as images of the day's humiliations chased each other through his subconscious. Since his breakdown this was a common end to his day but tonight there was something much worse perturbing him; something that the more he thought about it the more frightening it became. Every time he closed his eyes he saw the dead little face with the sly smile mouthing the words,

"…they tried to hide it from me today: but it knew me and called to me."

CHAPTER 3
WARNINGS

"There!!"

Rose was trowelling a post hole when Leonie shrieked and grabbed her arm.

"Look, he's there again, just at the edge of the woods, quick or you'll miss him. He flits about."

"It's probably just an interested local. Forget about it Leonie, love, it's just what you're having to put up with from Steve that's making you all on edge, let's have a good chat about that in the pub later, just us girls, eh?"

"Ok, you're probably right about Steve, Rose, but listen I'm telling you there is something really creepy watching us, watching me from over there and it's beginning to freak me out. Anyway I'm taking this sample from the fill back to the hut for analysis; maybe he'll disappear when I've gone."

Rose returned to trowelling at what she now knew in her heart was the entrance to her chamber. They'd made rapid progress on the preliminary exploration of Devil's Mound gathering enough evidence to establish it was considerably older than the village. The fieldwork and geophysical survey confirmed the centre of the mound was a hollow chamber.

The serene autumn continued sunny and warm providing optimum digging conditions and Rose felt they'd be ready to open the mound early next week. Yet despite all this there was a creeping, almost imperceptible change in the mood of the diggers, particularly Leonie.

"She was a bit sharp, Rose, she's been edgy since before the weekend."

"Well no one has more time for Leonie than me, but you know what she's like with men, gives out signals that she's anybody's. Then finding out rather abruptly that she was off with Steve didn't help. For all his charm he can be a callous bastard at times. Not that I'll have anything said against him going back the way we do."

"I don't think he means it, he just can't face any real commitment, not to his career, women, anything; he's never grown up. Lucky for Giles, he'd never be working as his number two if he'd any ambition or staying power! If you judge him in that context he's rather sweet."

"You're such a little pushover, Jan! Hey, maybe Leonie's right; I think I just saw her friend in the trees."

They were interrupted by Steve walking over to remind them they were scheduled to deliver their fortnightly Tuesday lecture for interested members of the local villages. Tonight's venue was the Windmill pub.

"Oh, and Leonie's just told me she feels sick so I've sent her home. I don't like to ask but would you be able to cover her bit about the finds, Jan? I'd really appreciate it."

He flashed his winning smile and Jan, pleased to be asked, agreed, ignoring the knowing smirk from Rose.

After Steve and Jan had left, Rose continued work until the long shadows cast by the setting sun made the trench almost too dark to see. However something was driving her on and she decided there was still time for a final attempt to expose the entrance. She knew she was quite alone when in a casual conversational tone, someone said,

"No, further to the left."

The voice, which was vaguely familiar, seemed to come from behind and she looked round surprised. There was nobody there; she stood up, looked all round: no one in sight.

It brought back the dream she'd had some weeks ago where she'd seen the mound in the distance and a voice had told her that it was special. It had been a warm friendly voice, like an imaginary best friend would have sounded, and she'd woken up knowing this was going to be her big break. In the dream the mound had been bathed in sunlight and she just knew that she would discover the academic riches inside, she would get the plaudits and after that the credit and reward she deserved.

Now in the shadows she wasn't quite as sure and for a moment she had the urge to get away quickly and follow the others but then began to think more rationally. It was her subconscious prompting her, a common feature in exceptionally talented individuals, and anyway the voice sounded friendly, it was helping her towards what she deserved. So she got back into the trench and began to scrape at the section further to the left.

***

That evening Steve, Jan and Rose pulled up outside the Windmill, a large modernised pub and restaurant about two miles away down a quiet lane by the side of the canal. The lecture, to thirteen people, went well and was followed by questions and contributions from the local audience. After the session finished and they were relaxing over a drink at a table in a corner farthest away from the bar one of the locals walked across and stood waiting for a pause in conversation. He was a heavy built man, with a ruddy face and faded pale blue eyes that seemed to focus on the middle distance. He'd massive calloused hands and was wearing an old greasy checked jacket over his farmer's overalls. He put a half full pint glass on the table breaking the flow of the talk.

"There's a few things I could tell you concerning that land you was pratting on about."

He paused to take a swig from his beer. Steve winked at Jan then said,

"We didn't see you at the talk; you could have made a most valuable contribution."

He grinned at Rose and Jan. The man ignored this and continued.

"That's because I weren't at the talk, I know as much as I care to about that place and what I've got to say's not for public entertainment. You might find it funny now but I don't think you'll find it as bloody funny in a few days."

Steve was about to say that he'd meant no harm but the man cut across him.

"Me family used to farm some land round there; never came to much and us sold up years back. Not a comfortable thing farming land that borders Devil's Mound. So we was glad to have sold. That place messes up any bugger that's daft enough to fiddle with it or spend much time there."

He paused as if struggling for the words to say what he needed to.

"It like, er, changes them, you know like takes the worst bits and grows them like it were manure, messes with their heads."

He came to a stop before blurting out.

"I know, seen it on our kid: seen what it did to me own little brother."

Then he paused and swallowed hard as if to control himself. Steve, who rarely noticed the emotions of others, used the pause to enquire with a smirk,

"The point of your story being?"

"Point is clever bugger, there's things you don't know, like how many fellers has killed themselves there over the years; how many car crashes there's been on that stretch of road and most of all why has nobody farmed on that piece of ground? Perhaps you've not noticed as how all them animals has been cut up round here these last few days since you've been messing with t'mound. I'd have thought puzzling that out would be enough to keep even a flash bugger like you busy for a while."

Steve had heard enough.

"Right, well, thanks for that fascinating exposition but as you said we're quite busy so if you'd excuse us."

"Don't worry I'm going but I hope you heard what I said because listen, you're not as bloody clever as you think you are and you've done yourselves no favours messing around with things that sensible folk turn their backs on. Well, I've done my bit now, can't say you haven't been warned."

He slammed his empty glass down onto the table and made as if to move off, then turned, looked closely at Rose and said in a quieter tone,

"You're the one, you're the one it's using: I'll bet it's you that found it."

Rose started to ask him how he knew but the man turned and walked away from the table and out of the pub. They sat for a while finishing their drinks. Steve and Jan joked about the man but Rose didn't join in. Steve teased her.

"Oh come on, Rose, you must have found all that 'Zombie Hills Have Eyes' stuff pretty funny. It was like an audition for *Scary Movie*."

"Perhaps, but it's been a long day and I'm tired, please let's go home."

By the time they'd packed up the minibus it was cold and dark with the moon fully risen. So cold that Steve had to scrape frost off the windscreen and they huddled inside their coats against the failure of the minibus's heating system to provide any warmth. Rose sat in the back as Steve drove and chatted with Jan in the front.

The evening hadn't gone the way Rose hoped; Steve, the selfish bastard, hadn't given her due credit for her discovery in his talk: typical. If life was fair she'd be dig director not Giles, a poor archaeologist, pathetic weak man with a failed marriage and no ambition. Just like her husband had been. Steve may be a good digger but he was like a little boy with no sense of responsibility, chasing after young girls then running away. She knew that if it wasn't for the glass ceiling in archaeology she'd be leading the Unit and they'd better watch out as she'd have them out of their jobs in no time. Looking at Jan laughing with Steve in the front seats she thought: look at the silly little tart throwing herself at the letchy waster. Leonie will be interested when I tell her tomorrow.

Thinking of Leonie brought her back to the mound; her mound. She'd called it 'my mound' once by mistake and Steve and Giles had made fun of her. Steve had called her Gollum and they spent the rest of the day calling out 'my precious' when she tried to talk to them and Leonie had giggled like those bitches at school used to. Well it was her mound, even the village idiot in the pub had known that and what's more she knew there was something in it, almost as if it had told her.

This last bit she'd rather not have remembered. It brought back the mysterious voice. She'd began to wonder who it was that Leonie thought was watching them when she saw they were passing Devil's Mound. Looking out of the window she tried to pick out the shape through the trees as the minibus drove past. Although most of the site was obscured by the fringe of trees, through a gap she thought she saw a flickering light moving around the mound. Then the bus was round the corner of the lane and the mound was gone.

***

Wednesday was the last golden day of that peculiarly elongated summer. Rose established the mound had been surrounded by a cordon of deep ditch when the chamber was built, and the entire feature had been covered by a heap of the earth taken from the ditch. She was sure that the entrance to the chamber, which she'd found further to the left, had faced a breach or causeway in the ditch. Whilst Leonie and Jan investigated the area between the causeway and the ditch she made the preliminary preparations for the opening of the chamber. All the team hoped they'd found a, possibly unique, Neolithic chambered tomb. Steve, as the established Neolithic expert, switched his attention full time from the village to the mound and Rose suspected that he would take over the excavation and relegate her to a supporting role. Leonie, who had become increasingly disenchanted with all aspects of the excavations and particularly with Steve, encouraged her in this.

"So unfair on you Rose, without you this crappy dig would have been wound up by now with nothing to show for it, just like all Giles's digs. And it's just typical of that selfish wanker Steve, takes what he wants and moves on. Thinks he can do what he likes on site; Giles would never dare challenge him on anything to do with excavation. If he ever does Steve just name checks all the high profile digs he's worked on and all the leading academics who consult him. If I hear one more mention of Khiroktia, Çatalhöyük or bloody Makriyalos I'll throw up."

She ran out of steam giving Jan the opportunity to interject,

"OK, but it must have been exciting to have worked at those places when you look at the way those excavations moved our ideas on. Anyway I think Steve's stories are really quite interesting, last night when we went to the pub he was telling me about…"

***

Rose wasn't listening, it was like they'd disappeared and she was in a different universe. She wasn't going to have Steve find the opening to her discovery, she knew exactly where it was; she'd seen it last night in a dream, if it had been a dream, she couldn't be sure these days.

But it was hers and she was now going to excavate it herself. Something had led her step by step to this discovery and she didn't want anyone stealing the moment. She'd told Jan and Leonie to investigate the pit at the other end of the trench. When they'd gone she clambered up onto the mound.

On the mound it felt good, where she was meant to be. At first the work went even more easily than she'd hoped, it felt almost like somebody else was directing her movements. Once she excavated down to the stone she switched to using a small trowel to try to expose a little of its surface. The feel of the ancient stone scraping against the steel of her trowel blade vibrated through her fingers and ran right up her arm. It gave her a luxurious sense of power.

But then suddenly, as the trowel found an edge to the stone, there came a terrible feeling out of nowhere that the ancient rock was trying to repel her efforts to expose it, that the stone itself didn't want her here.

She must have lost all sense of time because it had grown darker and there was stillness in the air like before an electrical storm. The conversation between Jan and Leonie in the trench sounded fuzzy and distorted, seemed to be reaching her across a long distance. She was dizzy now, maybe she should stop. Something was wrong: she didn't want to be up here alone any more. She'd go and join the others, but when she turned to look she couldn't see them any more. And there was something else here. Something urging her to keep going, the voice in her dreams: only now it wasn't like the best friend she'd always imagined and never had, it was harsh and threatening. Like the policeman who'd cautioned her when she'd accidently cut her ex-husband with that kitchen knife: cut him quite badly it turned out.

She thought maybe she was suffering from the heat, but when she tried to stop she could feel something deep inside under the stone pulling at the blade of the trowel, something stronger than stone forcing her to continue, just like the kitchen knife had forced its way into her husband's stomach. As her hand was pulled back into action it finally dawned on her that all her passion and intuition about the mound had maybe come from within it. Something in there had been using her; it wanted her to find it. It had guided her. She tried to call out but her voice, like in a nightmare, made no sound.

Then, through this confusion of dreaming horror she detected movement at the edge of the tree line by the estate wall: something was coming. Coming to stop her. She managed to turn her head to look. Yes there: there was something approaching: it had crossed over the wall. Funeral black like a rotting grave winding, distorted and elongated and above it the hideous mockery of a corpse white face that she couldn't bear to look at.

And then it hit her; this was what Leonie had seen, but it hadn't been stalking Leonie. It had been watching her, no, not just watching, it had been trying to warn her, to make her leave the mound alone.

The thing in the mound was more urgent now, pulling harder, frantic as it directed the trowel in her hand. Compelling her to release it, to release something she now dimly understood must never be set free. But she was beyond fearing that as she watched the thing from the tree line come capering across the ground towards her. Its perambulation was awful, disarticulated as if it was a thing of many pieces, only loosely jointed. But worse than that was the way it covered the distance, jerkily, at great speed and yet so horribly imprecise she could never tell exactly where it was.

She stood up to run but as she moved she felt the grass clutching at her legs as the earth pulled her down so that as she turned her upper body her legs stayed fixed. She heard cartilage tear and bone snap in her left ankle and she fell to her knees.

She shut her eyes, petrified, so she saw nothing. But she knew it had reached her, that it was on the mound. Beneath her under the earth, trapped in the chamber she heard something begin to howl. She didn't listen because the horror on the mound was so close.

Then it touched her and the feeling of that touch was so dreadful, so beyond description that death itself would have been better. So it was almost a relief when she felt herself tossed into the air to land broken and bleeding in the bottom of the trench.

CHAPTER 4
SEEPING THROUGH

Jan was labelling a finds bag in the trench and Leonie was having a ciggy break when they heard something squealing like a terrified child, followed by the sound of a body hitting the ground from a great height.

They turned and saw Rose lying splayed out, a smashed doll on the trench floor. Jan heard Leonie scream but made herself rush to where Rose was lying. How was it possible to suffer such injuries just from falling so short a distance? She was twisted and broken, sprawled across the trench, her right leg bent backwards beneath her and the left, a blood soaked mess sticking out at a right angle to the hip. Her fingers were bleeding and her fair hair matted from the blood streaming down her ashen face. She was whimpering with pain and her left hand was jerkily scrabbling at the base of her spine.

"Leonie run get help! Go on move now it's urgent."

Leonie ran and Jan tried to examine and comfort Rose, although unsure if she was fully conscious.

"Don't move, Rose, Leonie's gone for help. Please stay still, Steve will get an ambulance, you'll be OK I promise you."

But she didn't look OK and Jan was wondering how a simple slip down no more than five feet into a shallow trench could produce these injuries. She could see white splintered bone puncturing the skin through the blood covering Rose's right leg. She couldn't bring herself to look at the left leg protruding at such an unnatural angle so occupied herself looking for the source of the blood in her hair and speaking soothing words of comfort. She felt Rose reach for her hand and try to speak.

"Jan, don't leave me, mustn't leave me, get me away from here, it wants me, feeds off me."

Her voice faltered and she seemed to be drifting into a state of semi-consciousness.

"Rose, just hang on in there, love, help will be here soon and we'll get you taken care of in hospital."

She tried to speak again and Jan thought she caught the words

"Pushed me, warn Steve, warn him there's two things."

"Shush, quiet, love, stay still."

"Jan two things, not one two...my fault... tricked me, stop it, don't let it ou..."

Then Rose blacked out and a panicky Jan felt for a pulse.

It took the startled paramedics some time to decide it was safe to move Rose onto a stretcher and into the ambulance. Leonie went with her. Once the ambulance had receded from the site along the rough track that led to the road, Steve decided to close down work on the excavation for the day. As the diggers packed up he made the shocked Jan a cup of tea.

"What happened Jan, how did she manage to do that to herself?"

"I don't know, hardly seems possible. Steve, those injuries were awful, how could it happen? She must have twisted badly as she fell. I'm most bothered by the blow to the head; she wasn't making any sense when she blacked out."

"OK, once we've finished here I'll drive us to the hospital and see what's what, first I'd better share the good news with Giles.

***

In the scruffy gloom of the Unit, Giles was on the phone to Tim Thompson the historian and archivist they shared with the history department. He was preparing the documentary evidence on the area that would provide context and tenurial history for the site report.

"Yes, I'll have a pretty fair report ready for you next week. It's quite a tricky one this, you know there's no record of any settlement at all on any of those fields at the site. It would seem that since they abandoned the village almost two and a half thousand years ago no one's gone near it, very strange – it's good quality land. By the way, did you know there's rumours in the council offices of a dodgy scheme to develop it?"

"Yeah, get on with it please, Tim."

"Very well then, I'm going to conflate all the documentary and literary references into a brief report. There's a local legend about the mound that goes back a long way. It's meant to be a place to keep well away from. It's linked in with the history of Skendleby Hall and the Davenport family. The parish church even had a haunted vicar going mad and disappearing in the eighteenth century. The Davenports still live in Skendleby; not in the Hall, they sold that quite recently to a merchant banker or such like and were apparently quite glad to do so. Now that's strange behaviour from an ancient landed family don't you think?"

Giles was beginning to lose attention. Thompson's long rambling discourses had this effect on him. Then he realised Thompson's tone had changed.

"Still, the Hall's an interesting place, Giles, there's a small chapel with a most peculiar motto that translates as 'we guard that which watches'. It dates back to the fifteenth century. No one knows what it means and apart from this one carving in the stone in the chapel there's no other mention of it. The family, apparently, don't like to talk about it."

"Yeah Tim, very clever, it sounds like an academic fifteenth century joke."

"Sorry, I'm not with you."

"The quote, you know: it's a take on the roman satirist Juvenal's comment on Plato's Republic. *Quis Custodiet* and all that, you know, 'Who guards the guardians themselves.' Quite amusing. Anyway I'll look forward to your report. Bye."

Giles put down the phone with relief, a little of Thompson could go a long way. It rang immediately, this time it was Steve from the hospital.

When Giles arrived on site early Thursday morning the weather was showing signs of change, the sky was a paler blue and the sunshine hazy. The warmth of the previous weeks had been replaced by chill, the harbinger of winter. Giles found the change of atmosphere on site unsettling and it was not just his arrival that had dampened it this time. The previous Thursday the dig had been alive with the discovery of an ancient site within Devil's Mound. The post work visits to the pub by the whole work force, professional and volunteer, following brilliant sunny days had produced an atmosphere of holiday and bonhomie. The good humour on the site had been infectious. Now it was not only the weather that was chill but also the atmosphere. He'd expected the accident to Rose would have had an effect, but not this depressing. After all, the reports from the hospital were more positive than they'd feared initially; she would recover and maybe be up and about in a few months, although her mind might take longer to heal. And anyway, no one liked or trusted her.

He hadn't even had time to see for himself where the accident happened for his health and safety report when Jan asked if she could have a word. She led him away from the hearing of the other diggers.

"Giles, there's some things I need to tell you."

"OK, go on."

"What happened to Rose, well, that wasn't normal. No, don't look at me like that. For a start you can't hurt yourself like that falling a few feet. You should have heard what the paramedics said about it."

"Look Jan, people can get hurt by the strangest things. Listen, I knew a guy who got killed by an orange."

He hoped she'd laugh as he didn't really have time for all this, but she just got more agitated.

"Also, Giles, she said someone had done it to her, she wanted me to warn Steve and to tell him there were two of something."

"Well, if she was trying to warn Steve about two of something it must have been women. You can count yourself lucky he's not turned his charm on you yet."

He realised as soon as he said this it was a mistake, and for more reasons than just making light of Rose's injury. Her eyes filled with tears and she snapped, "she was lucky not to die. Have you seen how Leonie is? She thinks we're being stalked and all you can do is make silly fucking jokes. You're meant to be in charge, Giles. Try to act responsibly or at least have the decency to look like you care."

She fumbled for a handkerchief and, to stop things deteriorating further he said as if convinced,

"OK, OK, I hear what you say, I'll go and visit her in hospital, see if she's well enough to talk."

He walked off wishing he thought more about what he said before he said it. Why could he never get it right? He wasn't quite as insensitive as people thought and had already clocked the frozen atmosphere between Steve and Leonie. So he wasn't looking forward to the on site planning meeting that the four of them had scheduled for the afternoon.

In the event, to his surprise, the meeting started well, although it began to feel very cold in the draughty shabby site hut. He took great pains to handle the meeting with tact, steering away from any sensitive areas and after about half an hour they were behaving almost like they were a week ago. He wondered if this was partly out of respect for Rose, but by three thirty they'd managed to reschedule the last phases of the excavation and agreed to ahead with preparing to open the chamber sometime next week. He'd be able to put on some sort of show for Jim and his paper. He should have ended the meeting then but Steve had started.

"I know this sounds a bit weird but I did think of it before this happened to Rose. You know the way this thing was built. Well it's like it was never meant to be found, you get what I'm saying. These things were usually built to be seen, you know, they were a focus for the community. Spot the difference with this one?"

Giles was late for his next meeting and didn't want to discuss this now and especially not on site.

"OK Steve, but we won't know if that's true or not until we excavate it."

"But listen: there is evidence in the design, look I can show you, I've drawn it on a plan. Leonie just reach into the map draw and pass me the third drawing down?"

Leonie, sullen faced and puffy eyed, didn't answer, just pulled the heavy drawer open and reached inside, suddenly her face puckered up as if she was about to cry.

"You bastard, you fucking bastard, how could you? I hate you. I hope you die."

Giles watched astonished as she ran out of the hut; he saw shock on Steve's face and he moved over the other side of the desk and pulled the drawer right out. He thought he was going to vomit.

Inside the drawer, skewered to the wood by a heavy builder's nail, was a huge black crow. It had been dead for days and was in an advanced state of putrefaction. The flesh and feather around its beak was loose and rotting away but it still wore an expression of ferocious malice.

"Giles, it wasn't me, honest to God, I swear I'd never pull that type of stunt."

Giles put a hand on his shoulder, the thing horrified him but he needed to calm Steve and find Leonie. Steve wasn't easy to calm.

"It must have been that nutter in the pub, the one who tried to scare us. You were there, Jan."

Giles had no time to listen. He rushed out and found Leonie doubled up by the tool hut being violently sick. He walked over and began to gently stroke her back. She gagged and then said between retches,

"I felt it: my hand went into its stomach; it was liquid, mushy, disgusting, why?"

She gagged again but by now had brought everything up. Giles started to say

"I don't think…"

But she cut across him.

"I know. Now I've thought about it, he wouldn't do something like that, it's just I'm so angry with him, he hurt me so much. But if it wasn't him who was it? What's happening? Take me home. I'll never get this hand clean. Please I want to go home, I need to go home."

Giles handed her his car keys and told her to wait in it. He went back into the hut where Jan was soothing Steve.

"I'm taking her home, she knows it wasn't you, but best to keep it quiet. Look, you may as well pack up early."

He glanced toward the drawer which was still open and caught a glimpse of a sharp beak, decomposing mush and mouldering black feathers.

"Steve I don't like to ask but will you get rid of that fucking bird?"

He walked off to his car.

Steve and Jan watched, but before he reached it a battered Mini drove up the track and braked. A tall, slim woman with long dark hair and an ankle length black coat approached one of the site workers who pointed at Giles. Jan was reminded of an attractive and benign version of a Disney cartoon witch. There was a brief conversation during which the woman became animated and then angry. Then she turned and stomped away to her car, black coat streaming behind and high heeled black boots uncertain over the rough ground. Steve shouted across to him,

"What the hell was all that about?"

Giles looked fazed but eventually shouted back,

"God knows, she's called Vanarvi or something weird, claims she's seen the mound in a dream or something. I couldn't understand what she was on about, it's like she thinks she's some sort of witch, must be mad."

With that he climbed into his car and drove off down the track.

Jan looked worried.

"This place is getting too heavy, Steve; I think I'll be glad when we're finished here. The warning, that crow and poor Rose."

"Come on; don't take all that stuff Rose said about feeling something shifting around inside the mound seriously, that was shock and the effect of the sedatives they gave her."

"But what about what she said just before the accident?"

"Jan, you know that's because everybody's favourite older sister, Rose, puts too much extra in those cigs she smokes, that can't help her state of mind."

"Come on Steve, be serious."

"What you mean? That stuff about being pushed and a warning to the curious; it was banging her head, when she fell that did that, concussion that's all."

"No, not that, remember when we did that talk on the site at the Windmill. Well, on the way back when you and I sat in the front, quite romantic that by the way, Rose sat in the back looking out of the window into the dark. She said that as we drove past the site she saw some lights floating above the mound."

"Oh that's interesting 'cos when I was working on Çatalhöyük they did a survey of local traditions and superstitions. Locals left the mound there well alone, they reckoned it was haunted. At night there were lights moving around on the mound that were lost souls from the past. They knew nothing about the archaeology there, but funnily enough later excavation showed the mound was covered in ancient burials. They buried the dead under the floors of houses, perhaps to keep the things they feared where they could keep an eye on them. Interesting though."

Jan found herself wishing that Leonie was there to tell Steve to shut up about 'bloody Çatalhöyük'.

Sensing her mood Steve stopped his lecture.

"What's scaring you Jan, do you think we've got ghosts here too?"

He broke off for a moment as if looking at something.

"God, it gets dark quickly these days, and cold, come on it's time to pack up."

The light was fading rapidly, half the sun had dipped behind the Edge and in the distance an advancing front of wispy cloud, presaging a cold front, was picked out by the last rays of the sun in the violet twilight sky.

***

Around the same time, the Reverend Ed Joyce entered his study after a day of visiting sick parishioners. His last pastoral visit had left him feeling disturbed in a way he hadn't since the events in the Birmingham precipitated his mental disintegration. He'd visited William LaSalle, captain of the first eleven of the local cricket team whose pitch was on the other side of the field from where the archaeologists were digging. LaSalle's wife had asked Ed to visit, which surprised him as the man, a burly opening batsman, never attended church. But their house was near and he couldn't think of a reason to refuse.

They lived in Oak Tree Cottage, flanked by two great oaks near the ground. As Ed was opening the gate he heard a guttural grating sound and looking up saw a group of crows squatting on the thatch watching him. LaSalle's wife opened the door and gestured him in and into the front room. LaSalle sat in front of the TV drinking whisky; he looked pale and was clearly not pleased to see Ed.

"Listen Vicar, my wife insisted that I talk to you, but once I have then that's it, I don't want anything more to do with this even though I'd like to get me hands on the sick bastard of a practical joker."

He motioned for Ed to sit down and Ed settled into an armchair: he could see that despite his belligerent manner the man was scared.

"Last night I got a call that all the lights were on in the club house; of course they shouldn't have been, we haven't got anything on 'til Saturday night, so as nearest key holder I went across. The club was locked up but the lights were on, so I opened up and went in.

First thing I noticed was that the floor was wet and all the chairs had been piled up on the tables. Not tidily but in piles on top of each other, some of the arrangements seemed to defy gravity. The floor was wet because all the taps were on, not only the water but the beer taps too."

He took a swig of the whisky.

"Then I noticed the smell, the place smelt rotten, cloying, made me feel sick. So I poked around a bit and I saw that the wall by the toilets was smeared with something brownish red so I went over and piled up inside the gents I saw…"

He paused to take another swig of whisky and Ed noticed a sheen of perspiration covering his waxen face.

"I saw, Jesus, I can still see them, dead vermin; stoats, moles, weasels and the like all with their guts ripped out, blood and entrails smeared on the walls. Then I heard a sound over by the bar and I saw there was a fox head on it, grinning at me. I swear it hadn't been there when I went in. I'm not a man that scares easy see, I served two tours in Iraq but…"

He took another swig, finishing the glass and reached for the bottle.

"I got out of there sharpish I can tell you Vicar. Came home and called the police, and I would have left it there but my wife said you should know because there's too many strange things happening round here these days to be normal."

Ed stayed for a few minutes but LaSalle had nothing to add and clearly wanted him to leave. The wife thanked him and showed him to the door, where she quietly asked him if he did exorcisms like they did on

'Most Haunted' or if the diocese could get hold of someone like Derek Acorah. Ed had no idea who Derek Acorah was. He was still trying to make sense of the conversation as he closed the cottage gate behind him. Above him he saw the number of corvids on the roof had doubled. Across the lane the lights in the cricket clubhouse came on.

Back in the Rectory he moved to his desk and saw the box Mary gave him with its waxed paper package inside. He'd forgotten it but now he needed something mundane to calm him down. He picked it up and undid the ribbon. The packet was soiled with age and smelt of dust and decay. It contained some old parish newsletters and ecclesiastical magazines from the nineteenth century, of no great interest. Below these were a series of accounts of parish expenses from the same period. He was about to wrap it back up and consign the whole lot to the tip when he noticed there were some other papers below the accounts. He removed them and was faced by a small bundle of something older; aging manuscripts, handwritten in fading black ink. He was all too familiar with that spidery handwriting; it was Heatly Smythe's.

CHAPTER 5
FOG OVER THE CITY, DECEMBER 1st

Walking from the *Journal*'s offices through Albert Square Jim enjoyed the sentimental trappings of the festive season. The traditional European market was open, Christmas lights hung from street lamps and a giant inflatable Santa scaled the neo-gothic Town Hall. It was hardly past noon but the day was already gloomy with tentative wisps of fog. However, this, mixed with the aromas of spices, mulled wine and scented candles from the stalls, conspired to give a Dickensian Christmas atmosphere.

It was cold too, freezing cold, in sharp contrast to the Indian summer that had bathed the city up until Tuesday. Dodging through the crowded streets he turned down a narrow Victorian covered passage opening onto a small square: at the far end of which a group of young business types were studying a menu board outside the marble clad doorway of a restaurant.

The Trattoria inhabited one of the city's many defunct trading exchanges, relics of nineteenth century prosperity. Walking through the portico into the cavernous lobby he saw Giles sitting ill at ease on one of the fashionable, but very uncomfortable, low backed leather sofas. He needed a shave, his curly hair was a tangled mess and he was arguing with a man who had his back turned. As Jim approached the man stood up and he saw it was Derek Richardson.

"All right Jim? Finishing early for the weekend I see."

Jim ignored the jibe.

"Hi Derek, what brings you here?"

"Business: I've got a lunch meeting with Si Carver, was enjoying it too until we ran into your friend here. I was just explaining to him what a big mistake it would be to get too far the wrong side of Mr Carver. Worse luck for him, he's already made a start."

Giles, who by this time had got up and shaken Jim's hand, said,

"Not deliberately, Jim, it just seems that Mr Carver and the councillor don't have much time for archaeology."

"We don't have time for a lot of things and wasting taxpayers' money is one of them, but I'm a reasonable man so let me give you a piece of good advice before I go and join Si in the dining room."

Jim wondered what had been going on particularly as Richardson addressed his next remarks to him.

"Jim you'd better get it across to your friend here that this archaeology malarkey on Si's land is attracting undesirables onto the estate, there's disturbances and coming and goings late at night. This last week Si's noticed acts of vandalism: someone's leaving piles of dead vermin in the estate ground and it's attracting huge gatherings of crows. What's causing that then eh? And now there's all this bollocks about something important they've found that'll have to be saved. I don't think so. Listen, all this is getting in the way of an important economic development with considerable social benefits."

Giles broke in,

"So what are you trying to say?"

"I'm saying that patience is running thin and movers and shakers like Si have influence, which people like you don't."

Giles, angry himself now, said,

"Yes, but in a democratic society there are systems that protect our heritage."

"Yeah, well you can believe that if it makes you feel better."

"The historic landscape is an important part of our culture."

"Bollocks, who's interested in dead old things? No one, no one cares about that, what can the past or old stones change? Ask yourself this: when did you last see an archaeologist on 'I'm a Celebrity' or 'Strictly?'"

He turned aside and took Jim by the arm.

"Listen, Jim, I don't think you letting my Lisa take the pictures on that site is doing her any good, she's going strange again. Just make sure you keep an eye on her."

He turned and walked into the dining room to join Mr Carver and two minutes later they were ushered into the dining area in an efficient rather than welcoming manner and installed with drinks at Jim's usual table by the far wall.

A great domed ceiling towered high above the tables, so high that the modern lighting had to be suspended on wires that ran the length and breadth of the room beneath the dome; perhaps it was this that made the place feel cold. After ordering the set menu of pasta followed by meat in sauce, accompanied by a bottle of ink dark Primativo, they relaxed into their chairs. The place was quite full and yet, despite this and the background music of Italian crooners belting out Italian pop songs, it seemed strangely flat. Perhaps it was this that prevented Jim from feeling relaxed; in fact he'd not felt settled since leaving the dig last week and when his mind was unoccupied and drifting he fell prey to a feeling of unease. He was shifted from this morbid reverie by Giles finishing his beer in one large swallow and beginning to talk.

"I'll have another of those please. You know, Jim, this dig has gone from dull as Hell to a weird, possible page one feature, in less than a week. Five days ago we were dealing with the most boring village settlement in the universe, now we think we've found something unique from a much earlier period."

He was interrupted as a fresh beer arrived on the table; he took a swig that half emptied the expensive bottle, belched silently and then continued in a more disjointed manner.

"There's strange things happening; first the freak accident to Rose, which is going to keep her out of action for at least a few months, and then yesterday some crazy woman turned up at the site and warned us off, said we were meddling with things best left alone. She was mad as a badger shouting hysterical warnings; but the strange thing is she looked quite normal, in fact quite attractive and well, if oddly dressed; you know sort of soi-disant carnival."

His flow was interrupted by the arrival the starters. Jim, who ate here at least once a week, didn't recognise the surly waiter. This was unusual for as a regular, he expected a warm welcome and friendly service. This nuance was obviously lost on Giles who after a mouthful of pasta and an appreciative swallow of wine continued with mouth half full.

"Mind you, your mate Richardson was right about one thing: there are strange goings on. Rose thinks some maniac stalker attacked her and someone nailed a decomposing crow in one of the map drawers."

This image put Jim off his food, he found it hard to shake off.

Giles continued with his complaints until a different waiter took away the plates and refilled his wine glass. Jim, who had to drive out of the city through rush hour to the village suburb where he lived in the golden triangle of the tinted window Range Rover belt, thought this had better be his last. Giles on the other hand quickly finished his second glass and reached for a refill. The wine at least seemed to improve his mood.

"It's almost definitely a burial: probably Neolithic, where there shouldn't be one. So what's it doing there? The Iron Age inhabitants of Skendleby seemed to have moved away as soon as they found out what it was. They just covered it back over then went. After that no one seems to have touched the place. Strange don't you think?"

Jim was about to ask why he was so sure it was this earlier feature that caused them to leave when he realised they'd been waiting over half an hour for the main course. Looking round he saw the waiter who'd served them with pasta and beckoned him over. The man looked back, as if at someone standing behind Jim, and made a peculiar gesture with the first and fourth fingers of his right hand then turned quickly towards the kitchens. Just as he was about to complain Giles said jokingly,

"Look, that waiter just made the sign against the evil eye; he must think the Devil's here."

Jim, far from placated by this interpretation, summoned the Head Waiter, who, to his surprise, was singularly unhelpful, claiming not to recognise the description of the waiter as one of his staff. He did however promise to investigate the reasons for the delay to the meal as well as to bring another half bottle of Primativo that Giles had ordered. This didn't improve Jim's mood, he always paid. He also usually had to return to work or drive home so that most of the wine would be drunk by Giles.

Since the very messy breakup of his marriage Giles drank heavily and had adopted the habit of ordering more whenever he felt like it. These meals usually ended with Jim picking up a hefty bill and Giles basking in the temporary warm glow of alcoholic stupor.

Then two things that struck him as peculiar. One was that the original clock of the Exchange trading floor that dominated the wall he faced had stopped at the time they sat down at the table. The second was that a fair haired child sitting with a family party in the centre of the room had been staring fixedly at him, or perhaps something behind him, since he first became aware of her presence. However, the arrival of the main course and half bottle diverted his attention and as they began to eat, Giles returned to the source of his perplexity.

"So, we've got a pissed off team, a warped practical joker, a hostile landowner and a site that was meant never to be found."

He broke off to pour the wine and mop the sauce up off his plate with some bread, leaving Jim to reflect that according to his reckoning all the recent difficulties on site had occurred since the first investigation of the mound. Before he was able to articulate this Giles slurred,

"I've just time for an espresso and grappa before going back to the Unit. I may as well; I've nowhere else to go and won't see anyone till after the weekend. I don't suppose you'll go back to work; your weekend starts here right?

Jim admitted it would and they talked of his weekend plans. Later, paying the bill after hesitating over whether to leave a tip, he noticed that the clock had restarted and was showing the correct time and that the family party had left, as had Carver and Richardson.

They agreed that Jim and Lisa would be at the site on Tuesday morning to cover the opening of the Neolithic tomb and then parted. Jim felt that, in an imperceptible way, something had gone wrong with the day and he felt a sense of anxiety not lessened by the fact that as he walked through the thickening fog he felt he caught a glimpse at the periphery of vision of the surly waiter behind him.

The walk to the car didn't lift his mood as the fog steadily thickened. It being Friday afternoon the offices in the city rapidly emptied, disgorging thousands of people onto the streets with a common purpose: to get home early for the weekend avoiding the rush hour traffic. The pavements were clogged and in the smeary half light it looked like a dystopian vision of mass evacuation. The Christmas lights strung across the streets and from lamp posts flickered in and out of vision through the fog. Across the square there was the clatter and shouting from the European market. He jumped with shock at the sound of a klaxon as a tram emerged from the fog to his left, passed him at speed before disappearing into the murk again.

After experiencing the usual delays in queuing to get out at the barrier of the *Journal's* car park, he joined the barely moving queue of traffic heading for the main road south out of the city. Crawling through junctions and the virtually permanent road works, where no work ever seemed to take place and hundreds of forlorn cones narrowed the road, he passed the university's sprawling campus and eventually came to a dead halt at the junction with Plymouth Grove. The traffic always slowed to a crawl here and now it just stopped. Despite the fact that it was barely three thirty the combination of gloom and fog made it seem like the dead of night. The poor visibility didn't enhance the surroundings. To the left of the road stood the remains of a graveyard belonging to a church long since demolished after having been bombed in the war. This derelict open ground, enclosed by the remnants of decaying Victorian terraces and new university concrete, seemed lost and out of place.

The traffic refused to move and Jim wiped at the condensation forming on the inside of the car windows in an attempt to improve visibility. Presented with a choice of staring at damp, mildewed brickwork and stained concrete to the right or to the graveyard to the left he opted for the latter. What he could see of it through the fog was overgrown and decaying, the headstones blackened by soot deposited during the city's industrial heyday. It was the sort of place, he reflected, that you drove past without looking at but never failed to be aware of, even though the vision was marginal. Tonight his vision wasn't marginal although after a moment he wished it were. It was not so much the bleak vista of dark, unkempt headstones reminding him of Scrooge's grave in *A Christmas Carol*. Nor was it the air of neglect, decay and loss. It was that he thought he caught a fleeting glance through the swirling fog of a figure. It seemed as though a loosely articulated puppet was being jerked from one position behind a tombstone to another, the rapid awkward movement and poor visibility making it impossible to get a clear view. Indistinct or not, there was something peculiar about it as if it was trying to attract his attention. Jim was wondering if it was some trick being played by local kids when the traffic started to move. He accelerated slowly and looked back over his shoulder for a last glance but the figure was gone leaving only the fog and tombstones.

The thirteen miles home took the best part of an hour as the traffic snake crawled through the smeary grey and orange light. It was therefore with relief that he turned off the main road and followed the more sedate tree lined avenues that led to his home. The sense of satisfaction that normally enveloped him on arriving home on a Friday was tonight lacking. Even the light and noise that he encountered entering the house did little to lift him. His younger two sons and daughter were settled with their Friday treat, sweets, in front of the television, whilst sounds of a loud bass from upstairs informed him that their elder brother was expanding his already massive collection of bewildering music.

Walking through the book lined drawing room to the kitchen he found his wife listening to the Radio Four news and preparing the night's dinner. The Friday night dinner was the traditional rite of passage between the working week and the weekend. A leisurely affair with a couple of well selected wines after the younger boys had settled for the night, their daughter on Facebook and their elder brother 'hanging out'. But even the cheery greeting he received failed to rouse him and it was only a couple of hours later, sitting with an aperitif after a long soak in the bath, that his mood finally lifted.

Later that night unable to sleep, he sat in an armchair with a small whisky. The strategy worked and he began to drift into a dream ridden sleep in which something was looking for him in the fog. He was woken by the ringing of the phone and groped on the table for it assuming that there'd been some major event that his news editor wanted to clear with him. But it wasn't, at first it wasn't anyone: just silence and static. Then a voice.

"Jim Gibson."

"Who's there…Lisa, is that you?"

There was a strange laugh and then

"Guess what I've been doing…I've been looking through the footage we took at the sacrifice shrine. And we must have a problem with the camera, Jim, because it looks like they've already got out."

"What do you mean, sacrifice shrine?"

There was no answer just a brittle laugh, then a click, and the line went dead.

CHAPTER 6
'THICK EYED MUSING AND CURST MELANCHOLY'

Leaving the restaurant Giles moved through crowded foggy streets loud with the cheerful shouts of stallholders and office workers as he walked to the Unit's offices in the basement of the University. He needed the walk in the cold to clear his head and reckoned that it would be quicker than waiting for a bus. Like all weekends he felt down and lonely so hoped that someone would still be at work to raise his sombre mood and maybe make him a coffee. The grappa had been a mistake, he'd drunk too much and it would screw up his evening. The Unit was empty, his staff having left early. He walked down the stone steps and through the long main room to his small office, turning on the fluorescent lighting that flicked then came on with a blink and a humming sound which seemed much louder when the space was deserted.

On his desk he'd been left a note that read 'Claire rang, she's the woman who talked to you at the site on Tuesday; can you ring her?'

It was followed by a local number. Not the type of conversation he wanted right now but he put the note in his pocket. However, the memory of her took his mind back to the site: it was on good, well drained land in a rich agricultural belt yet since the village was abandoned about 300 BC no one had resettled it. Why? The surrounding fields were scattered with Roman, early and late medieval pottery but around the dig there was nothing. It was like some mega catastrophe had hit it: a type of metaphysical anthrax contamination that no one through the ages would talk about.

The only later evidence was the macabre record of a suicide in a thirteenth century document. He decided he'd get Tim Thompson to hurry up with his summary of the evidence. Then not wishing to dwell on it he decided to finish for the day as the emptiness of the sepulchral university basement was beginning to get to him.

Emerging into the deserted quad he saw the fog had thickened; the cold was intense. He thought he could hear ravens or crows calling to each other across the Neo-Gothic rooftops. They reminded him of the putrescent liquefaction of the dead crow in the desk. Shivering he crammed his hands into his jacket pockets and set off home. It wasn't a comfortable walk. Sounds were muffled by the fog and buildings and people assumed strange shapes looming suddenly in and out of vision. Just before he turned towards where he guessed the entrance of his road lay hidden in the fog he barged into someone.

"Hey pal, you can't walk through here; it's a crime scene, you'll have to cross back there."

His eyes focussed on a policeman with behind him others, partly visible, erecting a barrier round a patch of pavement; a crime scene and recent. He mumbled an apology and turned to retrace his steps but as they drifted quickly beyond sight he heard the snatch of a sentence through the cold dense air.

"Yeah, but not something like this, I'm fuckin' glad my kids are safe indoors."

His crumbling terrace house was in an area which had been a desirable inner suburb a hundred years ago. Now it was a no man's land inhabited by the poor and dislocated, intermingled with student housing, derelict wasteland and large dilapidated buildings some of which were boarded up but periodically reopened as squats and crack houses. All the families who could had moved out. But property was cheap here and this and the proximity to the university, attracted Giles and his wife to the decrepit house when they were post grads. Now Giles lived there alone and its disadvantages were more apparent.

Opening the door he felt the familiar stale rush of loneliness as the atmosphere of neglect and emptiness hit him. Since Sal moved out he'd let the place go to pieces and the house retained no trace of ever having been a home. He turned on the table lights in the large living room and flopped into one of the greasy brown corduroy sofas arranged around the walls. The room was littered with papers, books, CDs, vinyl and the remains of last night's TV dinner. The wall by the large sash window was dominated by two huge speakers, old fashioned and inelegant. In fact these had provoked the last in an increasingly bitter series of rows with Sal, which precipitated her departure. Needing some noise to dispel the claustrophobic stillness he picked up a compact disc called 'Band' and put it in the machine.

It contained the numbers he had to learn for the blues band he played in with old university friends. This band was another reason for the breakup of his marriage. He had, as Sal several times pointed out, failed to grow up. The disc contained two songs by a sixties blues group now featuring on adverts and suitable for his band to play in pubs when they managed to get the occasional infrequent gig. However, as soon as the first bars started to play he realised it just made him feel worse. He turned it off. The house was empty and desolate; the silence felt palpable. He needed someone to talk to. On the table he noticed the contents of the jacket pocket he'd emptied when he came in with the telephone message on top: he decided to give it a try. The number rang five times and then an answering machine clicked into life.

'The Vanarvi Astral Healing Centre is now closed but if you leave a number we will call you back.'

The voice was a woman's and, if it was the woman from Thursday, it now sounded a lot more appealing; husky in a sexy way. After a moment's hesitation he gave his name and number. In the kitchen he opened a bottle of red wine, catching a glimpse of his reflection in the glass of the cupboard. His sad eyes looked back at him confirming what a mess he'd become. He took the wine back into the living room, turned on the TV and settled back into the sofa. After three glasses any interest he possessed had evaporated and he drifted fitfully into a troubled sleep.

***

Tendrils of fog crept through the sash windows and began to pile up against the ceiling as he watched, unable to move. The fog began to slowly sink towards him. He could hear Sal washing up in the kitchen and although he shouted she didn't seem to hear him. He tried to tell her that the dark haired woman in the corner of the room shouldn't be there but wouldn't leave. The woman was sitting on the floor trying to tell him something he didn't want to hear. He thought he heard Sal say,

"She's the one you let out; she's going to bleed you."

Then the room got a lot smaller, in fact it was no longer a room and when he tried to stretch out his arms his hands immediately came into contact with cold damp stone. He was lying on his back on ice hard ground, frozen to it. He couldn't move and a crushing weight of stone was cracking his rib cage. He stared into the fog in panic, he could still see the woman's face drifting in and out of focus; she was both near and far away. Her features were indistinct; he saw only the shape of the long hair, glint of eyes and an impression of long sharp teeth.

Then something agonisingly sharp began to cut into his leg. The woman was holding a bloody flint knife. He started to scream but as he opened his mouth the fog poured into it wrapping itself round his tongue and slithering down his throat. He was making a desperate moaning sound but with no volume and with every moan breathing became more difficult as the fog slowly choked his lungs and his ribs broke. The agony of the cutting at his leg increased as the woman's face, laughing now, receded rapidly and disappeared. Now that the fog filled his mouth, throat and lungs it began to solidify. Breathing was no longer possible yet he still heard himself whimpering with pain and terror as he lost all control to panic and darkness.

Then, through the darkness, far distant, a ringing sound. It came nearer, grew louder until he jerked upright with a shock taking what seemed an age to recognise his surroundings and even longer to realise that he was staring at a newscaster's face on the TV screen. He'd spilt a glass of wine over himself and felt cold and sticky. There was still the ringing demanding to be heard and he finally recognised it as the phone. Groping round he located the handset and clasped it to his ear. His gasp of hello came out as a strangled yelp obviously confusing his interlocutor. He heard a woman's voice saying,

"Dr Glover, Dr Glover are you all right? This is Claire Vanarvi. You rang while I was out."

Giles had never been so relieved to hear a woman's voice before in his life.

"Sorry, I'd gone to get the week's shopping from Waitrose; I hope it's not a bad time to call."

As Giles began to recover his senses he found himself thinking that this was one of the nicest telephone voices he'd ever heard. Why had he described her to Jim as 'mad as a badger'? The voice, which he had subconsciously categorised as husky said in a slightly louder tone,

"Dr Glover, are you still there?"

Giles mumbled a response and the woman, whom he now thought of as Claire, continued.

"Thanks for calling me back. I realise I handled things badly the other day and must have come across as mad, but I do need to talk to you."

"No it's fine, thanks for getting back to me so soon."

Giles was by no means disinclined to talk. He was disorientated and needed female company so replied,

"Look, we could talk about it now if you like."

"No, I'd rather not if you don't mind, it's too complicated and not something we can do over the phone."

"Well, now would be good for me, I've got plenty of time."

"No, I'd rather not if you don't mind."

He replied drunk and peevish, without thinking,

"Well, you're the one who thinks it's important so why not?"

"Listen Dr Glover, I can't do it over the phone and I can't meet you tonight but we could meet over the weekend."

The mixture of frustration and booze brought out the spoilt child in Giles and he snapped back petulantly,

"Well I'm busy all weekend, this is the only time I can offer you."

"OK, I could meet you at the site on Monday."

"Can't do that either."

He could sense the exasperation on the other end of the line and knew he was being stupid and cutting off his nose to spite his face so offered Tuesday afternoon on site. He still sensed her frustration as she agreed but not before giving him her address in case he changed his mind about the weekend. The address was in Lindow, which gave him a brief flutter of unease making it too late to respond in a friendlier manner before she abruptly rung off.

He had good reason to remember Lindow: a celebrated archaeological find from the same Iron Age time period as his own site, but far more dramatic. He'd been a schoolboy volunteer with the team that unearthed a ritual killing preserved in the peat diggings of Lindow Moss. Known with characteristic gallows humour as Pete Marsh it was a particularly grisly find from an age when sacrificial murder had been carried out in an attempt to placate frightening and hostile gods.

He turned off the TV; silence reclaimed the room. The fog outside thickened as the events of the day hovered over him like a pall. His head was beginning to ache and the memories of the Lindow dig flickered, probing the edges of his consciousness. After half an hour of depressed torpor he decided to take a handful of pills and go to bed, but not before checking that the doors were locked and looking into every room in the house and under the bed.

For a time he lay awake listening to street noise and the old house settling itself for the night. He thought about how lonely he was and how he'd screwed up his life and those of everyone close to him even though they seemed to have moved on and started again. Eventually he dropped into an uneasy sleep with dreams populated by strange women, enclosed spaces and somewhere just out of sight the strangely grinning cadaver of Pete Marsh.

Having festered all day in bed on Saturday eating takeaways, and slept better that night, he awoke on Sunday, if not refreshed then at least able to function. The sky was deep blue and there was light frost on the roads and the few patches of grass in the square outside the house. So, after drinking a pot of strong coffee and smoking three cigarettes and a spliff for breakfast he started to rack his brain as to what to do with the remnant of the weekend. The problem was that his social life was blighted, he had no real friends so unless he made a special effort to organise something, or the band was playing, he tended to squander his weekends in solitude moping round the flat, watching TV, drinking and smoking.

Part of the cause of this had been a disastrous, short lived affair with one of his post grad students that he embarked on after Sal left. In the acrimonious aftermath of this he found most of his remaining social set had sided with his erstwhile girlfriend. He was reduced to a few old acquaintances, all of whom had wives and families and were fully occupied at weekends conducting self satisfied and inward looking activities to the exclusion of anyone else. Even worse, his extra mural activities with a student blighted his academic career and as a consequence he was now running an archaeology unit with no prospects and, since the recession and cuts to grant funding, less money.

Until, of course, the unexpected find at Skendleby. This, if it was interesting enough and he could muster the resources and energy to publish quickly, could, he hoped, restore his declining career. Maybe he could even sell it to television, become the first archaeologist on 'I'm a Celebrity'. That would show Richardson. It was the sudden shift in his train of thought that decided his day for him. He'd visit the site.

The drive to Skendleby lifted his spirits; the sun shone in a crisp blue sky although there were traces of gathering cloud over the hills. Once out of the city he followed the country lanes at the back of Skendleby Hall to the site. Parking his car at the end of a farm drive he followed the track across the fields. The excavation should have been deserted for the weekend but there were signs of activity. One of the site hut's doors was flapping open and tools and finds were scattered across the excavation. The earth around the burial feature was disturbed by a series of cracks around the suspected entrance. It looked like the site had been visited by vandals, a plague of moles and earth tremors.

On top of Devil's Mound there was something blackish at the spot Rose had been at the time of her accident. He wanted to be away from here but forced himself to investigate: on the mound he saw the eviscerated remains of two magpies. Their heads had been cut off and placed where the stomachs had been. The heads were angled down to make it seem they were staring through the earth into the chamber and as he looked closer in horrified fascination he saw their eyes had been removed and replaced by thorns. He jumped back in horror and rapidly backed away from the mound heart racing.

He paused to get his breath: what sort of thing would do that? It was obviously some type of warning but what did it mean? He walked back to his car and lit a cigarette, then glanced anxiously towards Skendleby Hall. Si Carver lived there and he wanted them off the site but would even a man like him stoop to this? The symbolic language of the warning belonged to a time when omens and the natural world meant more. Using social messaging and criminals would be more in Carver's line.

Then he thought back to Steve's story about the nutter who'd warned him off in the pub shortly before Rose was injured. This brought an image of Claire Vanarvi to mind. She'd been very worked up about the excavation and obviously wanted it stopped. Yet she didn't seem the type to resort to vandalism and criminal acts.

Now he was desperate to be away but first made himself ring Steve. He got an answering machine and left a message telling him to check the site over and get it cleaned up. Increasingly uncomfortable he kept looking back over his shoulder convinced someone was watching him from the tree line. He pocketed the phone, hurriedly secured the door to the shed and jogged back to the car.

He didn't want to return to his squalid lonely house so decided to check out Lindow. The drive along the back lanes didn't take long. He left the car in the small car park which served visitors to the common, crossed the road and followed the track across the Moss to the site where the body had been found.

This had been a major find and the nearest he'd come to making archaeological history. Yet he never felt comfortable with his memories of Lindow Man, a grisly and disturbing find. He'd been garrotted and pushed head first into a shallow pool of water on the Moss like the ones that he was now picking his way between. There'd been a thong of sinew wound around his neck, wound far too tight to be a collar, biting deep into the flesh. His head been dragged into a contorted position and two of the small vertebrae at the top of his spine had been broken. This was consistent, as the pathologists report stated, with simultaneous strangulation along with a heavy blow. Examinations of the head confirmed that in his last moments Lindow Man had received two heavy blows with a blunt instrument, which split the scalp driving fragments of bone down into the head. The brutality and frenzy of this attack had always disturbed Giles.

But it was the contrast between Lindow Man's sudden death and his life that was the most disconcerting; he'd led a prosperous and sheltered life. At the time of his death his finger nails were beautifully manicured. Why should such a well kept pampered individual have met such a savage death? These reflections now occupied Giles's thoughts all the way to the spot where he'd been discovered. The blackish pools of water shone dully as the clouds swept across the sky and the light darkened. This was not a place to hang about; so after a brief mooch round he retraced his steps.

Wandering back the sense of loneliness returned: he wanted to talk to someone who'd understand his mixed up feelings about the dig and his fucked up life. But of course there was no one. He worried that maybe his state of constant anxiety was the first symptom of a recurrence of the bouts of black dog depression which had been a feature of the last few years. His thoughts rambled; then he realised someone was talking to him.

"You ought to warn your friend that some of those pools he's walking across are quite deep."

The speaker was a middle aged woman, walking a dog and following the same path but in the opposite direction to Giles. As Giles explained he was alone he noticed the woman was peering over his shoulder at the way he'd just come. She obviously didn't believe him and said peevishly,

"Well he looked like he was with you! Yes, I saw him standing right next to you over in the middle of the

Moss a few minutes ago. He must have been with you: he had his hand on your shoulder."

She paused, looking disconcerted.

"Well, that's strange he seems to have gone now."

Giles suggested it had been a trick of the light, which had in fact changed over the last few minutes. The patches of sunlight were gone and the afternoon grown dark.

"I'm sure I saw a man with you, but I suppose you must be right, my eyes aren't what they were."

She paused again and he saw a flicker of uncertainty cross her face.

"Well, that's a relief because he looked most odd; almost like a scarecrow, dressed in some type of long black garment and…"

She looked across towards the Moss before gabbling,

"And he was moving in a most peculiar way."

Giles nodded then moved on; just as he crossed the road to the car park he turned round looking back over the Moss. He noticed that the dog walker had decided not to continue with her walk and was following only about 30 yards behind him and walking rather more quickly than the dog seemed comfortable with.

He briefly toyed with the idea of walking round the area to try to find the location of Claire Vanarvi's house but the Moss was bleak and desolate and instead he returned to the car. He leant against the fence with one hand as he scraped the mud off his left boot with a stick. Then he changed over and as his right hand grabbed at the fence it felt something squishy and soft. He jerked back in revulsion his heart racing as he saw, in front of his car, a line of small, partially decomposed field animals, mice, shrews and voles, had been strung up by their tails, dead on the fence.

"Christ where did they come from, they weren't here when I parked."

He stared at them in horror trying to wipe his hand on his jeans then got in the car and drove off as fast as it would go.

CHAPTER 7
OH GOD WHAT IS THAT WHICH STANDS AND WATCHES?

His last job of the day completed, a meeting of the ill attended church's 'young people for Jesus' group, Reverend Ed Joyce removed his clerical collar and moved with pleasurable anticipation into his study. He could forget about his parish, its peculiar worries and Richardson's crudely disguised threats to escape into the world of scholarship. In that world he was safe.

He paused to glance with just a hint of satisfaction at the poster from his first parish which covered the wall above the fireplace. It was a picture of himself in front of St Barnaby's church in Norfolk and underneath it was the legend 'Are you man enough to serve the Church of England?' Very appropriate, he felt, to put forward a role model that would encourage young people into the clergy. He felt that now he would have preferred it to read 'man or woman enough' but back in those unenlightened backwaters that would have been too modern.

He moved to his desk, unlocked its top drawer and extracted the sheets of stained and yellowing paper, wondering for a moment what impulse had led him to lock them away. What would these pages reveal that Heatly Smythe had considered unfit for Oriel College? Perhaps some record that might make his work on Heatly Smythe's prosaic, self satisfied letters exciting enough to attract publication. If it was a scandal, then perhaps some erudite reflexions of a moral nature from him could result in a work that would be both scholarly and populist. He rubbed his hands together in anticipation, took a sip of tea, opened a packet of chocolate digestives and sat down to read.

18th Nov 1776
Dear Sir,
Today I had thought to bestir myself from those melancholy humours that have of late shaped my inclinations, with an account of some of our local superstitions and customs in which you will no doubt discern echoes of Selborne. However, your maxim 'It is the hardest thing in the world to shake off superstition' echoing only too well ancient Lucretius, leads, I find, my pen in another direction. Alas I now find it hard to mock such antic foolishness as once we did when young before the fire in our chambers of reason at Oriel. I fear that what I have set down will not serve its purpose in extending our scientific correspondence but will remain hidden in the repository of my troubled soul.

    First you must understand that betwixt the fields that shape this parish and that of Woodford lies a stretch of ground unmarked by any sign of habitation or even the slightest trace of pastoral endeavour. This ground now amounts to waste although a countryman such as you would rapidly deduce that it contains all the prerequisites that would sustain a prosperous village and be a fit place to test some of the recent agrarian theories. Neither is there record of any habitation by the ancients, nor does any track or way cross it, despite the lane between the parishes taking many a winding detour round its periphery. My abode, well known to you from my epistles, sits a short way from the church at the end of the estate where the lane emerges from the wood on its quest to join the parish of St George's. Yet never in my years as priest of these two parishes have I seen a soul cross this land. The reason lies in local folklore, for in that field there is a feature called by the ignorant "Devil's Mound."

Yet, I fear I must confess, not only by the ignorant but also by the better sort, though it must be adduced that this counts for little in this forgotten and benighted part of the Kingdom. All in fact consider this mound to be the work of the devil and the fields surrounding to be cursed sufficiently strongly to imperil the life and mortal soul of any who would stray within its bounds. A view held even by the Squire who, you recall, betimes affords me the honour of his society. Though much disinclined to discourse upon the matter he will substantiate the belief with a list of events occasioned on those who through the years have attempted to assay such a feat. Neither will he be persuaded by my explanations of the new scientific understanding, so recently adumbrated by Mr Hutton in his exposition on uniformitarianism, of the forces which shape the earth. That in fact the mound is merely a consequence of the ancient sheets of ice that must at one period of antiquity have shaped the fields in which we live.

Alas such rational thought is of no avail in these parts where ignorance remains unchallenged if not venerated. The Squire asserts that the mound has some type of supernatural curator who watches it from the shelter of the woods that fringe the estate and which he is thought to inhabit. A tradition of the Squire's family has it that in the confused period of the reign of Richard ll one of his ancestors encountered this curator and was for his pains cursed unto death. But that before his death he divulged that the malign force that had struck him down in the prime of manhood was a form of evil yet more ancient even than the mound. That hereafter he and his descendants abjure and eschew any thoughts of visiting those fields. Signs of the curator, it seems, are rare but his appearance betokens an evil about to fall and is prefaced by strange lights that appear to float above the mound and between the trees. More on this matter he refused to speak of, although by now my curiosity was ignited. These past days my mind has much run on that conversation for reasons that I will set down on the morrow. But now there is a shadow moving amongst the trees and it grows dark. To dwell on such matters will, I fear, unsettle my sleep.

I thank you for the copy of Scopoli's work ascertaining the nature of the birds of the Tirol and Carniola that you sent to improve my mood following my recent indisposition. I fear that I am still too saturnine to have enjoyment of such diversion for, as with the Dane,

'I have of late, but wherefore I know not, lost all my mirth.'

I will bestir myself to the fireplace to while away some hours and take a glass of good Burgundy to encourage healthy repose and the hope of a better morrow.

I am, sir, your most obedient friend and servant.

21st November 1776
Sir,
I have, these last three days, been unable to bring myself to the task of writing lest that which I have tried to suppress should reawaken. Yet now it stirs! So this I will set down.

I had not long sat before the fire when I was disturbed from my contemplations by a loud knocking at the door, which, on being opened, revealed John Rundle carrying a lanthorne to light his way. His mother being in the last stages of a chest palsy and like to die required spiritual comfort in her last hours. The way was not far and he had brought his cart in which to convey us.

The night was cold, yet a crisp manner of cold, and therefore not unpleasant. I was in truth not too much displeased by this turn of events having been solitary of late and inclined to thoughts of morbidity. Mother Rundle rallied slightly at my arrival and I was able to impart some of the teachings of our Lord Jesus Christ, much to her comfort. In the damp and chill of her cottage it surprised me that she had endured this existence for so long. It must have been near midnight when she departed the sorrows of this world for the blessings of the next, secure in the knowledge of her salvation. Although John was willing to convey me back I considered it ill to separate him from his family and devotions. The departure of the blessed ever leaves an impression on those left behind and with mind much occupied I ventured forth to walk home. One of the few benefits of such remote livings is the comparative safety of the rude highways.

By the time I had reached within five minutes' walk of my abode and was passing the churchyard my spirits had begun to revive, such are the consolations of our Saviour. I decided for reasons which now elude me to walk through the churchyard and follow the path along the boundary wall of the estate house rather than to follow the lane. In this manner, I now believe, I was ensnared.

The sky was clear and the light of the moon radiantly illuminated my way whilst the firmament shone in all its glory. All was quiet in the churchyard, the neatness of which reflected well on the diligence of Mr Brigstock the sexton. In the stillness and gentle light I could see the vapour of my breathings precede me and in a mood approaching satisfaction I gained the ancient and rough wall that girdles the estate.

Being somewhat out of breath, I paused a moment to rest and, leaning on the wall, gazed over to observe the effects of moonlight on the woods. Through the trees, shining clear and bright in the distance, stood the feature the unlettered villagers call Devil's Mound, illuminated by moonbeams as was the case in the land of faerie in the books we read as children.

I collect not why the thought of a scientific examination of the feature came to mind but I fancy it was a remembrance of the works of Mr Aubrey and Mr Stukeley and their experiments on the burial mounds of our ancient British forebears from the time of the Druids.

Yet I confess not to have felt the temptation to assay such a task before this hour, or why I should attempt to refute my scientific classifications of the mound's natural origin. But indeed the thought of the practical application of natural philosophy dispersing the heathen darkness much cheered me and I returned to my abode with a lighter tread than that with which I had quit it.

On the morrow I rose to a bright morn with the early mist already dispersed by Phoebus's chariot as it rose in the east. The verdant sward was covered in a light hoar frost and, anxious to be about my work after my devotions and a hurried breaking of fast, I hastened with my measuring equipment to the estate boundary and from there to Devil's Mound. At the fringe of the woods I discerned but vaguely a very white faced fellow in black about some business of his own. Not wishing in any way to appear that my business was sub rosa I hailed him in the manner of an upright Christian. I received no answer but on turning to remind the fellow of his obligation to display respect to his betters I could find no trace of him.

I spent the period until noon pleasantly enough conducting a limited, but accurate, survey of the mound. It now seemed to me quite possible that it be a burial mound of the ancients although smaller than those of which we read and had recorded during our happy days of enquiry at Oriel. There seemed no evidence of the mound having been tampered with; so the possibility presented itself of my effecting an opening and gazing on a burial of the ancient type, pristine and complete with grave goods. I determined that in the afternoon I would return with pick and shovel and the aid of a willing labourer and drive a tunnel from the top to the centre of the mound. I whiled away the passage of my walk home with reflections of the monogram I would write and present to our old college library. This pleasant reverie was briefly interrupted by my catching a distant and fleeting glimpse of the surly fellow I had greeted earlier.

Having sent Mrs Wardle to fetch Mr Brigstock I fortified myself with some splendid game pie and cold hare washed down with half a bottle of good Madeira. Brigstock arrived and after I had complimented him on his labours in the churchyard I outlined to him my plans for the afternoon. To my surprise the fellow proved obstinate and refused to accompany me. When I pushed him further his manner bordered on the impertinent as he not only refused to change his mind but to suggest that I, as a man of the cloth, should have no such inclinations. I dismissed him from my presence and made a mental note to seek a replacement.

The hours of remaining daylight were few and remembering Virgil's advice on the 'hastening winter sun' determined to be about my business. The day had grown chill so donning greatcoat and muffler I hastened with my tools of excavation to the Mound. I was relieved to see no sign of the fellow lurking by the fringe of the woods but the fields enclosing the mound had acquired a sombre aspect. Notwithstanding I pressed on and identified a spot atop the mound to begin my passage.

Now it is a curious thing, but I am sure that when I left the shelter of the trees, the fields were in sunlight. Yet not five minutes later when I stood atop the mound posed to deliver the first blow to loosen the earth with my pick the sky was almost dark. Clouds had gathered out of a windless clear sky, with rapidity hard to believe. As I struck the first blow a fierce gust did suddenly blow up to such an extent that I was temporarily blinded by earth debris carried on the wind. Once my vision was recovered and the moisture in my eyes under control, I understood myself to be in the grip of a storm generated by some freak of nature and determined that I should postpone my antiquarian activities until more clement weather return.

I must own that I was by no means reluctant to have reached that decision as by now the atmosphere of the place had changed from the cheer of the morning and its desolation depressed my spirits. I collect also that large numbers of great black birds, which these last days have infested the churchyard, had gathered in the great trees by the estate boundary and commenced a harsh and discordant clarion.

I was much, I repent to relate, discomforted by these creatures, which the vulgar regard as harbingers of the tomb, so took up my equipment and hurried against the wind towards the gate in the estate wall. Just before reaching this sylvan shelter I felt, I know not why, a sudden and overpowering compulsion to turn round and regard the mound. I did so and saw to my shock and amazement that the top of the hump where I had stood had a new occupant. There stood a shape, a type of human form clothed in black, too far off to be distinct but the contrast between the black of the garments and the white of what I took to be its face was strangely terrible to contemplate. I confess I turned and ran for the woods. Once having gained the shelter I turned again to ascertain whether the occasioning of my alarm should have been imagination.

Would that it had, for what I beheld chilled my blood. Now it is a singular thing but it was the way that the creature moved rather than its appearance that heightened my alarm; terrible but insubstantial as if boneless though that appearance was. It seemed to gain distance in a series of awful twisting jerks, its apparel, like rotted grave windings, flapping round it. But even worse, and it was this that that caused my very blood to freeze, it seemed also to have arrived at its new place before it had left its last – to be both here and there at the same time. Its movement was accompanied by a sound like the creaking of old leather aprons being rubbed together or the beating of great ancient wings. For a moment I stood rooted to the earth with terror; then with a shout for Our Lord's protection I dropped my tools and fled.

22nd Nov 1776
Sir
Having written the above I felt disinclined to continue my epistle as the daylight was receding. It took the bustle and energy of Mrs Wardle's lighting of the lamps and candles to restore any form of equanimity. I dined on some excellent mutton chops, followed by a dish of toasted Cheshire cheese, and then retired with a decanter containing the remains of the burgundy to my study to peruse and correct the translations of Horace's Epodes which I have as you may recall recently effected. In this manner I whiled away some hours wishing myself with Horace on his estate in the Sabine Hills. I was indulging myself with the lines where he
   'Lightens all your ills with wine and song
   Sweet comforts for the ugliness of pain'
when Mrs Wardle knocked and entered to inform me that, as all in the house was ready for the morrow, she would return to her cottage. I heard her leave and was

therefore somewhat surprised when soon after she returned to inform me that behind the church, beyond the estate there were strange lights to be seen. I had no wish to leave the comforts of my study where the fire blazed and the candles shed soft light on the pages but could tell from Mrs Wardle's expression that as the shepherd of the local flock it was my duty to investigate. So, after having instructed her to send a message to the Squire, I left the study and with great reluctance robed myself and lightening a lanthorne set out into the night.

Outside the moonlight cast the shadow of the church tower in sharp relief and, after having assured myself that all was well, I, with as great a fortitude as I could muster, proceeded to the estate boundary whence I had returned in such haste that afternoon. Long before I reached the wall I could see the lights which had so troubled Mrs Wardle. They brought to memory the Jack o' Lanthorne of which we read with such fear, yet enjoyment, as boys. The lights appeared to emanate from the mound, around which they seemed to dance in a circular motion. My sight was too much obstructed by the trees to see clearly but I fancied that it must be some fellows up to no good. Yet no one from these parts would visit such a spot, even in daylight. The only person I had ever seen in the proximity apart from myself was he from whom I had fled this afternoon. At that thought the blood ran cold in my veins and I determined to return to the house and await the Squire and not remain like doomed Hector outside the Scaean Gate.

In the depth of night the trunks of the trees melded with the darkness but suddenly a patch of darkness separated itself from them and turned its white and awful visage upon me. It stood regarding me from a distance of no more than nine feet and on its face, the oddness of which I could not begin to describe, was the appearance of some manner of malicious and sardonic smile.

I was unnerved and unable to move. I knew this thing lived outside the will of our creator and that its disembodied malice would not be possible to contest. Slowly, it raised a limb from the folds of its awful rotting cloak and made an almost stately claw like gesture then with a sound like wind disturbing dry dead leaves it was gone. I knew the gesture spoke of my fate and with legs quivering I turned and for the second time that day ran. By the house I met the Squire with some fellows whom he sent on to the boundary wall. Myself he took inside and had me sit in my chair in the study. Having ordered Mrs Wardle to fetch brandy he addressed himself to me in the following manner.

'You look like you have seen the devil, Sir. Here drink this. My lads will go no further than the wall, what's over there is to be left alone. We keep to our part of this world, they keep to theirs. I've tried to tell you before, Sir, like it says in one of your books 'there are more things in Heaven and earth than are dreamt about in your philosophy'. Do not meddle. Leave well alone. One more thing, Sir, I like not the look of that solitary dark cloaked fellow that you have lately taken on to watch by the church. My advice is to send him from here.'

With that he departed leaving me to the terrors of the night. I hear the noise of wings, the crows, that filthy rustle of their great black feathered limbs. Surely not in the darkness. Oh God.

23rd Nov 1776
Sir
I proffer no salvation as I now collect that these letters will never be sent. I write only to let out that which I cannot inwardly contain. These writings I will secrete against the day on which they may prove of use to another soul that has tampered as I have, with that which is best left alone. I slept ill in the night, and such sleep as I had was wretched, nightmares haunted and filled with leathery rustlings that I could scarcely distinguish from reality. Whether I did rise in the night, pull aside the bed curtains and look out of the window to see the figure at the bottom of the garden amongst the apple trees or if I dreamt it is of no matter. Neither option gives me hope. Neither did the morn bring any cheer, the day being dull and cold.

It watches......

It watches from the trees and seems to come by degrees closer to the house yet when I direct Mrs Wardle's attention to it she sees or effects to see nothing. She has told me that she must away after luncheon to visit a relative who has taken sick and lives towards Poynton and may not return for some days. I believe her not. She may not see what I see but she fears. Yes, she fears. I darest not to church; I know he has been there!!

This evening I felt a disturbance in the shrubs by the window of the drawing room and fancied I heard dry laughter in the air. I shall not to bed tonight but bank up the fire in the study and remain there until morning. The great crows are loud again tonight: what do they sense?

I shall endeavour to beseech Almighty God to bring me comfort in the darkness. In the light of the day I shall send for a carriage. How dark it seems to be, O how dark.

Is he within the house? No, there by the lych-gate, he watches. How dark it seems.

What is it in the mound that I have disturbed? Where is the reason? Oh Lord protect and comfort thy servant.

24th
Oh God, what is that which stands and watches?

***

And that was how it ended. Ed Joyce sat in his armchair in silence for several minutes before he could tear his eyes away from the page. The ending was abrupt. The writing of the last section clearly deranged but the impression of horror was palpable; he could feel it in the room, with him. In fact so much so that he felt a reluctance to leave his chair and turn round in case there was something behind him. He knew that he was sitting in the same room in which Heatly Smythe had written these pages. Despite all his modern ideas about religious metaphors and symbols, there was in the journal a paralysing sense of terror and, like Heatly Smythe, he wished that the mound had been left well alone. During the rest of the evening he felt uneasy and waited until Mary was ready to come to bed. As he lay

sleepless in the dark the same phrase repeated in his head.
'Oh God what is that which stands and watches?'

CHAPTER 8
CAN THE DEAD SPEAK?

Hung over and frustrated with the mass of bureaucracy Giles was relieved to be told Steve was calling from the site. He hated Mondays, always spent either in the vast but dingy basement rooms of the Unit or even worse, in a series of tediously pointless meetings. An unusually excited Steve blurted out,

"Gi, we've located the entrance and we're not the first to find it."

"Hey great work man, tell me."

He lit a cigarette and leaned back in his chair, feet on the desk to listen.

"We'd only been on site about an hour when Jan broke through all the Iron Age shit and hit a new layer, an in-filled ditch and it's much older. Rose was right, Giles, we've got something: it must be a burial and I think we've nearly got the entrance. We could be in tomorrow."

"You sure? Jeez, that's great Steve."

"It's not all great: there's something odd about it: it looks like our villagers found it first and then sealed it right back up, even tried to restore it. Plus whatever is messing with the site hasn't stopped. But we can live with that a couple more days I guess 'cos we can excavate and be off site by the end of the week. I can have it ready and recorded by tomorrow. Seems you've got your five minutes of fame after all, Gi."

He asked Steve to meet him back at the Unit after work with more details and rang off.

So this was a special site. He rang the *Journal* and left Jim a message to be at the site with Lisa tomorrow by mid day, then settled at his desk to while away the grey hours of admin until Steve arrived. By six fifteen he was impatient, bored and was toying with the idea of leaving a message to meet at the Royal Oak when the door crashed open and Steve burst in. He brought updated site plans and photographs, which he spread on the table, hands filthy with excavation dirt. The grubby site plan showed clearly the excavated segment of the mound.

"This is the real deal Gi; a ritual site, and if it wasn't for the fact that there's no other evidence in the area, I'd say definitely Neolithic. It's like a hurriedly put together version of a chambered cairn although there shouldn't be one here. Look at the trench: it's the foundations of a wooden palisade. The fill is organic material and from the size of it, it must have been small tree trunks about 6 feet high screening the barrow and containing it. But look at this here, just between the trench and the entrance; it's the soil fill we found just before we packed up for the day."

He pointed to a darker patch on the plan about one metre from the entrance.

"We think that this is some kind of pit, maybe ritual. Jan and Leonie are going to have a closer look at it first thing tomorrow. From its position right in front of the entrance we think it's linked to whatever's in the chamber. But this is the weird bit, Gi, and I can't think of a parallel: the entrance has already been opened once.

"What we found isn't the original sealing. So what was it that made our boring villagers open it up then reseal it, and reseal it bloody quickly? It makes no sense. I mean it's been there all those years right next to them, so why suddenly break into it? But, from the evidence it's clear they not only rapidly closed up the chamber but then equally quickly reburied it under a great mound of earth. Why? Unless whatever it was they saw in there really freaked them so much they couldn't stand to be near the place any more. Hey, perhaps we should have accepted the offer from that sorry looking vicar."

"Yeah, well that's certainly different."

" Yeah and it gets even stranger because the earth covering the mound contains the latest dateable evidence on the whole site; so they must have re-buried it then immediately abandoned the village that had been their home for hundreds of years. So you and your reputation may have made it big time 'cos you've not only got an important find but you may have the makings of a horror movie."

"Yeah, whatever, but we'll get plenty of coverage."

Giles smiled as Steve moved back from the table to accept the cigarette he offered. He rubbed his eyes; the only light in the large basement came from the pool provided by the Angle poise lamp on the table. They smoked in silence for a few moments thinking what they could get out of this increasingly peculiar site. But the silence gradually became oppressive and when Giles suggested the pub and then a curry Steve agreed straight off.

The Royal Oak was cheerful and noisy as they entered, a good antidote to the gloom of the unit. Giles bought two pints of Pedigree and carried them across to the corner table. Steve swallowed half his drink in one go, carefully placed the glass back on the beer mat and leant back in his chair. Giles thought he looked pale, dirty and dishevelled, as archaeologists tend to do, but also troubled. After half an hour of desultory conversation and a second pint Giles was ready to suggest that they go to eat when Steve, having hesitated twice, started to speak more urgently.

"OK, I'd better tell you: had some trouble with the team on site, Leonie in particular. I think she's off her head and it's getting to the others. Maybe it's because we've been on it too long but the sooner we finish there the better. The tool shed was vandalised again last night only hours after I shut it when I cleaned the place up. Don't ever ask me to do that again."

"Sorry, Steve I won't, I was too strung out to do it myself."

"Yeah, OK, but listen: there's a dead fox inside, head was missing, smelt like it'd been dead for ages; wasn't there yesterday. What's all that about? And where have all those bloody noisy crows come from?"

He broke off as if to collect his thoughts.

"What's going on? Who's doing it? It's like the dig's being stalked. Ever since Rose started going on about the mound someone's been watching from that copse on the estate boundary. There's occasionally something like this on rural digs: you know, a combination of working with the long dead and morbid imagination. But even I feel someone watching when I close the place down at night and no one's got less fucking imagination me."

Steve's flow was interrupted by the ringing of his mobile. He answered and muttered a few words and then looked up at Giles.

"Can't make the curry, sorry, Gi, that was Anna, she's going to pick me up here in five minutes and wants to go and see a band at the uni. Just time for one more though."

As they were finishing the third pint a slim dark haired girl wearing tight jeans picked her way to the table and wrapped her arms around Steve's neck. Giles thought he recognised her as one of the history department's post grad students. Steve put down his glass and kissed the girl, pushed back his long hair, and got up to leave. Then he turned back to Giles.

"Oh yeah, almost forgot: I spoke to Rose today. Strange conversation; was glad when it ended, made my flesh creep. Soon as I walked in she hissed at me 'the dead can speak.' She was rambling of course, told me someone had got inside her head and led her to the mound. She was hysterical: tried to tell me about some dead thing in black that attacked her but she was shouting so loud a nurse came in and told me to go. As I was leaving she called out, 'don't excavate, it's what it wants: it's waiting for you, it knows, it's been waiting, it's beyond death, it was never alive.' I got out of there pretty fuckin' quick but I could still hear her halfway down the corridor."

He turned to go stopped for a moment and murmured:

"Sorry to just drop this on you but that's what comes with being in charge."

Giles said nothing just watched the dishevelled Steve and the slim hipped girl weave their way through the crowded pub to the door wondering how he managed to attract a never failing supply of attractive young women. Then he sat back with his drink thinking over Steve's unease; he was glad he hadn't told him about Carver and Richardson. He reached across and picked up a tattered copy of the evening paper left on an adjacent table, its front page headline screamed 'Violent maniac loose in south of city, streets unsafe at night.'

The piece reported a series of random, motiveless attacks along an axis leading from the area round the university along the main routes south out of the city. The police were baffled and had released no information other than a warning that the perpetrator was highly disturbed and that people on the streets after dark had to take special care. He was about to turn over and read further when he noticed that the paper had a small feature on tomorrow's excavation so he turned to that. Thinking of the excavation worried him: it was too hurried, almost as if something was pushing them to go too fast, he tossed the paper back onto its table.

Alone he wished he had a girlfriend like Steve always seemed to have. Any girl would do; in the pub all the women were either in groups or couples. He didn't want to return to his empty, shabby house so he drank on alone until closing time. That night he had the dream again: he was closed up in the frozen stone chamber with the frightening dark haired woman. It shook him up so much that he lay awake till five and then almost slept through the alarm.

***

Jim arriving early parked up the Shogun outside Lisa's flat and rang the bell. She was eating a piece of toast as she opened the door and unenthusiastically offered him a coffee. Jim noted the colourless flat reflected the void personality of its owner. Since her illness she'd maintained a strict routine that dictated the pattern of her life. It was this clinical desire for organisation which had made her first year as a freelance photographer successful. Well, that and the influence of her father. He sat at the pine table in the sparse kitchen and read the notice board on the wall where Lisa had written down all her appointments for the week. While he drank his coffee waiting for her to gather and check equipment he gazed around the flat.

It was a one bed-roomed apartment with combined living and dining space and a small bathroom, well maintained and decorated and yet entirely impersonal with no more atmosphere than apartments bought to let. No pictures, memorabilia or mess; nothing that spoke of the owner; a complete contrast to her parental home, which was filled with mementos of the career, interests and successes of her father, along with every modern trend in furnishing and conspicuous consumption.

Jim was trying to work out how the houses of the father and the daughter could be so different, occupying both ends of the spectrum from vacant to vulgar, when Lisa entered the room. Perhaps it was because he'd been thinking about her that made him study her more closely than usual. He saw, despite her attempt to conceal appearance, she'd grown up to be an attractive woman.

She did everything she could to disguise this, trying to fade into the background, unnoticed. It was like seeing someone for the first time and it jarred with his normal acceptance of her as just the daughter of a friend he'd known since she was a toddler. Lisa wore an anorak over her oatmeal sweater and Primark jeans. Her hair was scraped back into a pony tail with an elastic band and, as always, wore no makeup: like camouflage. There was no conversation: he finished the coffee and they left the flat, but there was something different about Lisa today: a type of impatience he hadn't noticed before and that she was trying to conceal.

In the car she reminded him in a bored flat tone that tonight was her father's pre- Christmas drinks party and attendance was obligatory. This party was a tradition. Councillor Richardson annually held what he called the 'first event of the festive season' at the beginning of December and intended it to set a tone of opulence that others would find difficult to match. Lisa was her normal subdued self during the drive and some of this transferred itself to Jim. Perhaps it was the thought of having to put in an appearance at Derek's party, which would painfully extend what was already going to be a long day. He'd lost interest in the site and was irritated with Giles, who seemed to operate on two levels: either self pitying sponging off him or an almost manic enthusiasm for the dig evidenced by the tone of the phone message he had left.

When Giles first the idea of the *Journal*'s exclusive coverage of the excavation he'd been carried along by the persuasive manner. Yet, this morning, Giles told him that despite their agreement, there was to be coverage by the local TV news and maybe other coverage drummed up by the university coms people. He was reflecting on how most of his old friendships brought him little pleasure these days when he realised they'd reached the estate boundary. He steered the

Shogun down the bumpy track through the trees and parked up behind one of the Unit's minibuses. He helped Lisa get her gear out of the car aware of a rustling noise above him growing in volume. Looking up he saw that the crown of every tree was packed full of dark black crows.

The day was cold and sombre without any trace of a breeze, the atmosphere seeming to muffle the sounds of the dig. At the entrance to the site an unusually animated Steve was in conversation with two mud splattered young women who he could vaguely place as Jan and Leonie. Not a conversation, a heated argument and Jim wondered how people could get so worked up about scraping about in the mud to find bits of pot and bone. By now he was close enough to hear Leonie shouting.

"What else do you need to make you understand, Steve? Rose was attacked, I'm being stalked, a vicar wants to exorcise the site and someone's leaving long dead animals and birds all over. I can still smell that fucking crow on my fingers."

"Leonie, chill: you only need to hang on for a few days then we're away."

"Steve, how fucking stupid are you? The villagers walled this thing up to hide it and then ran away 'cos they were terrified, and you, you want to open it."

She threw her trowel at his feet and rushed off towards the mound. Jim saw she was crying. Steve placed an arm around Jan's shoulders and she momentarily rested her head against his chest only to quickly straighten up when she saw Jim watching. Steve removed his arm and greeted them.

"Sorry about that, archaeologists can be as temperamental as actors; actually it's your visit that caused it. Leonie thinks we should postpone excavating the barrow until after the pit's been investigated. She thinks it has some sort of ritual function warning anyone who wants to mess with the entrance. Claims that it will only take them another day and that what they find will help us when we open the feature.

"But Giles is dead set on opening it today so you, and the film crew over there, can record it. Anyway it's too late in the year to excavate properly so the sooner we get the thing opened up the sooner we get off this site and that's what most of us want; it's too cold and dark to be doing this type of work in December."

While he was talking Giles appeared, clean shaven, reminding Jim of how he used to look before his problems.

"Hey, Jim, you're just in time,"

The clean cut Giles called out,

"We're almost ready to break through into what we hope is a unique Neolithic barrow. Steve thinks it's like a really small version of the Five Well Chambered Cairn. But the real deal is that this one is in a location unlike any other. Congratulations, you're about to record history being made."

The journalists followed Giles who continued to brief them as they crossed the forlorn and neglected village excavation. Clustered around the entrance of the mound were most of the diggers listening to Leonie. She was standing on the edge of the pit waving her arms and shouting.

"Look, you can see why we shouldn't do this: it's entertainment not archaeology, we're messing with something we don't understand."

As Giles reached the mound Leonie turned on him and demanded,

"Listen, Giles, please delay opening the chamber until I've excavated this pit."

Giles was angry; she was challenging him in front of the press. He noticed the film crew was filming the scene and he didn't want human interest, he wanted the coverage to record a major discovery. He asked calmly as he could.

"Why Leonie? What difference would that make?"

"You're meant to be an archaeologist, you should know: if you open the mound before the pit you destroy evidence and lose what it can tell you about the mound."

"Don't worry we'll be careful."

She spat out at him,

"Right, then here's the real reason. Once you've seen what I find in it you won't want to go anywhere near that chamber."

And he shouted back,

"Now you're being hysterical."

Steve pushed past Giles reaching out to Leonie, trying to calm her down.

She turned and slapped him hard across the face then strode across to Giles.

"I'm leaving this dig, it's a mess. You do what you like, do what you fucking well like. You can't screw around with this type of thing. You bloody fool; do you still not get what happened to Rose?"

She burst into tears and half ran towards the site exit with Jan calling after her.

Jim turned to Lisa, she was laughing.

It took Giles and Steve about half an hour to calm people down and reorganise the opening of the chamber. During this time, while Lisa was checking light settings and working out the best camera shots, Jim, feeling like a spare part, stood by the site boundary looking across to the woods which bordered the estate. His attention was drawn to a movement or disturbance at the edge of the woods. He was trying to make out what it was when he was tapped on the arm and turning round saw Jan, hands deep in the pocket of her coat and with sloped shoulders, looking diminutive and defenceless.

"Mind if I talk to you?"

Jim had to resist the impulse to put an arm round her like would with his children, he asked her,

"I can see how upset your friend is but I don't understand all the stuff about the pit and the chamber."

"She thinks they're linked in some way and the pit's a warning. What we found down there is pretty disturbing. It's been filled in a deliberate way; it's sealed in a series of different layers. Each of these layers contains fetish objects: things of power that have been deliberately placed in context. But what really freaked Leonie is that not all of the finds in this pit are Neolithic; some are contemporary with the village. This means that before they covered the feature over they'd found this pit directly in front of the entrance. It bothered them enough to replace it as it was and to add their own power fetish for extra protection.

"Leonie's sure we've nearly reached down to what's really buried in there. She thinks its part of the villagers' attempts to keep whatever's inside that feature buried. So we should delay opening the chamber until we excavate the pit. She feels it so strongly it's freaking her out, stopping her sleeping, she's sure it's not just her imagination. She says we're being watched from the woods over there; thinks she was followed home last night. She's overwrought and strung out, but I guess we all feel a bit that way now."

Jim could see Jan was almost as scared as Leonie. To him it was no big deal if the photos and story in the *Journal* were a day late. So if it calmed things down he'd suggest putting back the opening until the excavation of the pit was finished to everyone's satisfaction. He was just about to suggest this to Jan when there was a shout from over by the mound.

"OK, get ready, we're going in."

CHAPTER 9
THE OPENING: JIM AND LISA

Giles was standing with his back to the mound explaining to the semi circle of journalists, excavators and interested visitors how the feature was going to be opened. Behind him crouching by the entrance was Steve with Lisa close up holding the camera. Jim found himself at the back having to stare over people's heads and shoulders to get a glimpse of the entrance. It was too late to stop this now but when he turned to tell Jan he saw she'd disappeared. Then he saw her small hooded figure standing over at the perimeter fence staring towards the woods.

Giles hyping it up: introduced Steve as one of the world's leading Neolithic specialists. Jim thought maybe Giles had missed his true vocation in life and could have made a career promoting media events. All the same, he felt a sense of unease mixed with distaste for the way this was being conducted; ironic considering Giles was turning it into some type of media event for the benefit of his paper. He briefly entertained the image of a celebrity opening; perhaps the footballers and wags whose mansions were close by would be available. Then the small crowd surged forwards and he saw Steve had started.

The work on the entrance had stopped at the point where, theoretically at least, only a few loosely positioned large stones remained between the outside world and what the scientific survey suggested was a small passage leading to a burial chamber. Most of the preparatory work had been completed so Steve's task should, therefore, be largely cosmetic taking only a few minutes. This would allow a shot of the opening followed by a shot of Steve entering the chamber. What followed would depend on what the chamber contained and whether it was in a fit state to be filmed. Whatever the result, Jim had reserved a full page, which would largely comprise colour pictures. The *Journal*'s readership would not want too much archaeological detail and if the chamber proved either not to exist or to contain nothing of note, then the piece would work just as well as local interest focused on personalities at the site.

He began to feel the cold and realised they'd been watching Steve for fifteen minutes. The murmurings of expectation had ceased as the onlookers shifted from foot to foot shuffling and stamping about in the still, cold air. It seemed that between the entrance and the chamber the short passage was partially filled with rubble; not a promising beginning. The fifteen minutes extended to forty-five and Jim began to think that, not only had this been miscalculated, but that the whole event had been a waste of time. He could see Lisa becoming increasingly frustrated and biting at her finger tips and Giles crouched by the entrance, shouting at Steve,

"Come on, Steve, get a move on it's freezing out here."

There was a piercing scream.

***

Later, when Jim tried to recall the scene he could never quite get the sequence. It seemed distant; almost as if everything happened in slow motion or the participants were wading through treacle.

The scream came from behind him in the parking area. He turned and saw a rapidly moving woman in a hooded coat with long dark hair. She was shouting and gesticulating as she ran up on to the path that led through the village excavation to the mound. Striding across the mud in long dark boots, coat flapping around her legs, she reminded Jim of a strangely elegant scarecrow. He heard her shout,

"Dr Glover. Stop. You've got to stop. You don't know what you're meddling with. Please, please stop this now."

Jim supposed that this must be the woman Giles had described as 'mad as a badger' in the restaurant. Close up she was extremely attractive, if inappropriately dressed for a mad rant on an archaeological site.

A loud yelp of pain came from the direction of the chamber and Steve staggered out, hands clasped over his eyes. He lurched a few steps towards Giles who threw his arms out to support him. The elegant scarecrow pushed her way through the confused onlookers towards Giles at the epicentre of the drama.

Jim caught a scent of perfume as she passed and then had to blink his eyes closed. A violent tearing wind had suddenly risen blowing directly out of the mouth of the chamber, howling across them, whipping dust and debris up from the site into their eyes. When he opened them and blinked through the tears he saw the TV cameraman on his knees holding his face. The mad woman had reached Giles and was haranguing him while Giles, obviously unnerved, was trying to support Steve.

They made a bizarre triptych, the long hair of Steve and the woman being whipped and mingled by the ferociously strong wind, with Giles at the centre turning his head rapidly from left to right trying to calm Steve, listen to the woman and look towards the mound. He seemed desperate to watch something at the entrance, Jim remembered Lisa.

Lisa, where was she? Now for the first time Jim engaged; Lisa was his responsibility. Jan grabbed his arm and pointed.

"Your photographer, she's gone into the chamber, I saw her near the entrance when Steve came out. Look she's gone in!"

Jan had to scream so her voice could be heard above the rising noise of the wind, which had blown her hood back and caused her hair to stream back behind her in the flow of dust and larger detritus that was blinding them. Above them hundreds of crows circled, cawing and screeching.

By the entrance Steve and Giles were struggling to stay upright and the mad woman was shouting with increasing urgency. But her words were being blown away flying rapidly with the wind to Jim.

"She's in there. She's gone in. You have to get her out now, get her out, get her out, go and get her out now you fool. Go."

Giles went stumbling bent double into the whirlwind that was blowing straight out of the mound's entrance leaving the woman to support Steve. Jim saw him disappear through the entrance and into the chamber. The woman followed, leaving Steve, still clutching at his eyes. She stopped a few feet from the chamber, turned her back to it and stood blocking the entrance to anyone else. She was still shouting but the wind had risen so violently that he couldn't catch even the fragments of words. But her meaning was obvious; she stood eyes blazing, legs braced and arms stretched out at her sides like an image of crucifixion. Her hair and clothes were blowing wildly; she was now the centre of the storm and an impenetrable barrier to the chamber.

The crowd had turned and was running for the site gate to escape the storm. Above, the air was swarming with great black birds circling high up cawing and watching as the diggers tried to hold down and secure flying evidence and equipment. The vortex of the storm circled the chamber driving the stinging freezing hail the gale had summoned. Steve was helped into one of the site huts with the blinded cameraman leaving Jim, Jan and four or five others standing anxiously watching the entrance.

He wanted to help Giles but was afraid to cross the possessed woman guarding the entrance to Hell's mouth. Then, after a few moments, which felt like ages, Lisa appeared, being pushed from behind by Giles carrying a flash lamp. Giles was dazed but Lisa was laughing, reluctant to leave the chamber, she was more animated than Jim had ever seen her.

For a moment she and the woman stood face to face, locked in an intense stare, then Jim took her by the arm and half led half dragged her away to the car, surprised at her strength.

The site was rapidly emptying; he could hear Giles shouting orders to cover up the entrance and secure the evidence. Jim called in to the site hut to check on Steve. He seemed uninjured and whatever had been afflicting his eyes seemed better; he was talking to Jan, smoking and sipping a coffee. He waved to Jim, who carried on pulling Lisa towards the car. At the site gate he turned to look back towards the chamber. Standing in front of it were Giles and the woman in the wind and freezing hail. They seemed impervious to the elements, locked in an intense conversation in which she gesticulated constantly whilst Giles appeared to stand motionless, head bowed, arms dangling at his sides. Above them the birds, battered by the storm, wheeled and shrieked.

Although barely three o'clock it was dark when Jim unlocked the Shogun, pushed Lisa into the front seat and strapped her in. As he steered the car back down the track to the road he was aware she was shaking. He turned, thinking she was crying, and saw she was silently laughing to herself, shoulders heaving.

"Lisa, are you OK?"

"Yeah, really safe innit."

The strange reply surprised Jim; he expected her to be upset not amused. They drove on in silence; once away from the site the wind dropped and Lisa started to sing to herself quietly. It was better than conversation he supposed but when he tried to listen all he could pick up was the cadence of a repetitive chant, without words he understood or any discernible tune. So he drove on with something like an ancient dirge sung backwards filling the car.

It was not until he had almost reached her flat to drop her off that he asked.

"Lisa, what happened back there? What did you see inside?"

CHAPTER 9
INSIDE: LISA, STEVE, GILES

Steve settled expertly into opening the chamber but he still felt distracted. Why had Leonie slapped him like that? Their scene had been over ages ago and was never more than a bit of fun, she must have known that. There shouldn't be any problems and all he'd been doing was trying to calm her down and stop her making a fool of herself. Leonie was always up for it, which was what he liked, but grounded and easy going. He thought that Jan, who was more emotional, would be more likely to over react. True, everyone was getting a bit crazy on this dig but once the chamber was excavated they could shut the dig down and move to the Unit to plan publication. He realised he very much wanted to shut this dig down and move on. His emotional, or more precisely, sex life, was getting too complicated and he was beginning to feel that soon everything would go pear shaped again.

He didn't like this site, they were being watched and someone was fooling around with the site at night so his job as site director was more complicated. He resented being phoned up by Giles and told to go and clear up after the sick vandals: it made him feel uncomfortable and exposed. Why would someone bother to travel out here to break into the huts and disturb the diggings and sections? The stuff with the dead crow in the desk had been the last straw; it freaked Leonie so much she even believed someone followed her home at night and, although she'd not said it, he knew she thought it was the stalker who watched from the trees.

Despite his scepticism he was uneasy, but, ever the true professional, he continued meticulously with his work. It wasn't as easy to open the chamber as he'd thought. The problem was the passage behind the entrance which was half filled with rubble. Giles's planning and preparatory work hadn't allowed for that. Typical. Giles had been chivvying him for the last fifteen minutes to hurry up and at last he snapped back at him,

"I'm not Howard Carter opening the tomb of Tutan fucking Khamen for Lord Carnarvon; I'm on my hands and knees trying to unblock a poxy little passage in the freezing cold. So give me some space and shut the fuck up."

The thought of Tutankhamen and the associated curse was unfortunate bringing back Leonie's premonitions. He worked on thinking this was really crap archaeology. They shouldn't be digging like this; they should be going much slower leaving time to record the process. Everything was too quick; Giles was usually so methodical, too methodical: yet here they were putting on a show for the local media, digging an unknown feature at breakneck speed. This was show business not archaeology.

Without warning the crudely fashioned stone he was handling suddenly shifted and dropped down away from him as if pulled from the inside. There was nothing beyond it just ancient space. He was in!

He never understood what happened next. He saw a faint light on the floor and something moving in the dark space beyond the gap. He heard a soft, voluptuous moan ahead of him and was hit in the face by a fierce stinging blast of grit-laden stale air. He was blinded. The rough wall he was crouching against began to crumble. He felt something push him and he stumbled frantically out holding his eyes. The world seemed to have changed. It was as if the blinding wind from the chamber had followed. What had he let loose? He started to scream, then felt two hands grasp him and Giles's voice in his ear.

***

Now Lisa's time had come: she saw Steve stagger out holding his eyes and behind him the open passageway. She was impatient, the fool had messed around too long checking he wasn't missing or destroying evidence, as if that mattered. Now he was out of the way and the entrance to the chamber was hers. She'd felt a growing compulsion as they argued stupidly about whether to open the chamber and she burnt with frustration. Hanging around while Steve wasted time messing about slowly over the poxy evidence she'd lusted to kill him, taste his blood, but that would have to wait.

He was gone and the chamber called to her. The smell of damp earth at the entrance was replaced by odours of dust, age and decay as she crawled down the short cramped passage. By the light of Steve's flash lamp abandoned at the entrance she saw the crude stone walls. Before her was a low opening, a doorway supported by a crude, stone lintel. Through the haze of disturbed dust and sediment in the passageway and by the light of the lamp she crawled and stumbled through the opening. Inside there was an uneven, flag stone floor and the roof narrowed to a point about five feet above. In the centre of the chamber were two large rocks covering stick-like debris and she was about to direct the light at this when she heard the noise. It was like a distorted form of singing or chanting, high pitched, foreign, as if it were running backwards. It hit her with a jolt like lightening and she felt dizzy. Without knowing how, she found herself sitting slumped against the chamber wall.

The noise had gone now but the feeling of light headedness was growing, she was going to faint. She thought she'd passed out yet she could still feel the chill cold of the stone floor penetrating her buttocks and thighs through the thin denim of her jeans. Then there came a sensation of ecstatic merging with the chamber which seemed to expand and contract in the light of the flickering lamp now flashing like a strobe.

Then: she was flying - a dark sky lit by the crimson of a great fire. Beneath her, figures composed of light and shade moving round the flames in a jerky circular dance passed in a swirl of colour as she swooped over and into the heart of oak woodland. She sucked greedily at the smell of early summer and blossom and fresh new leaf, the smells of release and freedom. Drank in the colours of young green shoots and white petal. In a clearing below she could see a smaller fire with figures, some crouched and tied, lit clearly by the blaze, a woman in a long white robe, bare arms, long dark hair, and eyes ablaze. She held a stone knife and all around was the the sound of soft sibilant chanting. Then the sensations of power, magic and pleasure. The feeling of release like the moment before wetting the bed in a childhood dream or the wonderful first seconds on the cusp of orgasm, the firelight on the wild pack laughing as the sing song chant grew in intensity to a paroxysm of ecstasy. In the frenzy of the dance she saw her dark haired summoner approaching. They danced towards each other, danced into each other: merged, became one

"Lisa, Lisa are you OK? Lisa, speak to me."

The sensations receded: a pedestrian, peevish voice penetrated her consciousness. The feeling, colours and sounds were gone, replaced by Giles shining the light in her eyes, an expression of anxiety on his stupid face as he half carried and half dragged her from the chamber. Outside, there was the wild ecstatic wind spreading mayhem and poor dull Jim standing next to the witch. A glimpse of that vain fool Steve in the hut unaware of what he'd set in motion: the new order that the ancient chanting carried by the storm was spreading. The slow languorous return of warmth cradled in the soft leather seats of the Shogun. Then sensation: the sensual glow of heat, after millennia of cold, of looking through fresh eyes, the feel of new flesh with its suppleness and texture, the languorous comfort. But, best of all, freedom and power with the rapture of vengeance still to come.

***

Giles stumbled into the chamber, Claire's words ringing in his ears, and crawled along the passage towards the beam of light. Where was Lisa? She had obviously broken through into the tomb. Despite his concern the archaeologist in him took over. This was a unique feature: a type of Neolithic barrow or cairn like the Five Wells cairn but much smaller, this was special. He entered the chamber with a frisson of excitement observing the crazy paving effect of the laid stone floor covered by a ridge shaped cairn of local stone. In the centre of the floor directly facing him was the final confirmation of his speculation.

The crouched skeleton of an adult, partly visible, weighed down and crushed by two huge stones. It was only then he noticed Lisa slumped against the right hand wall with her mouth agape and her legs twitching as if suffering a type of seizure. It took about a minute to revive her, during which Giles became increasingly uncomfortable with the chamber. He felt an urge to get out but forced himself to stay with Lisa.

When she finally came to, she showed neither signs of recognising Giles nor of having suffered any discomfort. She looked like she resented him, hated him even. He manoeuvred her to the entrance and turned to retrieve the flash lamp. By its light he noticed some fragments of pot by the skeletal feet, and, glinting in the lamp's light, a well constructed and sharp, flint knife.

Once he'd dragged Lisa out he was surprised she was able to walk unaided. She walked off without a word pausing only to exchange brief but intense eye contact with Claire. By the time Giles was fully out of the entrance Jim was bundling her off to the car park. He was excited by the find but reluctant to re-enter the chamber. Claire seemed not to have moved since he entered the chamber but now turned to him eyes blazing.

"You fool; do you know what you've done?"

CHAPTER 10
INSIDE: CLAIRE AND GILES

Claire had intended to arrive earlier in a final attempt to persuade Giles to stop the excavation. Despite their previous two difficult conversations she felt the type of connection with him that occasionally happened with strangers for no logical reason; she knew he was troubled. Last night her sleep had been disturbed by a recurring dream in which a frightened child or young woman was contained in a dark space whimpering, but every time Claire tried to help her she was prevented by a feeling of dread which woke her with a start. These constant disruptions to her sleep pattern lasted until the early hours of the morning and she slept through the alarm clock.

She had a consultation with a client in Nantwich that morning who claimed she was suffering from a psychic disturbance in the garden, claiming to see a dark figure in evening dress emerging from the shrubbery at odd hours of the day and night. Claire's diagnosis was that the woman was bonkers but clearly distressed and having arrived late for the consultation she found herself leaving even later. The sun was shining on Nantwich as Claire climbed into her car after a final discussion on the etiquette required for dealing with a formally attired apparition with a penchant for lurking in shrubbery

She drove rapidly towards the motorway consoling herself that it paid well and financed the expensive pair of boots she'd bought the previous day and decided to wear for the consultation. The drive was prolonged by road works near the airport and by the time she was clear of these she was far later than she'd expected. Between the road and the motorway clouds obscured the sun, by Lindow the day was sombre, chill and bleak. When she eventually reached the dig the pall of the weather was matched by her rising sense of anxiety, which the massed crows in the tree tops did nothing to diminish.

She parked in the lane, walked rapidly to the site thinking, as she hit the mud of the excavation, how impractical her outfit must look. She saw the spectators crowded around the mound at the far end of the dig. Now she knew what was happening and began to scream at Giles to stop. Before she reached the crowd she knew she was too late.

She didn't see Steve stagger blindly towards Giles, or the entrance to the chamber open but she felt the effects: the rush of dark malignant air bursting from the entrance, scattering and blinding the crowd. Something had escaped: she felt its malice as well as the bite of the gale as it reached her, pushing her back towards the car park. She sensed that something unnatural in the vortex of the storm recognised her and cursed her.

Pushing through the crowd she saw the slim form of the photographer slip into the passageway. Forcing herself through the gale she ran to where Giles was supporting Steve in his arms. Now she could see the passageway to the chamber gaping open and recognised the source of evil, and destruction.

She screamed to Giles to get Lisa out and then stood in terror with her back to the entrance to prevent anyone else following. No one tried and she noticed almost all the onlookers, disturbed by driving hail and wind, were rushing to disperse. As the gale reached a pitch of intensity she felt, as much as heard, a wild delighted ululation that seemed to come from the clouds above her head and disappear towards the woods at the estate boundary.

She turned and saw Giles emerging from the chamber leading a girl. The girl shoved him off and walked quite confidently towards her. As she passed Claire she stopped and stood for a moment staring fixedly, the trace of a malicious and knowing smile on her lips. But it was the eyes that held Claire paralysed: they were triumphant but ancient and unspeakably evil. They were the only eyes that truly saw and understood what had happened here. In that stare Claire felt the jolt of pure hate, like a blow that turned her bowels to liquid.

She was terrified and defeated by the presence of something so powerful that any of her skills were no more use than a baby's toys. The creature released her from its gaze, smiled and walked off. Claire staggered back to her car feeling sick and hadn't driven far when she had to stop and throw up at the side of the road. She'd always believed in the power of goodness and thought that absolute unconditional evil was rarely seen in the world. Now she'd seen it and her world had changed.

Giles and Jan supervised the closing down of the site. The wind and hail subsided and the afternoon brightened but they felt disinclined to work on. Neither of them felt the urge to explore the inside of the chamber. That could wait until tomorrow but they had to close it up to secure it for the night. Giles was the one who reluctantly crawled again down the passage to temporarily reseal the burial chamber. He shone his light through the opening and its beam played across the broken pile of bones under the rocks and then a camera lying on the floor by the wall where Lisa dropped it. He quickly recorded and bagged the flint knife and some sherds of pot and carried these and the camera, which he noticed was turned on, outside and handed them to Jan. He sealed the entrance and returned to the site hut.

There was no one there, even the birds had deserted the trees, and he was alone. The site felt empty. There was a genuine change of atmosphere but in his present state of mind Giles couldn't tell if this was an improvement or not. He closed the shed, left the site, padlocking the gate behind him, and walked to his car. On the drive back to the Unit his mind was blank and he was scarcely aware of the journey. It was only when he was parking up the car in the darkening university quad that the flicker of unease that had been his constant companion these last couple of weeks began to trickle back into his consciousness.

In the Unit Steve and Jan sat drinking coffee liberally laced from the bottle of rum in Steve's desk drawer. Steve, hollow faced and gaunt, turned to Giles.

"I don't know what happened today but that was the worst archaeology I've ever seen. We broke every rule in the book. It was treasure hunting not excavation and I'm finished with that site. What you made me do has ruined my reputation."

Giles patted him on his shoulder wanting to ask him what he'd seen when the tomb fell open but knew Steve wouldn't tell him and that he didn't want the answer anyway.

"Take him home with you, Jan."

She helped Steve to his feet; neither of them had taken off their coats so they moved directly to the door. As they walked away from him Giles noticed a long streak of grey had appeared in Steve's long unkempt hair. Must be dirt from the passage he told himself. The camera was on his desk and it occurred to Giles that whatever footage Lisa had taken in there he'd be able to view. The idea of doing that in the deserted Unit seemed unappealing so he shut it in his drawer and set off after the others. By the time he'd locked up and emerged into the gloom of the quad they'd vanished.

Driving back through the inner urban dilapidation one thought continued to circle round and round his head. Why hadn't they continued the dig? What had happened to make everyone behave so oddly? On any other dig he'd worked, such a find would have archaeologists queuing up to explore and record the chamber. Here some hail and gusts of wind had sent them home.

But rationalise as he might, he knew Steve was right; it had been rubbish archaeology, not their normal method or procedure. The way they behaved, the crap archaeology, the abandoning of the site: that wasn't their normal modus operandi. It had been a collective lapse of reason and they'd all danced to different tunes conducted from elsewhere. This made him think of Claire, who, after accusing him, had disappeared into the night. What was it she thought they'd unleashed?

CHAPTER 11
THE DISC

The cordoned off crime scene at the end of his road had acquired the obligatory pile of teddy bears and floral tributes. Above them the crudely written banner that a police woman was removing, read: 'The Godless are punished, the night is not safe.'

The world was going mad. His empty house offered its usual dismal welcome and he was relieved to be distracted by the flashing of the answer machine. He pressed the button and after some traffic noise heard:

"Giles, it's Leonie, you made a big mistake today, something bad is coming for you. I'm scared and I'm leaving; don't try to contact me, you won't be able to. You need to warn Steve. He opened it, he's in worse danger than you and tell him......tell him I shouldn't have slapped him."

There was a pause then, as an afterthought:

"Forget about the pit, leave everything now: don't touch it, don't touch anything."

The line went dead. Giles walked into his gloomy twilight living room and slumped into the sofa. Outside it was dark but the room was eerily illuminated by the orange glow of the street light in front of the window. He turned on a table lamp and saw the mug and bowl from his breakfast on the coffee table by his feet. The house, like always, was filthy, it depressed the hell out of him, but he was too weary to go out or tidy up. The day was a disaster and the excavation a disgrace. Plus, if that weren't enough, according to Claire Vanarvi he had managed to let loose some demonic entity that should have remained confined: brilliant.

His thoughts were picking up the familiar trail of self pity, sketching out his favourite theme: the acts of a well intentioned individual, himself, being thwarted at every turn by an unfeeling world. He found this strangely comforting and had just reached the point where he quoted T. S. Eliot to himself: 'Between idea and the reality. Between the motion and the act falls the shadow.'

He'd forgotten the rest so took down his battered copy of Eliot's collected poems from the shelf and carried it through to the kitchen. He opened a bottle of red wine, filled a large glass and returned to the sofa.

Slouching back with his feet on the coffee table he took a large swallow of the nasty, yet appealingly cheap, supermarket Merlot. The book had fallen open at the last page of 'The Wasteland' with the words 'These fragments I have shored against my ruin' underlined in pencil. He found the beginning of the poem, finished the glass and refilled it. Immersed in this familiar state of melancholy he was able to reflect with grim humour the irony of having chosen a poem whose first section was called 'The Burial of the Dead'.

He'd always thought 'The Wasteland' was a poem designed to suit the thought processes of an archaeologist and was savouring the line 'for you know only, a heap of broken images where the sun beats' when he heard the sound of dripping water. By the time he reached the line 'I will show you fear in a handful of dust' the sound was disturbing his concentration.

It must be from the bathroom upstairs; he went to check. As he reached the bathroom door the sound of dripping changed to a steady flow of water cascading into the bath. He paused for a moment with his hand on the door, this upper landing was only lit by a dirty skylight; it was dark and shadow filled. He'd meant to replace the landing light bulb but hadn't got round to it. The noise of splashing water increased and for a moment he thought 'what if someone's in there?'

But when he'd got back the house had been all locked up, no one else had a key, so the idea of an intruder relaxing in the bath was ridiculous. Still, as he hurriedly pushed open the door, his first motion was to quickly flick on the light switch and disperse the darkness. The cold tap was running, slowly admittedly, but at too great a volume to have just happened unaided. He'd never liked the bathroom. His strongest memory of it was the night Sal left and he'd slumped half drunk in the bath feeling the cold emptiness of the house envelop him. But at least then the bath behaved itself.

He turned the tap off telling himself that he must have left it on, even though he clearly remembered he hadn't had a bath that morning, and headed for the door. As he was pulling it closed behind him he heard a drip and turned in time to see the tap slowly rotate and the drip become a trickle. His nerve snapped,

"Stop it, stop it."

The sound of his voice, hysterical though it was, steadied him. He stared at the tap, it was still turning and the flow increasing. He heard himself say,

"You're only a tap, you'll do what I bloody tell you."

He grabbed it in both hands and turned it as far back as it would go. This was difficult as fear made his hands sweat and his heart pound. He began to back towards the door only to come back and give the tap one extra tight turn. He left the light on in the bathroom but removed the key from the key hole, firmly closed the door and locked it from the outside.

Returning to the living room he was no longer in the mood for poetry and introspection. He turned on all the table lamps but left the curtain open. Outside the street lamps had gone off; why was that?

He tried to tell himself that he was overreacting to his time in the chamber. He noticed his guitar on its stand and decided to practise the numbers for New Years Eve when his band had one of their increasingly infrequent gigs. After searching unsuccessfully for the practice disc, he remembered he'd left it in the player so pressed the play button and waited for the music.

In the silence it seemed the room was waiting; then a static hiss began to bleed out from the speakers followed by the sounds that can be heard in any empty room, the odd creak, the distant sounds of traffic, footsteps upstairs. Odd, Giles thought, I don't remember this.

Then a sound of distant blurred voices, a faint babble of sound and a whooshing noise like the wind. The hairs on the back of his neck stood up; something about these discordant sounds made him very afraid. Then the noise was cut by the sound of a woman's voice, sibilant and distorted but clear. A sequence of words in a lilting chant, a foreign language and strange cadenza like the disc was running backwards. The sequence of words was repeating itself against a background of static, white noise like that picked up by radio telescopes tracking empty space. The voice was growing in vehemence and the chant chilled Giles to the bone, he'd never heard anything so filled with despair and hatred. Where had this come from? He knew what had been on the disc: not this, never this.

He listened: the same short phrases, a pattern perhaps fifteen seconds long, the cadence of the voice lifting towards the end. White noise was still audible but the terrible voice grew louder, repeating with increasing shrillness. A short repeated threnody rising in volume to a pitch of frenzy. At the climax a final shriek. Then, just white noise cut off suddenly by the last few chugging bars of a blues number.

He switched the disc off with fumbling fingers. The silence of the room gripped him like a shroud. What was happening, how had it got into his house? Maybe it was a mistake, some interference on the disc. The music had finally started so perhaps it had cleared itself up.

He froze, hesitating, his hand hovering over the play button, then with an effort of will he pressed it and waited for the disc to start in the same agony of stillness in which he waited for a penalty to be taken, or a doctor to pronounce on test results. The hiss bled out from the speakers, please let it be music, but it wasn't: the first stair creak of background noise, then microwave interference and finally the voice. Hearing the chill sibilance slide over two phrases of the repetitive chant mesmerised by the otherworldly venom his blood froze.

"Christ, I let it out and it's followed me."

Now even the sound of his own voice was freaking him; he hit the off button and jumped back from the machine as if it could bite and hovered by the door shifting from one foot to the other frozen with panic.

How long he remained performing this terrified jig he didn't know, but gradually a semblance of coherence returned: he needed someone to calm him down and explain what was happening. Averting his eyes from the CD player but not turning his back on it, he crossed to the phone and dialled Claire Vanarvi. To his relief she answered immediately and he poured a mixture of fear and gibbering down the line.

She'd been a good choice being used to the deranged and, although what he was gabbling made no sense, she recognised he'd reached the end of the tether.

"Dr Glover, stay calm and bring the disc here to me."

"What? Touch that thing, you must be mad."

"The disc itself can't hurt, just take it out of the machine and bring it to me, stay calm you're quite safe."

By the end of the conversation her soothing voice calmed him sufficiently to extract the disc from the deck. Without daring to take his eyes off the malignant sound system he groped his way backwards to the front door, got out of it and careered wildly out onto the dark street. Behind him in the deserted house all the taps began to run.

His hands shook as he unlocked the car: where should he put the disc? He didn't want it where he could see it but if he put it on the back seat he wouldn't know what it was doing. He settled on the glove compartment, tossed it in and closed the door.

Once the mechanical task of driving took over he began to calm down a little and by the time he turned off the motorway heading towards Lindow he was sufficiently in control to stop glancing over his shoulder at the dark. He located Claire's house, an old gentrified terrace in a lane facing onto Lindow Moss.

He'd frightened himself like a child and he was about to make a fool of himself in front of a woman who already had a low enough opinion of him. He stuffed the disc into his pocket and with as much control as he could muster he walked down the narrow path to the front door. The terrace had a small well kept front garden and through the curtains of the front room a warm and soft light suggested a subtle and calming ambience. After ringing the bell and waiting for the door to open he thought, too late, about his appearance and also what she would look like in her own house and even what she would be wearing. His own clothes were dirty from the excavation; he felt sweaty and anxious and could detect a rank body odour seeping out from under his coat. He breathed into the palm of his hand to check if the suspicion that his breath smelt foul was correct and realised unhappily that it was.

The door of the house opened and she stood there in a soft white woollen dress, long dark glossy hair falling over her shoulders, backlit by the subdued yellow light he had noticed from the road. Clean, soft, warm and inviting. Giles felt a childish desire for comfort and security matched by a long forgotten impulse to cry.

***

Claire heard the doorbell and paused for a while before opening it. She hadn't been surprised by the call; the disaster at the dig had terrified her, but wondered at the wisdom of inviting him here. He was unreliable: creating havoc in his mad rush to excavate the mound. But even someone as boorish as he was must have been affected by the extraordinary events of the afternoon. His performance on the phone bordered on hysteria but his fear of the disc increased her unease; what had they let out?

Eventually she opened the door and seeing him blubbing on her doorstep she felt pity so brought him in and put him on a sofa in the living room.

***

To Giles the difference between their homes couldn't be more pronounced. The room was clean, comfortable and softly lit. It radiated space and well being, its colours coordinated, the walls hung with pictures and tapestries, the polished wood floor mellow with age scattered with rugs. He recognised the strains of the Brahms Sextet coming from the speakers in the room's corners. She poured him a glass of chilled white wine, which from the label on the bottle he identified as a Sauvignon Blanc, and sat watching him as he drank. Never had he been more aware of the gulf between the screwed up mess he'd become and someone else.

On her first visit to the site she seemed wild and mad: now their roles were reversed and he sat trembling in dirty clothes in her clean home. He tried to tell her about the disc but failed to make sense, managing only to hand it across to her. She understood she was dealing with a man on the verge of nervous exhaustion and further dealings with the disc or any other of the day's proceedings would be counterproductive. What he needed was sleep but that wouldn't be possible until he was relaxed.

She refilled his glass and went to draw a bath infused with calming oils which she directed him to supplied with a large warm bath towel. When he'd gone she went into the pantry at the end of her kitchen and opened the door of her herbarium. Satisfied with the ingredients she prepared a drink disguised as a type of herbal tea and took it upstairs and told him to drink. When she returned to the bathroom in ten minutes he was relaxed and sleepy. She handed him the towel and left to prepare the spare bedroom having decided before sedating him that he was in no condition to return home that night. By the time a quiescent Giles had slipped between the clean sheets a feeling of languor was suffusing his body, and shortly after his head touched the pillow he was asleep.

Claire went downstairs to the living room and picked up the disc. Something had been let loose as her dreams foretold and this was part of it. For a moment she considered locking it in a drawer until the morning, then she got up, inserted it in her music centre and pressed the play button.

CHAPTER 12
PARTY NIGHT

"Dad, you've been in like forever, hurry up I need to wash my hair now!"

Jim's soak in the bath was interrupted by the voice of his daughter pitched in the wheedling tones perfected by adolescent offspring. He realised from the tepid temperature of the water he'd lost track of time. Wrapping a towel around his waist he left the peaceful sanctuary of the tub and re-entered the chaotic world of family life. His daughter pushed past into the bathroom slamming the door behind her. Whilst he was dressing in the bedroom his youngest son shouted at him through the door, "Dad, Mum says to hurry up or you'll be late" before thundering up to his lair on the second floor from where the bass sounds of a music system turned up loud began to boom down through the floor.

Jim ran his hands through his hair and inspected himself in the mirror. The reflection staring back at him reminded him of his father; how this had come about he didn't know but he seemed also to have inherited a wardrobe of sports casual clothes. Unless he was dressed in his work suit or for a formal do he looked like any one of millions of anonymous pretend golfers. It didn't matter what he chose to wear it always happened that he was perfectly turned out for the nineteenth hole and as he hated golf, and only ever played as part of his work or hospitality duties, the thought stank.

He wandered downstairs, where son number two was sitting at the large kitchen table in front of a spread out pile of school exercise books, to be greeted by a cheery 'you look nice dear' from his wife, who was over by the Aga stirring something in a large stainless steel pot. This scene of domesticity made him want to sit in the ancient leather armchair by the side of the kitchen's chimney breast and pour himself a drink. However, Alice repeated that he was late so, after a perfunctory kiss and a ruffle of Liam's hair, which evoked nothing but an 'aw dad leave me alone will you' type of shrug, he wandered into the hall and picked up his car keys. After a shout of 'bye, I won't be late', which went unanswered, he left the warmth of the domestic hearth, carefully locking the front door behind him.

Outside it was cold and dark with driving conditions on the narrow country lanes treacherous. He hated Richardson's parties: pretentious affairs with people he didn't know or like but to whom he had to be polite. For Derek this was the whole purpose of the parties, which he described as 'the place to be seen'.

Jim didn't want to be seen and Alice always found an excuse not to come, usually the children. He knew it would be at least three hours before he could excuse himself and leave. All things considered it had been a rubbish day. He'd thought about the excavation whilst soaking in the bath, but being an unimaginative man, categorised it as one of those things that just happen, like the peculiarly bad service on the day he and Giles had eaten in town. The thought of that made him feel hungry and he cheered himself with the memory that the hospitality chez Richardson was lavish and there was always an ample and expensive hot and cold buffet.

The drive took him past the site and through the woods on the fringe of the estate but in the warmth of the car, listening to Classic FM, he scarcely noticed. Turning into the lane of large detached new houses on the small exclusive estate where the Richardsons lived, he found it difficult to find a space to park. About fifty or so cars occupied every inch of the lane leaving only narrow gaps at the exits of driveways. Most of the cars were Mercs, BMWs or Range Rovers with obligatory blacked out windows and many, he reflected morosely, bore personalised number plates of the worst self advertising kind.

He could hear laughter and music from behind the tall hedge. Every window in the house was brightly lit and the standing lamps flanking the long driveway illuminated the gardens. The front door was open and he entered unnoticed into the bustle and noise. In the hall he was met by Janice, Derek's wife, all blonde curls and spangly dress, carrying a champagne bottle, talking to a man with a polished shaved head and a diamond attached to his right ear dressed in a suit that Jim thought would cost more than he earned in a month.

"Jim, this is Si Carver, he's the new owner of Skendleby Hall."

"Yeah, and you won't recognise the place after I've got to work on it."

Jim pointed out that they'd already met.

"Yeah, of course, Williams, no, Gibson, isn't it? You edit the local rag. I hope you've thought seriously about how you're going to support my development by the Hall, maybe a petition or something."

Jim said that he was still thinking about it.

"Yeah, well you need to think quicker if you want to send someone to cover my strictly-invite-only Christmas Eve party. Real A list event that'll be, come yourself if you want, everyone who matters will be there: I've asked Rio, Wazza, the lot."

Then he saw someone more interesting and moved off leaving Janice to escort Jim through to the large kitchen where the drinks were laid out. He noticed that since his last visit all the carpets had been removed and replaced by an expensive wooden floor and that new ash blonde wooden furniture and shiny leather sofas were scattered about the house. The lighting, as always, seemed too bright coming from crystal chandeliers in the centre of all the downstairs rooms except the kitchen. Acres of bright space and expensive furniture gleaming with minimalism but a brittle and impersonal feel, like a show home suffering compulsive makeovers.

In the kitchen Jim recognised a few lost souls he saw here every year and whose names he never remembered. He helped himself to a glass of wine and stood by the kitchen sink, leaning against a work surface taking stock of his fellow guests. Some slinky young women and sharply dressed young men but a fair smattering of men dressed like him for the golf course, expensive V-necked sweaters in pastel shades and logos worn with red trousers or unnatural looking ironed jeans. Oddly, there was no sign of Derek, whose presence was normally unmistakable and whose voice tended to dominate proceedings.

He took his wine into a conservatory of barn-like proportions where, on a huge table, was a vast array of dishes ranging from lobster salad through cassoulet to Roquefort and crusty bread. He helped himself to a large plateful as much to stop feeling like a spare part as out of hunger and began the usual excruciating process of trying to eat standing up. Whilst doing this he fell into conversation with a couple of other misfits adopting similar strategies. The music from the front room became louder and the noise level began to make conversation in the conservatory difficult. This was unusual at Derek's well regulated and formulaic gatherings. He was on the point of suggesting to his companions that they get another drink when he was accosted by Derek, who took him by the arm and led him out of earshot to the far corner of the room. Derek was not operating in his normal manner of assured bonhomie; he seemed rattled and strangely vulnerable.

"Listen, Jim, I warned you about those archaeologists: I don't know what happened to Lisa on that jaunt of yours today but you'd better put that food down and go and speak to her."

He was red faced and talking very quickly.

"When she came back she was lively, animated, and, as you'll soon see, different. At first it was all right, in fact a nice change from her usual morose self, but now she's making an exhibition of herself. I tried to speak to her but she bit my head off and turned very nasty, now she's like a mad thing."

He then steered Jim to the front room and the music. In the centre a group was dancing while everyone else watched. Lisa was the focus of attention although Jim only recognised that it was Lisa after he looked a second time.

Her hair was down and she was dancing with her arms above her head and laughing at two men dancing with her. She was dressed in a tight glittering gold top, a very short skirt and thigh length boots. His first reaction was one of pure admiration, she looked provocative and very sexy, with much longer legs than he'd previously noticed. She also looked out of control. This took thoughts of attraction out of his mind and he felt embarrassed and alarmed.

"Get her out of here and take her home."

Derek's voice was urgent as he pushed him through the periphery of the throng towards the dancers. Any uncertainty about how he would approach Lisa was unnecessary.

She danced clear of her two partners and swayed towards him, her arms tracing snaky patterns above her head watched by everyone in the room with interest and amazement. This type of floor show was not expected at Derek's.

Her eyes were sparking in a way he'd never seen. She placed both arms round his neck, lifted her right leg and entwined it around the back of Jim's and, clinging to him, continued to sway suggestively to the rhythm of the music. She was encouraged in this by the applause of her entourage. Breathing into his ear she ground herself against him and slipped a hand down to his groin.

He didn't feel embarrassed or aroused as his objectivity told him he should, he felt very afraid. He was being humiliated: it was deliberate, threatening and spiteful.

He tried to pull away but she positioned his right leg between her thighs and was sliding up and down it like a pole dancer. Shouts from the crowd urged him on and it was clear that there were some in the room who envied him as they clapped along with the beat. A fit looking young man in a sharp suit with a huge lump of gold on his wrist, standing next to Si Carver, shouted,

"Go on, granddad, fucking give her one."

The spectators cheered but the scantily dressed sexy young woman whom they saw was very different to the spiteful presence that he felt smothering him like poison ivy.

"Lisa, stop being stupid, let me go, your dad wants me to take you home."

Lisa removed her hand from his groin and placed both hands on the sides of his head holding his face close to hers, looking into his eyes, her mouth open and her tongue flicking across his lips. Suddenly she seemed bored and released her grip.

"Fine, Jimbo, I'm ready to go, this is so boring, take me home. But you've missed your chance now, you won't get another."

She disentangled herself and without a backward glance walked straight through the crowd to the front door, ignoring her father. Jim turned to make eye contact with Derek, who merely gestured to the door and turned back towards the kitchen, obviously relieved the social embarrassment was over.

On the road a clergyman locking his car stared at them. Lisa laughed and pulled up her skirt, flashing at him. In the car she didn't speak and it seemed to Jim her performance had been an act which she'd now dropped. He felt both unable and disinclined to open conversation, worried about what direction it might take. So they drove in silence through the dark countryside with the headlights playing on gaunt trees and open frosty spaces. Jim would normally have played some music but remembering his recent brush with music thought it wisest not to, so the only soundtrack to the journey was the hum of the engine punctuated occasionally by soft giggles from the passenger seat.

When they arrived at Lisa's apartment she opened the passenger door and then turned towards him. He saw that the already short skirt had ridden right up and just before he turned to avert his gaze she slid across the seat towards him.

"Now's your chance to find out if I'm wearing knickers, Jimbo."

He was conscious of a hand behind his neck and warm breath on his face. Her lips brushed his and he felt her tongue flick across his lips and up his cheek to the lobe of his left ear. Then a sharp, piercing stab of pain which made him shriek. Lisa wriggled out of her seat.

"Think yourself lucky, that's just a token. You got off lightly 'cos you're harmless."

Then she slammed the door and walked off, laughing, towards her flat.

Jim sat in a state of shock and then, desperate to be away, turned the car round and drove quickly off. He'd crossed the old pack horse bridge and turned onto the Silk Road before he managed to regain a normal breathing pattern. There was a tearing pain in his left ear lobe and when he touched it his hand felt the unmistakably warm stickiness of blood.

She'd drawn blood. Why? What was about? He felt so upset and humiliated that he almost missed his turning down the lane that skirted the Skendleby estate and led towards the safety of home. He turned sharply causing the car to slide on the icy surface, which he corrected with some difficulty. This immediate problem caused by driving helped him to recover his senses and an element of his old pragmatism returned. He was wondering what to tell Alice when he got back. He'd have to explain being home so early with his ear bitten through and the collar of his shirt soaked in blood.

The car was still slipping about on the road surface even though he was driving with extreme care and he noticed a strong wind had sprung up. The boughs of the trees on either side of the road were swaying and twisting wildly in the full beam of his headlights. He slowed at the sharp bend by the estate's gate house where the road began to slope down to the woods. This stretch of road had started life as a track through a wild and vast forest but as the woods had diminished, replaced by farm land, the track had become a metalled road. Alice always said the wildness of this area had never been completely subdued and the spirit of the old primeval forest still survived.

Then he saw something remarkable: the trees on either side of the narrow road were being shaken violently by the wind and yet, picked out clearly in the headlights and seeming to hang motionless in still air, were some crumpled beech leaves. These were moving slowly to a far different rhythm from that of the rest of the wood. He watched fascinated as the leaves circled each other caught in a state of unnatural, suspended animation. They held a hypnotic quality and Jim was aware of nothing else apart from these dead fragments of the old wood and their strange courtly dance. Then they suddenly froze and hung motionless in the night air in front of the windscreen, clearly picked out against the dark of the night. For a moment time seemed to stand still; then he was through them as if he'd passed through a bead curtain hanging in a doorway. The car slewed across to the side of the road and come to rest in a passing space by the bridge.

He turned off the ignition, engaged the handbrake and sat in the still darkness listening to the thudding of his heart, hoping he'd not had some type of stroke or epileptic seizure.

Someone was watching; a figure standing at the fringe of the woods, picked out at the furthest reach of his headlights. The dark trunks of the trees merged with the torso but a white face caught in the uncertain light was staring at him. Then it was gone, leaving Jim reminded of the surly waiter who'd gestured to him in the restaurant.

Too shaken to continue his drive and needing fresh air, he opened the car door and got out. Outside the warm and comforting interior of the 4x4 the night was cold and, despite the shelter of the trees, an icy wind viciously whipped across his face.

Through the trees towards the excavation he had an impression of light and in his state of bemusement he walked towards it. Within the wood it was less windy but darker. The light from the headlamps didn't penetrate beyond the first two or three metres. This thin spur of woodland, fringing the road, looked idyllic in daylight. But at night it was unnerving and uncertain underfoot. He stumbled towards the edge of the tree line where the fields that flanked the dig began. The scrunching of twigs on his progress through piles of dead leaves disturbed the silence as he lurched between the rough and ancient trunks of the oaks. He could hear the stream nearby rushing over its stony bed sounding like a torrent further distorting his perspective. By the time he reached the stone wall of the estate he could feel sweat trickling down his back and his heart pounding.

Across the fields the dig lay abandoned for the night, and there, strangely illuminated at its edge, was the tomb. An insubstantial dark figure was perambulating across the fields towards it moving with a type of gait that seemed to defy any natural laws of movement. A peculiar process was propelling the figure without it taking anything recognisable as a step. Watching it filled Jim with a sense of terror he'd never experienced in his life, not even in his worst nightmares.

Then, as he feared it would, the figure stopped and slowly, deliberately, turned its head; Jim stood rooted to the ground, time stalled. An awful white face fixed its gaze upon him and Jim comprehended it knew him. The face was hideously distorted but the expression of gleeful malevolence was stark and Jim felt it like a blow. Then, in a curiously disarticulated gesture, it slowly raised one of its arms and pointed an unnaturally long white finger at him.

He was cursed, marked for death or damnation. It hit him like a blow, short circuiting his nervous system. It was this spasm of horror that released him from the spot and sent him stumbling and gasping through the woods towards the lights of his car. He drove away: tonight he'd been served a warning and he was going to heed it.

CHAPTER 13
ANCIENT ECHOES

"It's been a macabre exercise this one."

The flat nasal accent belonged to Tim Thompson leaning back in his tilting chair beneath the 'This is a smoke free area' sign lighting his pipe. He looked like, and played up to, the stereotype of a dusty academic: untidy hair, beard, glasses and even a brown cord jacket with elbow patches which he must have had specially made. So he blended in perfectly with the dishevelled and untidy surroundings of the Unit's main research room. The site review was being conducted without any great enthusiasm from anyone except Thompson.

The conference was taking place later in the day than scheduled because Steve and Giles had turned in late. Steve had sat up drinking rum with Jan, not gone to bed until four and then overslept, whilst Giles had slept very soundly but woken late in strange surroundings feeling like he'd been drugged. It was, therefore, not until two in the afternoon that the review had been able to commence. Neither of them felt at the height of their academic powers and both were irritated by the pungent odours of Tim Thompson's pipe smoke suspecting he smoked it out of sheer affectation. But they were morbidly eager to hear his report of the site documentation as what they'd just encountered had left them confused and uncertain.

"What's most interesting," Thompson continued once satisfied that the pipe was fully alight, "is that since the village site was abandoned there's not a single shred of evidence of any subsequent settlement despite it being in an excellent situation. So we have evidence of a well established village being suddenly deserted not later than about three hundred BC, which, by the way makes it contemporary with the sacrifices at Lindow Moss. After that, nothing. Strange don't you think?"

He paused for effect and to relight the pipe, which had ceased smoking.

"However, the unoccupied site continues to have a recorded history and a frightening one at that. There's a passage in volume 24 of the *Folklore of North Cheshire* published 1832 that records a generations-old children's rhyme about a soul-stealing devil peculiar to Skendleby. Then there's the journal of Montague Heatly Smythe, Vicar of Skendleby between 1771 and 1776. An Oriel man with time on his hands he was a friend of Gilbert White, you know, the one who wrote *The Natural History and Antiquities of Selborne*. This journal looks like his attempt at the same thing. He published some of it privately and it is now archived in the library of his old college and very dull reading it makes.

"However, the last section deals with local legend. One of the legends deals with a series of lights that appear by Devil's Mound, and bring disaster to anyone who sees them. Up to this point the journal is written as a series of eloquently discursive, if pedantic, letters to a friend or colleague, probably White. The letters are reasoned, rational and slightly sceptical but become increasingly morbid in tone.

"Then they just finish: the last one is dated 16th November 1776 when he suddenly disappears from the parish, rather like your Iron Age villagers. He returns to his college, where he is considered distinctly odd, spreading wild tales of haunting and the Devil. There's a note in a friend's journal expressing concern and then Heatly Smythe disappears from the records. The circumstances of his death are unknown but suicide is likely.

"I believe some later instalments of the journal are missing and I'm trying to locate them. In fact there've been problems with a number of vicars in this parish, including the present one, who has a strange past. Anyway, I digress."

During this speech Thompson's pipe was again extinguished but he was sufficiently engaged with his subject to ignore it. Giles and Steve were also engaged with this in a way they wouldn't have been before the excavation. Their normal approach to Tim was to make fun of him and his evidence. The game was to pretend to take what he said seriously and then extend it to ridiculous levels until he realised and lost his temper. They were experts in this game of 'Wind up Thompson' and derived a childish pleasure from it, but there was no pleasure now.

"In fact," Tim continued, basking in their undivided attention, "for an uninhabited spot it seems to attract a surprising amount of human misery. Amongst the medieval records I came upon a Calendar of Inquisition post mortem from the Chester Archive dated 26 September 1283 which recorded the following:

'John de Balnea of Adlington hanged himself on St Mary Magdalene's day. He took off his clothes and fled to the park of Skendleby close by Devil's Mound and there as one frenzied, hanged himself by a cord from a hazel. No one else is guilty.'

"So we have prima facie evidence of a suicide in the Middle Ages which names your site. Also archives of the old Macclesfield Gazette record a disproportionate number of suicides in the vicinity, for instance in 1922 a local JP who was an amateur local historian and archaeologist hanged himself in virtually the same place and for no apparent reason and there's plenty of others.

"In all the records I have not found one shred of evidence of habitation or life but plenty about death about which there is a great deal more in the report. Odd for a deserted spot, don't you think?"

The silence which followed the presentation of the documentary evidence was broken by the entrance of Sophie, the Unit's secretary, with a tray of coffee. Giles noticed the streak of white in Steve's hair was spreading; it wasn't dust, the hair had lost its colour overnight.

Steve led the next stage of the review and Giles, who knew most of it, let his attention wander. Suddenly, irritated, Steve paused pushed his grimy fingers through his rapidly whitening hair and snapped at Giles,

"Perhaps you might try and listen to this bit: I'll keep it short to match your attention span."

Giles thought it best to let this go and Steve continued.

"Neolithic cairns take ages to make, fact! They're in use for centuries, fact! They are in high visible positions in the centres of population, fact! Well this one was thrown up in one season using a ragtag of materials and techniques in an area where no one lived. It was used once in a way that no other ever was and then it was hidden. Short enough for you, Giles?"

Giles said nothing, just let him carry on.

"And get this: these features are usually orientated so they face the rising sun at midsummer yeah? Well, ours is orientated at the setting sun at the winter solstice. This was special magic. Think of this too: our Iron Age tribe is so frightened when they find it they carry out some of their own propitiation rites then they re-bury it and move. I think they move to Lindow Moss because contemporary with this are the sacrificial bodies we found there. In other words they had to keep on sacrificing because something still scared them shitless."

Giles had heard enough.

"Steve, get on with it and stick to the facts you seem so keen on."

Steve started to react then controlled himself and continued in a more measured tone.

"Fine, I hope this is factual enough for you. These features are traditionally associated with ritual, but it's as if this one deliberately seeks to pervert the ritual. It's got nothing to do with any idea of rebirth. This isn't about dying, it's about being kept dead."

Tim Thompson, who'd never been on site, unlike Giles, was enjoying this and chipped in,

"Just like an M. R. James ghost story like 'Oh whistle and I'll come to you my lad'– spooky, spooky."

"You wouldn't joke if you'd been there yesterday."

Giles could see Steve was angry, his face drawn and white.

"See how funny you find what they found today. When the team from the university went in to record the interior they realised the body had been weighed down by two massive stones placed on its chest. Now why would they have done that?"

"To keep it locked in there" Giles replied quietly.

"Got it in one; to make sure whoever it was they buried stayed that way. We know whoever was put in was already dead or about to be killed, but they still feared her resurrection. I know this is unscientific but I could sense that fear when we excavated the chamber, we all could."

Giles put his hand on Steve's shoulder, an unexpectedly sympathetic gesture.

"Take it easy, Steve, getting so tightly wired isn't going to help."

Steve shook the hand off but calmed down enough to light cigarettes for him and Giles, took a couple of deep drags and continued.

"I'm OK now but listen, I have seen something similar to this but not in this country. Whilst finishing my doctorate I was working on sites in Cyprus and Crete. I worked with Le Brun and the French team on the Neolithic settlement of Khirokitia. It was a large village settlement of stone built houses on a hill, far larger than anything here but also much, much earlier, the village started off in about 7000 BC. They buried their dead in pits either outside the huts or often under the floor of the huts, their idea of keeping it in the family I guess.

"But in some of these graves the bodies had a large stone quern which had been deliberately broken placed across the chest before the grave was filled in. Le Brun reckoned this was to prevent the dead from returning to the world of the living. Some of the Cypriot archaeologists were scared enough to wear charms to ward off evil. I've still got one; I think I'll try and find it. But that site didn't feel anything like this one does and I should know, I contributed to one of the published papers on the site, *Fouilles Recentes a Khirokitia, 2001*. You can look it up if you like."

"Yeah, I think you may have mentioned that once or twice."

Giles managed not to smirk.

"So we have a unique archaeological feature which its builders went to extreme lengths to keep hidden. Maybe it'd be better if we hadn't found it."

"Yes, but we have found it."

Steve ignored him and continued.

"Have you seen my hair, it's bloody well turning white, you can see it happening and look what happened to Rose. She went on and on about excavating and once we begin she gets attacked, like her usefulness is ended."

"Come on Steve, she slipped."

"Have you seen her recently, Giles, bothered to visit? Can you explain those injuries? She's off her head raving about not daring to close her eyes for fear of what she'll see when she opens them."

Giles didn't want to think about it so didn't reply, leaving Steve to continue.

"I can analyse the evidence but I don't really want anything more to do with the site until I've had some decent sleep and got myself back together; we've been overdoing it."

"Steve, look at it rationally; there was a freak storm, some hysterical behaviour and you got some dust in your eyes. Yeah, we're dealing with a ritual feature and the people who built it were obviously frightened by it. But it's easily the most exciting find of the decade, and we don't want anyone else getting the credit for it. So we can put up with a few unusual happenings until we're done. You'll feel better tomorrow so let's go to the post grad club for a few pints and plan finishing it off. Once you and Jan excavate that ritual pit we can close down the site and spend the rest of the winter writing up one of the most important excavation reports of the century."

Giles bought drinks but couldn't stay as he had a preliminary planning permission meeting regarding the use of the site post excavation. So, having calmed Steve down and persuaded him to excavate the pit, he headed for the council offices.

The meeting started badly when he realised Councillor Richardson was in the chair, and got worse as he had to sit through a flashy presentation on the benefits of developing the site by two highly paid consultants from an advertising agency. Giles watched as Richardson skilfully asked them a series of questions purporting to dispute some of the ad-men's claims but actually giving them an excellent opportunity to provide further proof of the scheme's benefits.

He was then given only five minutes to present the case for preserving the archaeological evidence before Richardson questioned him.

"So, Dr Glover, you're telling us that all the economic and social benefits, not to mention jobs, in a time of recession are outweighed by a small pit with some bones in it? I wouldn't try saying that to a bloke who's been out of work for years if I were you."

The other members of the panel were still laughing at this when Giles replied weakly,

"That's not what I'm saying. What I am informing the committee, Chair, is that there is much about this feature we don't yet understand."

Richardson sniggered,

"So you want to prevent essential social and economic regeneration to preserve something that you don't know about. Listen we've heard an excellent and detailed proposal of the undoubted benefits of this private capital scheme. You're opposing it on the grounds that you don't know what you're talking about. Well, that's why we're so happy to pay the high taxes that subsidise your department."

This produced another laugh round the table as intended and Giles realised there was no point in losing his temper so said as calmly as he could,

"That is not a fair representation of what I was saying."

Richardson cut him off.

"Talking about what's fair now, are you? Tell us what's fair about all the trouble your dig's caused. You should see the complaints we get, what's fair for the people who need work and homes? What's fair for Mr Carver, whose land you're sitting on and who is prepared to invest good money in the public interest?"

Giles realised the questions were rhetorical; he'd be given no chance to answer and this was confirmed as Richardson announced there would be a five minute comfort break followed by the next agenda item. Giles picked up his bag and left but Richardson caught him up in the corridor.

"Hey, you remember who pays your salary. Because if you get in my way again I'll make sure you don't have one. I told you in the restaurant there's winners and there's losers. The winners have the power and the money and the losers like you - archaeologists and the rest of the work-shy public sector, well they're the past. And you can't afford enemies like me, especially with your record, understand?"

Richardson said this with a contemptuous smile on his face. Giles felt himself blushing with embarrassment, he wanted to wipe the cocky grin off his face but he'd been intimidated and humiliated so he just nodded and slunk away. He was leaving the building ashamed and furious when his mobile rang but it wasn't Claire like he'd hoped, it was Jim.

"Giles I saw something at the site last night, something bad is happening, I need to talk to you."

CHAPTER 14
THE SHADOW FROM THE PAST

After the final shriek of hate and terror screamed from the speakers Claire sat paralysed in mortal dread. She wanted to get out of the room and not come back, but she couldn't and anyway it would follow her.

So, heart pounding, she forced herself to stay in the room until she was controlled enough to lean forward and press play. Familiarity didn't make it easier; it was worse even though this time she anticipated the increase in vehemence and the terrifying end. It was a curse but how had this foul, long dead, entity escaped onto the disc?

Her house, painstakingly created as a haven of spiritual healing, was violated and abused. She couldn't deal with this alone. There was only one person she could turn to in this crisis: she needed Gwen. She thought briefly of Giles sleeping upstairs; he wouldn't wake for several hours. She checked her watch and was surprised it was nearly four in the morning. She'd sat down to listen to the recording before midnight, where had the time gone? Leaving a note for Giles, she slipped the disc into her pocket and silently left the house.

Just after five she reached Oswestry without realising how she'd got there. It was far too early and she was mentally dislocated, so turned the car onto the forecourt of an all night truckers' café. Outside there was ground frost and she shivered as she stumbled towards the entrance.

The place was empty except for an unshaven man in a dirty leather jacket dozing in the corner. She sat for an hour as her tea grew tepid and her life unravelled.

She thought she'd managed to submerge or lose her psychic awareness or 'the gift' as her mother had called it. But the disc had brought it all back in a rush of shock and fear. The last ten years she'd devoted her life to trying to establish a spiritual peace and calm and share it with others. Now something was reaching for her, something far worse than the restless dead that blighted her youth.

As a child she had been what Gwen and her friends termed a 'sensitive'. Her only awareness of this had been a series of terrifying dreams, or would have been dreams if they'd occurred when she was asleep. But they didn't, they happened at any time of the day prefaced by a feeling of dread, a clamminess of the skin and a sick headache.

These experiences led to bizarre behaviour ranging from self harm and attacks on others to bouts of solitary weeping. Her mother referred her to a series of doctors and specialists who diagnosed a range of ailments covering the spectrum from brain tumour and epilepsy to pathological disorder resulting from the early disappearance of her father. Nothing worked and as Claire grew older the more disturbed she became. By her teens she'd been expelled from three schools for a variety of offences ranging from aggressive sexual behaviour and bullying to threatening her teachers, most of whom regarded her with fear and loathing. At sixteen she was beyond all control and, although academically bright and, during her quieter periods, capable of being charming and generous, was regarded as a threat to herself and everyone else.

But before the authorities organised themselves sufficiently to section her she absconded from the temporary care home and disappeared. The eighteen months that followed were the darkest Claire experienced. Life on the streets of London led to petty crime, abortion and being run by an abusive pimp and only ended when her volatility and capacity for violence proved too much even for her clients. She joined a caravan of New Age travellers and anarchists but her concept of freedom was too extreme even for them and, during a free festival on the Welsh borders, they dumped her and fled. It was there, crouched in the entrance of an alternative lifestyle tent, drugged and feral, that Gwen found her.

The years that followed she scarcely remembered, but gradually she calmed down and the appearances began to diminish. She started to regain some control as the cocktail of therapies, natural medicines and spiritual techniques that Gwen used to counter her disturbances took effect. By the age of twenty one she was part of the loose association of psychic healers that composed Gwen's collective, and one who was understood to have particular skills. However, Claire was reluctant to push these skills too far, for her the main purpose of the process was to keep calm. This worked. Over the years she succeeded in building up a circle of clients and a strong reputation in the psychic healing community. Now this finger from Hell had tracked her down, the horror had returned. Here she was once more; panicked, lost and on the run.

This time, however, she had someone to go to. She fastened her raincoat against the cold wind and left the sterile yet somehow comforting shelter of the cafe. After having lost herself in the one way system of Shrewsbury town centre she reached the house tucked away in a maze of old streets by the fallen church of St Chad's.

Gwen seemed strangely unsurprised by her turning up unexpectedly and ushered her inside. She inhaled the familiar slight smell of cat pee that always seemed to linger in the house. Gwen led her through to the kitchen, took her coat, made her sit down. She sat on a pine chair in the Victorian kitchen and watched Gwen as she made the tea. Gwen looked just the same, dressed in a charity shop man's black suit with a white open necked shirt and Dr Martin's boots. Claire had never known how old she was but people reckoned that it must be near seventy. Tall and bulky with short cut grey hair; everything about her appearance was belied by the sound of her voice, which was delicate and refined. Gwen brought the tea to the table, rolled up and lit a herbal cigarette.

"So it's back then?"

Claire choked out a few words then, fumbling about in her pocket, produced the disc and passed it across.

"Somethings terrible is loose; its essence is on this disc, it's hunted me down – listen to it."

"Finish your tea, dear, then we'll listen together. Two heads are better than one."

They sat in an uneasy silence and listened as the chilling voice began to reach out into the four corners of the room. Gwen hit the off button.

"No, I can't listen to this, but I know someone who might."

She took it out of the machine, put it in its box and then into a drawer, which she locked.

"No real need to lock it in, the disc itself is neuter, but the message is dangerous. You look dead beat and need to sleep but first you'd better tell me everything that's happened so we can work out what to do."

Haltingly at first and then with growing fluency, Claire related the story of the dig and Giles. Being able to talk to someone who wouldn't react with scepticism or incredulity was a relief. Beginning with the burial dream she explained how, on first meeting Giles, she knew he was the unwitting agent of the entity inside the mound and that his life was linked with hers. She found it difficult describing the opening of the chamber and the paralysing stab of terror she felt when Lisa directed that foul gaze, full of hate and recognition, at her. More difficult to explain how Lisa's eyes formed her mental image of the thing on the disc. Then, when she'd finished, she felt tears welling up and cried for the first time in years at the relief of no longer being alone with this burden.

She hardly resisted as Gwen led her upstairs and ushered her into the well remembered bedroom where the rehabilitation of her youth had begun. Gwen helped her undress and get into bed and stroked her head as she drifted to sleep. A sleep resulting partly from nervous exhaustion and partly from Gwen's knowledge of the herbal remedies that Claire had, hours earlier, applied to Giles.

Leaving the door open Gwen went downstairs to think. When Claire had appeared damaged and wasted at the entrance of her healing tent so many years ago, Gwen knew it wasn't chance. Although not possessed of Claire's gift, she was highly perceptive and sensed the thinness of the curtain separating the material world from the one that could only be intuited.

She'd taken Claire in and tended and loved the unlovable and vicious being until, bit by bit, the gifted, caring and beautiful young woman beneath the surface was slowly excavated. Partly because her own youth, which had fluctuated between Crowleyesque sexual magic and Gardnerian witchcraft, could have gone the same way, but mainly because something deep inside told her it was predestined that she find the girl. After sitting and thinking she began to make phone calls.

Claire woke to late afternoon sunlight streaming through the curtains being drawn back by Gwen. She'd slept soundly and for the first time in days without dark dreams. Gwen put a mug of tea on the bedside table.

"Don't worry, this one won't send you to sleep. Then get into the bath I've drawn. I've left some of your old clothes out. Choose some you like because when you're dressed we're going out."

She washed her hair and luxuriated in the bath, feeling the tensions ease from her muscles. From the pile of her old clothes she selected an outfit of black jeans, t-shirt and black wool sweater which she remembered from her Goth period. By the time she got downstairs it was dark. Gwen handed her a coat and ushered her out of the house.

The night was clear and cold with a full moon rising. They picked their way through the side streets to the town centre. Wyle Cop was decorated for Christmas with lights and Christmas trees suspended between the medieval and Tudor buildings. The streets were crowded and everything was cheerful and reassuringly normal.

They wandered around for a while then climbed up the steep medieval street under the shadow of St Alkmond's church, passing a group of kids sitting on the gravestones drinking from cans; this gave her a pang of nostalgia. Gwen stopped at a gap in the passage and descended some steps to a small Italian restaurant in a church crypt. She ordered the set early evening meal and a litre of the red house wine then said,

"We're going to meet a man in a pub, not an ordinary man and certainly not an easy one. He was in the papers some years ago in connection with an exorcism he attempted in an old building just a few yards from here. The epicentre of the possession was a young girl; it was too powerful for him and went badly wrong. It broke him, there were allegations of abuse and he left the church. Such a pity, he was a beautiful and charismatic man. Now he's damaged and lives between a room here and a remote cottage on the Herefordshire/Welsh border. He's become a twitcher, spends his time bird watching. Oh, and he's got the disc. I gave it him while you were asleep."

Claire started to protest but Gwen held up a warning hand.

"You have to trust me: I trust him, we were close once but sadly not in the way I needed, he's not that sort of man."

The Jolly Boys pub was down a narrow cobbled lane opposite Bear Steps. It was part of an old seventeenth century terrace occupying an even older site. Inside, apart from a lit-up fruit machine, it looked as if it hadn't been touched since the 18th century. The walls were timber, wainscoted up to shoulder height, and above that the white painted ceiling was yellowed by past years of smoke. A narrow passage with small rooms off it surrounded the central bar area. Inside the smallest and dingiest of these, in front of an open fire in an otherwise empty room, sat a shabby black suited figure. He had an unhealthily red face, patchy white beard, bitten fingernails and was nursing a pint glass. He glanced up as they entered and Gwen said,

"Claire, this is Marcus Wolf, I'll fetch some drinks."

For a while, basking in the warmth of the firelight they exchanged stilted small talk. Gwen noticed that Marcus Wolf and Gwen had more of a shared past than she'd imagined; they also had similar accents. When Claire mentioned this Marcus ascribed it to a similar background of public school and an Oxford College. For a man of solitary disposition he seemed perfectly at home chatting in a pub. This and his sense of old fashioned manners, which she found quite touching, made him seem most unlike Gwen's billing of him as a damaged recluse. But when Gwen asked him about the disc he changed: picked up his glass and drained the last half pint in one slow draught. Claire watched his Adam's apple bobble with each gulp as if he were having trouble swallowing and saw his hand shaking as he replaced the glass on the table. He sat silent for a moment, turned to Claire and said.

"I wish you had never brought this abomination to me. You have no idea how foolish you were to accept this disc or how dangerous it is. Someone let it out and you've spread it. Didn't you realise it was looking for you?"

His voice was now agitated and querulous.

"Whatever's on this is in other places too, you can count on that. It's ancient, evil, and it hates, all it needs is something to carry it, something to possess where it can gestate and grow until it resumes its full power. For all we know it's already done that and this is just an echo on a disc. What have you unleashed?"

His voice grew louder and as he finished he brought his hands hard down on the table knocking his glass onto the floor. To Claire's surprise it didn't break. Gwen placed a hand on his shoulder and Claire asked,

"But will you help me?"

He took a deep breath and reached down to pick up the glass, then in a quiet voice said,

"Forgive me, I shouldn't have shouted or called you foolish, it's just that I had hoped never to encounter anything like this ever again. I'm not sure I can cope."

Claire took one of his hands in both of hers.

"But you will help?"

"I'm not sure I know how any more."

"But you will try to help?"

"Try to help? Yes, I have no choice, I have to help you now: you've dragged me into it, it knows you and now it knows me. I've no other choice. But I fear you have implicated me in something that will complete my damnation."

He held up his hand as if in a strange blessing then delivered his chilling final words.

"But mainly I will help as I fear for you, Claire: because for you I think the end will be worse and could stretch beyond this life."

CHAPTER 15
RITUAL, THEORIES AND WARNINGS

"Oh God, Steve, there's another come quick."

Jan was crouched where they found the body. It was a fairly shallow pit, and over the years the strata had been disturbed by tree roots and animals digging. Inside they'd found the skeleton of a man. All organic material had been broken down but from damage to the bone structure it was obvious he hadn't died a natural death. It looked like he'd been killed, thrown into the pit and covered in great haste. This was substantiated by the presence of a broken bracelet of jet beads scattered over the body, obviously broken either in the struggle or during the hasty internment. Whoever owned the bracelet hadn't realised it had been lost or been too frightened to enter the pit to recover it.

Steve joined Jan as she delved beneath the level that comprised the last resting place of the skeleton.

"There's something under this, something much older."

Steve climbed into the pit and they filtered and sifted through the dry ancient earth. Before long their cold numb fingers uncovered some fragile scattered bones. Side by side through the sunny winter afternoon they gradually, piece by piece, exposed a ruined young life, the complete skeleton of an adult male whose skull had been severely fractured by a blow from a heavy object. They sat at the pit edge, the smell of dry earth, rotted vegetation and death in their nostrils, staring at the pathetic remains scattered below them in silence. Steve brushed dirt from his hands and said so quietly that she could hardly hear,

"I suppose this winds up the season's digging. He must have been one of them, the Neolithic builders. I wonder why they chose to kill and leave him here like this. Christ, Jan, a full Neolithic skeleton in this context and we found it, the type of thing you dream of."

He stopped, touched his hair where it was turning white, then stood up feeling the stiffness in his knee joints and held out a hand to help her saying,

"This should give Giles plenty to oppose the commercial development, it's a mega find."

He looked again at the fragments of fragile bone, pale against the dark earth.

"All the same I wish we'd never disturbed it, never found it."

"But now we can reseal it all and get away from here. Steve, the dig's over!"

"Yeah I guess, perhaps."

As the red sun sank behind the trees to the west they wearily left the pit and trudged to the site office. Their shadows dragging behind them like two giant stains reluctant to leave the pathetic remains.

During the afternoon's work they'd spoken only when necessary and then about the minutiae of fine trowelling. They thought of nothing except the next fragment they'd uncover. As the other workers put the site to bed for the night they sat in the hut with a mug of coffee, both thinking of the lonely body buried alongside the stone axe that crushed its skull.

"We'd better ring Giles and tell him what we've found; he'll probably want to come out in the morning.

A good result, but not a particularly cheerful one. You and Leonie were right about the pit, it did offer clues."

"Like a warning to the curious? Yeah, we thought it would. Can you imagine what the villagers must have thought when they dug that grave for their own sacrifice and found someone had beaten them to it? I bet they knew then they'd made a big mistake messing around with the chamber. We should have left it alone, Steve. The witchy woman who came to the site to warn us was right, so was Leonie."

"Forget Leonie, her hysterical behaviour just about sums up why we're in this mess. Look, yesterday I felt like that, but today it doesn't feel so bad, we all let our imaginations run away with us starting with Rose and look where that got her. Like Giles said: we're professionals. We uncover and explain the past in a rational way. We're scientists."

He faltered as if unsure, then carried on.

"You know the empiricists who show what the past was really like in all its prosaic and tedious detail. Here we got worked up and made to dance to the demands of a rubbish local paper. We've let ourselves be turned into poor archaeologists; tomb raiders. We even tried to open the chamber in the middle of a freak storm. OK, we seem to have dug up some grisly exhibits but we've also jumped to some pretty quick conclusions."

He accepted the smoke she offered but couldn't stop talking, the words pouring out, running away with him.

"One day we're sifting through the mundane life of a small village, no big deal, next thing we've jumped into the script of a horror film. We acted on assumptions; we've no concrete evidence that the villagers left when they opened the tomb. We just let ourselves get carried away, all of us. We need to get a grip and just take time to examine the evidence. When Kathleen Kenyon found the infant sacrifices sticking out of that wall at Jericho she didn't run off screaming and call for a priest to exorcise the bogey man. She painstakingly excavated and then developed some hypotheses on Neolithic rituals in the Middle East that proved the basis for her future work and a benchmark for others. That's what we should be doing because what we're faced with here is probably just the same."

He'd spoken with feeling borne of uncertainty and frustration, but having finished he realised he'd made sense: they'd let the atmosphere of the excavation cloud their judgment and hype their emotions.

For a time they sat in silence sipping coffee as the rest of the crew finished tidying up the site and drifted off home. They heard the shouts of goodbye and the rumble of the Unit's minibus starting up to ferry the workers and skeletal remains back to the Uni. The silence over the site was complete, the sun had sunk and the darkness was gathering. Suddenly Jan grabbed his hand,

"Listen."

"Listen to what?"

"Exactly, that's just it, there's nothing to hear: those bloody birds have gone."

All the same Steve didn't want to hang around but nor did he want to abandon the wall of rationality he'd built. Caught in this halfway house of uncertainty, his parting shot lacked conviction.

"Things have got so bloody ridiculous that I'd even begun to think that what I saw in the tomb started to make my hair turn white."

"But Steve, love, it did."

***

Driving back to the Unit Steve had plenty to think about. Despite his rational explanation there were aspects of all this that still disturbed him. He'd spent the last forty-eight hours putting events into some type of perspective that fitted his sceptical nature and academic training. He was not only a far more skilled excavator than Giles, but also a better scholar. His published works, limited as they were, reflected the rigour of his mind and the breadth of his experience. He understood the Neolithic fear of the waking dead.

In their cosmology there was no tangible barrier between this world and the spiritual world. Shamanism and hallucinogenic trance provided their explanations of the universe; their buildings and daily life reflected this. Neolithic belief and reality couldn't be separated, belief was daily life. This led to a psychology where believing was seeing, not the other way round.

Working so closely with this particularly gruesome manifestation of Neolithic culture had infected them all. They'd got into the wrong frame of mind by the time they opened the chamber. Their openness to suggestion had been heightened in the way a warm up man will work a studio audience or a religious cult.

So they failed to recognise the natural phenomena coinciding with the opening of a chamber. In his case he should have remembered that the change in air when opening a long sealed chamber can result in a sudden outgoing draft. That's what damaged his eyes. He should have remembered Howard Carter noted something similar on opening Tutankhamen's tomb. He hurriedly parked this remembrance of Carter and the curse at the back of his mind. What he had to remember was to consider only evidence not supposition.

They hadn't conducted the excavation rationally and he blamed Giles. Well, Giles and himself, because it was his own fault he had ended up working for a second rater like Giles. He should have been more ambitious, at least that's what Anna told him as they lay in bed last night unable to sleep. Thinking of Anna reminded him of how supportive Jan was being. Clearly she wanted more than friendship and was hurt by his refusal to go home with her for dinner. Attractive though that was, he couldn't afford further complications.

Thinking of Jan brought him back to the site. There had been something different about it today. He and Jan worked well, methodically and undisturbed. As it grew dark they'd wanted to leave but only in a normal way. The site hadn't been messed about with overnight; there'd been no feeling of being watched or constant anxiety, it was like something had gone.

He looked up suddenly at red lights and noticed that in his self absorption he'd driven past the university. He decided to pack it in for the day and go home. On the way he'd pick up a bottle of wine and a takeaway and ask Anna to come round. He'd had enough archaeology for the day, he needed an antidote.

***

Bathed by the crepuscular light of the Unit's main office Giles was preparing notes on the final few days on site. The report of two burials in the pit hadn't surprised him. The evidence was beginning to add up. The pit was a warning which they'd ignored. He felt jittery. This had been compounded partly by the peculiar phone call from Jim, whom he was due to meet later, but more so by his inability to contact Claire Vanarvi. He decided to try her number again but as usual got only the answering machine. He settled again to the notes when Tim Thompson entered the room carrying a camera.

"This is the one that your photographer left in the chamber. I thought I'd have a look to see what's on it. The stills of the opening don't tell us much; but its facility to take video clips must have been running when she was in the chamber. There's a few seconds of very strange footage. I'll connect it to your PC and we can look at it in more detail. I can't quite make it out on the camera, the screen's too small."

Giles didn't much like the idea of returning to the tomb at the time of its chaotic opening but something had happened in there, maybe this would explain it. Thompson selected the video clips, clicked the mouse and sat back to watch.

A strobe lighting effect filled the chamber. The camera jerked its focus towards the fragile skeletal remains under the heavy slabs of rock, which seemed to be the source of the light. Then it shifted. For a tantalising second two figures converging in a brief spasming motion, filled the screen. Then there was just one: Lisa, shuffling in a type of trance. A few indistinct seconds of footage in a tomb built five thousand years ago and never meant to be opened.

"Not conclusive but rather interesting don't you think?"

Tim tried to sound amused but Giles knew he wasn't as he fiddled with the controls to replay the scene. They replayed it twice more and eventually managed to freeze the image at the point where the two figures seemed to merge. It was difficult to see where one figure ended and the other started but there was an image of one face turned towards the camera. By the dark shade of the hair alone it was obviously not Lisa. The film moved forwards to end in Lisa's shuffling dance. After that they weren't inclined to watch it again.

"It's obviously just a trick of the light but for a moment there were definitely two figures, but we know that's not possible. Most odd."

Tim Thompson appeared less confident as he said this; his eyes flicking towards the dimly lit corners of the room as if there was something there. Giles didn't instantly reply, the face on the screen was familiar and not only from his recent nightmares. Then he said,

"Yeah, most odd, Tim. She's out, first on disc then on film, now she's walked right out of the bloody chamber and we let her. That tomb wasn't meant to be found. I've been thinking about this ever since Steve did his 'I've worked on every important Neolithic dig in the universe' bit."

He paused a moment thinking of the figure on the film.

"To them the dead were an important part of daily life; they helped maintain order and stability. Their tombs weren't graves like ours; they were central to life, designed for high visibility as the focus of a redemption mythology and the crowning glory of their society. Notice any difference from the one that we've just uncovered?"

Giles looked at Tim Thompson, who'd, for him, remained silent and attentive for a long spell, then continued impelled by the sudden burst of intuition the film clip had generated.

"The place is the key; they travelled there for a purpose. It's a place they kept away from, a place to hide things that frighten them. The rock slabs that weighed the body down weren't only to keep her from coming back to life but also to prevent her from moving on to the spirit world. They put the tomb here because it was a place where no one would ever come and release her. This was an evil place long before the tomb was built."

"That's pure crap, Giles. You can't be certain of any of that, you can't be certain that the villagers left immediately after finding the tomb, it could have been months or even a couple of years after. The evidence would equally support either hypothesis."

"Yeah, OK, it's not possible to date it exactly but don't you think it's strange that this is also when the Lindow sacrifices started?"

He didn't want to talk about his certainty that the entity on the film was the face in his dreams and the voice on the disc.

"You're working too hard, Giles; you need to get out more. Listen, ancient history deals with sources full of references to the supernatural or religion; it was a catch-all for everything that couldn't be understood. Come on, lighten up. I only showed you the film because I thought it would be an entertaining way to end the day."

He faltered, unconvinced by his own logic then continued in a softer tone.

"It's late, you go home, Giles, I'll lock up; you look pretty well done in and I'm sure when we examine this in the morning there'll be a rational explanation. I don't think any mention of ghoulies or ghosties will cut much ice with our professional colleagues when we publish."

Giles grunted goodbye, collected his coat and left the Unit. In the quad he paused to phone Jim but before he had time to key in the number, the phone rang. This time the voice at the other end was Claire Vanarvi and he remembered why the face on the camera had seemed familiar. But this was replaced by a flood of relief at hearing her voice, the strength of which surprised him.

"Giles, sorry to have run off and disappeared like that but I needed to check that disc out. I've given it to someone with more experience in these things, someone I think you need to meet."

"Fine, but where are you?"

"On the way back from Shrewsbury. Can you meet me at the house later tonight? About eight thirty – I could fix us something to eat."

"Yeah, I'd love to. I've got to meet someone first but I can do that en route."

"Great, see you later, bye."

He phoned Jim who asked to meet him at The Hanging Man, explaining that he'd rather not have the conversation at home.

When Giles arrived Jim was seated at a table in front of the fire talking to a group of red faced men in suits obviously stopping off on the way home from work. Seeing Giles, he got up and met him at the bar.

"Thanks for coming, Giles, I'll get you a pint and then we'll go into the lounge, it's quieter in there."

The lounge shift had obviously gone home as the room was empty. Jim carried in the drinks and they sat in the furthest corner like conspirators.

"What's up Jim?"

"I've had a strange evening."

He paused then said brusquely,

"Look, we're not going to do a feature on the site. I'm sorry but it's clear that someone doesn't want us there. More to the point Lisa's had a relapse; it must be due to what happened in the the chamber. Steve should never have let her in there on her own. Now she's out of control. She disrupted Derek's party prancing around like it was a pole dancing joint; she was drunk, barely wearing anything, and in the car when I dropped her off she did this to my bloody earlobe."

Giles had noticed the red puncture marks on Jim's right ear and been idly wondering whether it was some mid life crisis induced attempt at ear piercing gone badly wrong.

"I had some trouble explaining it at home although the kids seem to think it's funny. Derek's worried about her. The neighbours in her flat called the police out yesterday because of the noise and odd goings on. He thinks she's had another breakdown but this time it's manic rather than silent. Derek's actually frightened of her; and he doesn't scare easily. I've never known him like this. He even suggested that perhaps something's got at her because of his plans to develop that land.

Now he's trying to get her to go and see that pleased-with-himself vicar again."

He stopped and finished his pint and looked so unlike his normal self that Giles felt moved enough to thread his way through the crowd to the bar to buy refills. He had to wait whilst all the regulars were served first, the barmaid using their first names, and began to think longingly of Claire Vanarvi's house. On returning to the table Jim charged on with his story.

"But what really decided me to pull out of this business is the practical joker who I ran into the other night after the party; almost gave me a heart attack. Something's going on at that site. I don't know if it's some sort of protest over Derek and Carver's plans or what but I don't want anything more to do with it.

"Look at the reports we've carried in the *Journal* these last days: random attacks, cut up animals, buildings broken into and defiled. I couldn't sleep last night, all this was going round my head. Then I began to think about these attacks that the police can't work out; not that they're telling us half the story; they've even doubled up patrols for their own safety."

He picked up his glass and took a swallow and Giles saw his hand was shaking.

"I wasn't going to tell you this, Giles, but now I can't stop myself; my chief crime reporter says if you plot these attacks on a map they stretch from the university to Skendleby. It's true; I tried it last night, a trail of random vicious attacks linking the dig with the diggers. You've started something running and I don't want anything more to do with it, I've got family."

Giles thought of the crime scene only a few yards from his front door. They drank up and left the pub; in the car park without really knowing why, Giles said,

"There was some weird footage on Lisa's camera."

"Well, if I was you I'd get rid of it Giles. Someone has an unhealthy interest in that site and it's brought nothing but bad luck. Someone is warning us off and I don't think it's only Carver. Perhaps that mad woman of yours is part of it."

He paused for a moment then reached out his hand and gently held Giles by his left shoulder for a moment in a hesitant but genuine gesture. Then he finally got out the thing he'd brought Giles to the pub to tell him.

"Listen, something very wrong is happening, something that you started; it's scaring me and I've covered plenty of atrocities in my career. I'm out of this, I can walk clear but I don't think that you can, there's a chain of events and you're part of it. Watch out."

He got into the 4x4 and drove off. Giles felt relieved for Jim in a way, almost glad he hadn't told him that something that shouldn't exist outside of comic books was tearing his modern existence apart. He didn't want to think any more in case he conjured something worse, so he stood for a moment taking deep breaths looking out over the fields at the outcrop of the Edge picked out in harsh relief by the rising moon.

CHAPTER 16
QUIS CUSTODIET IPSOS CUSTODES

About the same time Jim was driving home, his connection with the dig severed, Reverend Ed Joyce was sitting in his study nervously fingering the box containing Heatly Smythe's final epistles. It had been several days before he could bring himself to consider re-reading the manuscript. During that time it ate away at him, exacerbated by events at the cricket club where members were refusing to go alone after dark and doubling up for bar duty. Ed thought it was only be a matter of time before he was asked to perform an exorcism. The club president had sent him images of weird pyramids and pinnacles formed by chairs on the table tops when the club house was locked and empty. He'd also sent him a shot of the club house roof, its ridge tiles occupied by a line of grim black corvids whose unswerving ghastly stare intimidated members.

People in this quiet backwater now double locked their doors at night and there was increased demand for crucifixes and ghost hunters on the internet. He'd even been invited by a cable station he'd never heard of to appear in a show that combined cookery and the supernatural. It was hosted by a psychic chef who cooked dishes specifically appealing to the manifestation as an integral part of exorcism. These images tormented Ed as he lay awake at night.

He suspected the events at the club were connected with the excavation and that Heatly Smythe's journals contained the key to understanding what was happening in the Parish. He was sure Davenport knew far more than he'd admit: he'd been very unhappy at the refusal to have the site blessed. Ed felt only relief at not having to perform some travesty of an exorcism under Davenport's steely gaze.

Davenport was the connection. The squire in Heatly Smythe's account who warned him off the mound was Davenport's direct lineal ancestor. They feared the mound then and they still did. Suddenly with a flash of clarity he understood the significance of the carved stone motto in the Davenport family chapel. It had seemed a rather charming example of aristocratic idiosyncrasy. Not now. 'Guarding the Watcher' brought vividly to mind Heatly Smyth's last terrifying words 'Oh God what is that which stands and watches?'

That there was corroboration for Heatly Smyth's disturbed scribblings he found even more unsettling than the manuscript itself. He thought he'd caught a glimpse of a ragged shadow flitting through the trees at the fringe of the graveyard at twilight after evening service but told himself it was just stress-fuelled imagination. This disturbing train of thought led him to the Rectory and, in particular, to the study, where he now was.

He was getting himself into a state about superstitious belief. He was an agnostic, modernising cleric only because he lacked the capacity to believe and had sufficient understanding and self loathing to admit this to himself. So he maintained the church carried a moral message but needed to be seen as a branch of the social services. It followed that the church's message was conveyed through parable, or as he preferred to call it, metaphor, and as society became more enlightened the supernatural elements of the church's role would diminish. But this was no comfort to him when he was scared and in his heart he knew it came a very poor second to the real thing and that he was a worthless priest.

So why was he so disturbed by a tale that might just as well have come from the pen of M. R. James as from a parish priest suffering from stress? He'd read the document again, but this time more analytically. To prevent any strain to his eyesight he turned on the bright strip lighting in the room. Normally when working at his desk he preferred the softer and more intimate table lamp. Also, he moved his chair so that his back faced the wall and not the door.

It didn't work; the second reading was worse. Much worse: because Heatly Smythe, at times, was rational and even optimistic. His descent into terror was quite sudden and yet to the end he was clear about what he saw. After the second reading he felt an overwhelming urge to share the contents of the document with someone, but not Mary; that would be too close to home and she'd assume he was suffering another episode.

He needed to talk to Nigel Davenport; persuade him to shed some light on this. Once decided on this course of action he felt better. Davenport would probably know of some family tradition that would put a logical slant on this and they would end up laughing and for once he wouldn't mind being the butt of the joke. He replaced the papers in their box, grabbed his coat from the hall and stepped out into the night.

The new Davenport residence was a large, modern detached bungalow standing on the edge of what had once been the village green. He strode out purposefully and as he passed under the lych gate he remembered the disjointed phrase of Lisa's, 'they tried to hide it from me but soon I'll see it and know it.'

The recollection made him shudder and brought back seeing Lisa as he arrived late at Councillor Richardson's party. She'd been getting into a car with a middle aged man. At first hadn't recognised her, she had her hair down and was dressed in a skimpy outfit; very revealing and not like her. His attention had been drawn to the shapely long legs when she lifted her skirt to deliberately expose herself to him. He knew she was taunting him but found himself painfully aroused: so much so that he had needed some time to regain control before he could enter the party.

The memory filled him with shame but fortunately he had no further time for reflection on lust and remorse as he'd arrived at the gate of the Davenport residence. The bungalow was large but without ostentation save for the family crest subtly picked out above the front door, but without, he was relieved to note, the motto from the chapel. Davenport opened the door and Ed experienced the usual increase in his heart rate.

Not a tall man although strongly built, Davenport exuded command. He was dressed, as usual, in a tweed jacket worn over checked shirt, yellow tie and dark green V-necked jersey. With his thick iron grey hair and the type of neat moustache once favoured by young officers he looked exactly what he was, a scion of the landed aristocracy. Something that had no place in Ed's vision of a modern society but which when confronted face to face seemed uncomfortably more solid than anything else in his metaphorical cosmos.

Davenport greeted Ed politely, fixing him with his customary stare, which, as always made him feel inadequate. He was shown into a large living room where two dogs dozed in front of a real-flame effect gas fire and after some pleasantries and parish business, raised the subject that was troubling him.

"I've been wondering about the idea of the blessing for the excavation, Sir Nigel."

He hesitated over the use of Davenport's first name, it felt over familiar and almost impertinent. Davenport, if he had any feelings on the matter of familiarity, didn't reveal them but clearly didn't want to discuss the excavation: his eyes bored into Ed's.

"You tried your best, Vicar. Not your fault, best not waste any more time on it."

"Yes, quite so, but actually there is something else that made me want to…er…to seek your advice."

He faltered a moment and then continued, trying to keep his tone as light as possible so he wouldn't look foolish.

"Mary cleared out the storeroom in the cellar where the detritus of the centuries has been stored; you know how these things accumulate."

At this point he paused and gave a little forced chuckle as if what he had said was amusing but it was clear that Davenport neither cared about how things accumulate nor found it the least bit amusing. So, feeling increasingly uncomfortable, he stuttered on.

"Yes, well never mind, anyway would you believe it? She found some jottings of one of my predecessors, Heatly Smythe."

Davenport's gaze remained steely.

"I know that you are well aware of the volume on his writing that I am preparing, Sir Nigel, and have on occasion been kind enough to comment and even encourage."

'Oh, for Christ's sake, stop it, Ed' he said to himself feeling his face colour up at this self induced humiliation He avoided looking at Davenport's face as he nervously attempted to reach the point of his visit, but had he been looking he would have noticed a brief change in the intensity of his gaze.

"Yes, it would appear Heatly Smythe became quite agitated about the mound that they have now excavated and he suffered some sort of mental breakdown. The writing becomes deranged and rather disturbing."

The combination of the memory of Heatly Smythe's terror and the steady gaze of Davenport conspired to make Ed's discomfort grow and he could feel the palms of his hands clammy with sweat. Davenport at last deigned to reply,

"Well I wouldn't pay too much attention to that either, Vicar. He was a strange chap by all accounts. I'd get rid of any later rubbish that he wrote when he was ill and confine yourself to his jottings on natural history."

"Yes, I am sure I will, but in these last entries he writes about the Squire, your ancestor, telling him about Devil's Mound."

He found that the local name for the mound came too readily to his mind these days.

"The Squire warned him off the mound but also hinted that he'd seen someone watching the churchyard. Heatly Smythe felt that there was something troubling the Squire of which he was reluctant to talk, and I was…er…wondering that, bearing in mind your curious family motto, er…you know…perhaps, whether you could shed any light on this."

With that he floundered and stopped failing to meet the unwavering gaze of Davenport's pale blue eyes.

"Well, if I were you, Vicar, I'd follow my ancestor's advice and leave well alone. Stop poking around in the nonsensical rumblings of Heatly Smythe; you have no idea where they might lead you. Anyway time's getting on and I'm sure there's a great deal you need to do, so if you have finished your tea, Vicar, I'll show you out."

This was said with finality and Davenport stood up and ushered him to the door.

"I'll look forward to hearing your sermon on Sunday as always, Vicar, thank you for dropping by, goodnight."

With that Ed was outside the door in the cold night, none the wiser but less composed than when he'd arrived. Davenport had been as authoritative as ever, but once the mound had been mentioned he'd shut the conversation down. However it was clear that his knowledge of the Heatly Smythe incident was greater than he was prepared to admit. Davenport had given him nothing so he'd made a fool of himself as usual. With cheeks still burning with shame Ed returned down the driveway past the swept up piles of autumn leaves now beginning to glitter with frost. Deep in unhappy thought he wandered back towards the Rectory.

Just by the lych gate a shiny black Range Rover with blacked out windows drove past him, stopped then reversed. It pulled up alongside, the electric window descended and Ed caught a glimpse of a passenger with long, scraped back, blond hair, draped in gold, texting on a smart phone and beyond, a mass of flashing lights on the dashboard. The driver leant across her and Ed thought he recognised him from Richardson's party. He looked to be in his late 30s with a polished and shiny head, reminding Ed of the Italian dictator Mussolini.

"Hey, from the look of you, you must be the vicar, we've not met before but I'm your neighbour, Si Carver. We live in the Hall. I was going to have someone ring you but this seems as good a moment as any."

The voice was harsh and graceless, Ed begun to return the greeting but Carver cut him off.

"Now listen, I'm pissed off with the goings on in your churchyard. I bought this place for peace and quiet, put up electric gates and security. Your bloody bells waking us up on Sunday are bad enough but I didn't expect to have these types of problem from the church, know what I mean?"

"I'm sorry Mr Carver you have me at a disadvantage, I'm not sure what you're talking about. I'm the Reverend Ed Joyce by the way, call me Ed. Perhaps we'll see you in church one of these days."

"No chance, what sort of loser do you take me for? Now listen, I paid good money for this place. We moved out of town to avoid low-lifes and all that stuff going on round your church. I want it stopped understand."

"I'm sorry, I still don't…"

Si Carver interrupted,

"These last few days there's been lights in the churchyard, people coming and going, bloody great birds, tramps, dossers, all types of scumbags. We've had people climbing over the wall into the estate grounds. My people found animals, dead, ripped up where I'm having a golf course put in. How would you like that in your church, eh?"

Surprised, Ed stammered,

"But we have no plans for golf in church."

Carver ignored him, his voice louder now.

"And I've seen someone at night in them trees. There's nothing at the back of us, just those archaeologists wankers, but at least they're gone at night. So it must be some of your church youth groups yeah? Or that tramp who hangs around the graveyard by our boundary wall who I suppose you give money to; typical that is, encouraging scroungers not to work. Local police are no bloody use so I'm telling you. Get it sorted, understand?"

"Forgive me, Mr Carver, but I believe we are at cross purposes…"

But he got no further, Carver was shouting now, his face red. Ed, and doubtless his passenger, felt the spray of spittle from his mouth with each expostulation.

"Cross purposes: fuck off. It's your fucking churchyard, your fucking problem, so you sort it yeah? You deal with it and do it quick; 'cos you wouldn't enjoy getting the wrong side of me. Do you get me?"

Ed was correct in his assumption that the last question was rhetorical as without any further courtesies the window ascended and the Ranger Rover moved off carrying the blonde passenger who had neither moved nor acknowledged Ed, just sat chewing gum and texting with an expression of vacant boredom. He noticed that its number plate bore the legend SI 2. He watched the rear lights recede into darkness, slightly shaken by the aggressive rudeness of his new neighbour. Worse, however, were the thoughts that followed. What was it in the churchyard by the wall, and what were the lights? No one else had ever reported anything and he hadn't been disturbed. His mind was drawn back to the very things he was trying to forget: the Heatly Smythe manuscript, the lights and the thing that watches. Carver may well have been describing what Heatly Smythe claimed to have seen.

He saw to his alarm the reversing lights of the Range Rover approaching him. Again the window descended to reveal the blonde still texting and Carver's angry shiny face.

"And now you've really got me going, Next time you try to bless that fucking field I'll stick that fucking cross right up your arse yeah? I told Richardson to tell you to support the development, we want those tossers off the site and you're encouraging them. Do you know what this is costing me? What this is fucking costing? Do what Richardson tells you or next time I won't be so reasonable. Comprendo?"

Ed was still staring into Carver's eyes in astonishment as the window ascended and the car moved off at speed. He reached the front door of the Rectory, went inside and called to Mary but she wasn't back from a trip to one of the theatres in the city; the closest she came these days to her old acting career.

The house was cold and empty and he felt the familiar flashes of panic and anxiety that heralded the return of his illness. This country parish had been intended as rehabilitation from the problems in Birmingham. But fear and anxiety were again beginning to direct his thoughts again towards madness and the false refuge of suicide. He stood in the stone flagged hall and started his deep breathing exercises. After some minutes he'd calmed down sufficiently to think more clearly. He went to the medicine cupboard to find the tablets that slowed him down and soothed his mind. However, the evening had another surprise for him. The phone began to ring.

It was Richardson.

"Vicar, have you seen Lisa? She seems to have disappeared. I don't know what you talked to her about but, since then, she's changed for the worse. She came back from photographing that bloody site spouting all types of strange rubbish about flying and sacrifice – turned up at the party out of her head, dressed like a tart – I had to get Jim Gibson to take her home. Anyway, she's disappeared, I thought she might have come to see you, she kept mentioning the graveyard and a tomb, not that it made much sense. At first I thought well, at least she's talking; but it wasn't a change for the better, it was…"

His voice faltered and what Ed heard next he wasn't even sure was directed at him. It sounded like Richardson was talking to himself.

"Shouldn't have let her on that land, it must be me it's after."

His voice trailed off leaving Ed thinking it was the first time he had heard Richardson sounding anything less than assured, then he said more audibly,

"Anyway if she turns up, ring me and keep her with you for God's sake."

The phone went dead and silence regained its dominion over the Rectory. Ed, lost in the silence, resumed his deep breathing then moved back into the kitchen to find his tablets. He took two with water, switched off the light and turned to leave the room. Through the window he could see the churchyard stretching away towards the estate wall. He stood for a moment, looking out towards the shadows, trying to slow the beating of his heart, telling himself that soon the tablets would kick in and Mary would be back.

He began to recite the order of Sunday service to regain control of his mind and was just beginning the prayers when he saw something dark and ragged disengage itself from the shadows. It paused for a moment and seemed to stare at the Rectory, or more precisely, at him; then it was gone, merged with the dark. Somehow he was sure it meant him to see it and that its movements were quite deliberate; it was the understanding of this that caused what was left of his nerve to snap. He ran from the room wrenched open the front door and rushed panicked into the night. After a few desperate paces he hit something solid, two arms grasped him.

"Steady, man," said Nigel Davenport.

CHAPTER 17
UNE NUIT EN ENFER

Davenport tried to calm him like he would a child, then shepherded him back through his front door and sat him down in the ancient kitchen armchair. He moved to the sink, filled the kettle and made a pot of strong tea.

"Here, drink this, Vicar; you seem to have got yourself in a bit of state. I thought when you left earlier that you weren't yourself so I thought I'd just look in on you."

He placed a hand on Ed's shoulder and continued in a far more sympathetic tone than Ed had heard before.

"I suppose that perhaps I was rather brusque. It would have been better if you'd not got yourself involved in any of this but as I put you up to offering the blessing I suppose I owe you some sort of explanation. A pity you found those papers; that was just dammed bad luck. But the good news for you, Vicar, is that none of this is your affair, you've just blundered into the wrong place at the wrong time. Just like Heatly Smythe. We failed to help him; perhaps we'll do a little better for you."

Ed sat in the chair feeling the hot tea warm him whilst Davenport's steadily delivered monologue along with the tranquilisers gradually settled his nerves. It was not so much the explanation that did it, he'd rather just try and blank the last few hours from his mind, it was more the reassurance of Davenport's calm and authoritatively timbred voice.

"You may be surprised to learn we were quite relieved to be out of the Hall, despite the fact that my ancestors have held it in fief to the Crown since the fourteenth century. The present Hall is relatively modern, early sixteenth century, built on the site of its moated predecessor. But of course, as a local scholar you know all this. Glad to see a bit of colour coming back to your cheeks, you looked white as death out there in the graveyard."

It was true that the Ed was now breathing steadily and looking less cadaverous, but Davenport must have noticed how he kept turning in his chair to look at the window as if anxious something was outside.

"You must keep something a bit stronger in the Rectory, Vicar; point me in the right direction and I'll fetch us a real drink."

Ed indicated the dining room and Davenport left the room to return with two large tumblers of whisky. He handed one to Ed and continued.

"You've lived your life as a Christian; you're a minister of the church. Yet you seemed to be surprised you have to deal with the supernatural; I'd have thought that went with the job. Now, for the first time, you've encountered real evil."

Davenport paused and took a large swallow of whisky; the silence of the kitchen was broken by the ticking of the clock.

"Make no mistake, Vicar, evil exists; my family have lived with it for centuries. The Bible warns us of its presence. It's real, Vicar, not an analogy or metaphor as you like to preach, now you've experienced it and it's knocked you for six hasn't it?"

Ed, confused and shaken, nodded an acknowledgement but made no attempt to speak. The ticking of the kitchen clock sounding unnaturally loud as he sat listening clutching his whisky tumbler until Davenport said,

"I've never seen anything myself. Felt its presence though in the Hall; scared me when I was a boy. We've never really understood what it is but the family tradition is that we're meant to watch it. Problem is the family fortune sank so low we had to leave the Hall; all this listed and graded building stuff makes them impossible to maintain. I never thought I would be able to let someone else move in without warning them. But you must have met that creature Carver.

"The Hall wasn't even for sale when he turned up trying to buy it, and after about half an hour of his talk about money and being a winner and all the 'punters' he'd fleeced, I thought, why not? Not a very Christian thought, Vicar, but if anyone deserves what the Hall conceals, it's him. But now that the archaeologists have started meddling I feel that something's been disturbed, something that maybe even he doesn't deserve."

Davenport settled into one of the aged Rectory kitchen chairs, stretched out his legs, and having balanced the whisky tumbler on his stomach, continued.

"Because of a freak event during the Wars of the Roses my family inherited a legacy that we never wanted. Ironic isn't it that during the last of the medieval wars at the threshold of modern times we acquired an ancient curse. Because that's what it is, Vicar, and I can see from your lack of disbelief this comes as no surprise to you, perhaps it's even a relief. About three hundred and fifty years ago my family tried to get this curse lifted, with disastrous results, since when our fortunes have declined. So, since then we've left it well alone and tried to steer unwelcome busybodies away from here."

He took another drink, smiled then said,

"Sadly the most persistent meddlers have been the local clergy: men with enquiring minds but too much time on their hands, like your friend Heatly Smythe. We feel rather badly about him, perhaps we should have warned him off more strongly before the damage was done. Now here you go following the same dangerous path and in a way I've encouraged you.

"I, like my father and grandfather, never wanted to know much about it or the role we are supposed to play. Leave well alone was our policy, but no matter how much we try to ignore it, every fifty years or so something happens to remind us it's there. Now that damned pipeline has stirred everything up, brought in the archaeologists. I used all my influence to oppose the route of the pipe and prevent the archaeologists getting permission to dig. All to no avail.

"So, when Carver turned up offering to buy the place, we cut and ran. I tried to persuade myself that we left because we couldn't afford the upkeep but that wasn't the real reason. The real reason was centuries of dread. I have no heir to leave it to so it would have left the family anyway. So better Carver than someone half decent."

He took a sip of whisky, leaving Ed to reflect he'd never heard Davenport speak at such length before or with such directness. He found himself breaking the silence that hung over the kitchen permeated by the ticking of the clock,

"So the motto, then, it has some relevance?"

"Not a motto Vicar, a punishment, and as I said earlier tonight it's best to leave it well alone while you still can."

He seemed to have finished but then said,

"I'll tell you one last thing. After that, Vicar, you need to shut your mind to it or move away to another parish, perhaps an urban one where you can throw yourself into some type of social work, because that's your real interest isn't it? Not God as a reality in people's lives."

Davenport got out of his chair and walked across the dimly lit stone flagged kitchen floor. By the window he paused and stared out into the night. Ed had the impression that he might even be doing this for effect, to add weight to the advice he was about to deliver.

"Listen carefully to this, Vicar."

He corrected himself.

"Ed, rather."

He took a sip of whisky and began.

"Whatever it is out there, it's ancient and unknowable, not of our world, maybe not even our universe, and its contact with us, the living, is never less than misfortune. When I was about fourteen, my grandfather talked to me about it. He was not a communicative man, he'd commanded a battalion on the Somme, was decorated for it. You follow my drift? Men like him were not easily shaken and he had deep religious beliefs of the type we don't seem to encourage these days, unquestioning belief. In his philosophy there was evil, modernity had not quite replaced superstition. One day he took me for a walk round the estate boundary, beating the bounds he called it. I remember we stopped to lean on the wall looking over the fields towards Woodford, where our archaeologist friends have been so busy. He told me our family and the mound were linked, that back in the middle ages we disturbed something better left undisturbed."

Ed noticed that the volume of Davenport's voice had diminished and he was speaking more haltingly as his narrative progressed; the ticking of the clock seemed louder.

"I didn't much care to hear what it was that should have been left undisturbed, even at that age when curiosity takes you in every direction. But he told me the family tradition: there was something guarding or watching the mound in some way linked to us. It was here long before we were and it would be here long after we'd gone. Stay clear. That was all he said, not enough to explain but enough to tantalise. I think I understand him better now. He died rather badly shortly after."

Davenport paused and Ed suspected he might be grappling to control his emotions.

"Now there's no more family Hall and, after me, no more direct family so at least the circle is broken. Take a break, Vicar, go on holiday and get away from here for a bit. Ah, I hear the front door, I've stayed too long, and I'd better be off."

He turned to leave the kitchen and met Mary coming in radiating a cheerful normality from another world.

"Squire Davenport, how nice to see you. I don't think you've visited us before. I hope Ed's been looking after you."

"Yes, very well, thank you, Mrs Joyce."

He turned to fix Ed with a level stare,

"I've enjoyed our little evening together, Vicar; now don't forget our discussion. I'll let myself out. See you both on Sunday, goodnight."

Ed particularly appreciated Mary's company that night. She, as always, made him feel secure and gave him strength and comfort. However, when she suggested they go to bed, 'busy day tomorrow', he remained in the kitchen alone. He even, most unusually for him, refilled his tumbler. The night had frightened him and he was gripped by a presentiment that the events of the day were not yet over. So when the phone rang at eleven forty five he was shaken but not overly surprised.

"Hello, St George's Rectory, the Reverend Ed Joyce speaking."

At the other end of the line there was silence, then some creaks and whooshes of white noise but the feeling of a presence of someone there. Then a strange distorted voice began a chant in a language he couldn't recognise. Ed was about to replace the handset when he heard a throaty giggle and then a familiar voice.

"I saw the way you looked at me outside the party, trying to look up my skirt, not what we expect from a man of God."

Then more silence which Ed broke.

"Lisa, where are you? What do you mean? Your father is worried to death."

A harsh laugh interrupted him.

"You don't know where I am but I'll tell you where I've been. I've been with them, dancing on the tomb. I'd have asked you to join us; you could have had me there. Except you wouldn't have been man enough, would you? Not a pervy little hypocrite like you."

Again there was nothing but the remote sibilance of the chant and a sound like the distant sea and he thought she had gone, then a human voice again.

"But I know where you are, little Ed. I could call on you any time, and perhaps I will when you're alone at night. Would you like that? Do you play with yourself when you think of me; my father used to."

"Lisa, please, you must stop this nonsense at once. Tell me where you are so I can inform your father. This act has really gone far enough."

Then the line seemed to be interrupted by background sounds like a radio station shifting its frequency, white noise or static, a wind rushing. Lisa started to speak again, she sounded different.

"Ed, I think that something's…"

Then the voice changed and he heard the other voice again but this time much louder. He was sure now it was a chant or ritual dirge, like no other he'd heard, in a language he couldn't understand. Some kind of warped mantra; constantly repeating, the voice growing in harshness and malevolence. He stood trembling, holding the phone, unable to either speak or put down the handset, caught frozen in the spell of the voice. It grew in volume becoming increasingly shrill and disturbed until, with the start of a shriek, it was abruptly cut off, leaving Ed listening to the rushing wind noise until the phone went dead. He continued listening to the dialling tone until with a lurch he threw down the handset. He shakily filled the whisky tumbler and downed it in one then refilled it and sat slumped at the table.

In the early hours of the morning Mary woke to find her husband missing and his side of the bed cold. She went downstairs to find him. There was a light on in the kitchen and the sound of a voice. On the table an empty bottle and in the armchair hunched up with his hands clasped behind his knees rocking backwards and forwards was Ed. His lips were moving as he repeated over and over again,

"Most merciful Father protect us, God have mercy on us, deliver us from evil.

CHAPTER 18
SOMETHING WICKED

On his way to Lindow Giles stopped at an expensive, pleased-with-itself wine merchant. The assistant wearing a long apron and white shirt reminded him of a waiter in a Parisian bistro but was far more attentive and, before Giles could regain control of the situation, had persuaded him to part with £39 for a bottle of Amarone. Giles wondered if this was an entirely suitable offering for a first meal with a woman he hardly knew designed to discuss events that disturbed them both and for which he was responsible. Ten minutes later still smarting at the cost of the wine he parked up in the nearest space to the cottage he could find noticing that cars already parked had accumulated a thick rime of frost. It was December but he'd not got used to the rapid grip of the cold that followed the seemingly endless summer. Shivering he turned up the garden path to the front door.

Claire opened the door, pecked him on the cheek, an encouraging start, then led him into the large single room that along with the kitchen occupied the whole ground floor. Again he was relaxed by the aura of the house, the soft lighting and candles and the smell of spice and lemons. She was wearing an ankle length white cashmere dress over soft leather boots and he noticed that her hair was newly washed and slightly perfumed. A small circular dining table was laid for two at the back of the room beyond the fireplace where split logs were blazing.

"Sorry about running off and leaving you last time Giles. Ah, Amarone, that's a very generous accompaniment to a light supper, or perhaps you were expecting something more?"

She took the bottle from him with a light, slightly brittle, laugh and moved through to the kitchen. He watched, admiring the way the dress emphasised the curves and suppleness of her body. She returned with a glass of white wine for him.

"Here, drink this whilst the Amarone breathes. Cheap but acceptable and don't worry, I'm not going to drug you like I did last time."

They ate the meal, a plate of vegan antipasto then a fragrant risotto, against a backdrop of light, forced conversation punctuated by embarrassing silences. But, by the time it was finished and half the bottle of Amarone had been drunk out of beautiful hand blown goblets, Giles felt more relaxed. They left the table and its candles to finish the wine sitting on a sofa in front of the fire.

"I've left the disc with a friend in Shrewsbury. He says it's toxic but thinks whatever possessed it has moved on. Now he wants you to arrange for him to meet the girl."

"What girl?"

"The photographer, of course, the one who went into the tomb alone and came out changed."

"Why, why would he need to see Lisa? Listen she's disturbed enough as it is, she had a history of mental breakdown before all this started. In fact the photography was meant to be some kind of therapy. I'd leave her alone."

As he spoke he remembered Jim's description of Lisa on the night of the party.

"Giles it's really important we see her. Marcus thinks there's a strong link between her negative energy, the opening of the tomb and the disc. You said yourself the disc re-formatted itself on the day of the excavation, that's what brought you here the first time remember? Whatever's been seeping out over the centuries polluting Skendleby is now free. We know it's on the disc but where else is it? Think about it, your photographer's the obvious target: a damaged, empty shell, nothing but negative energy, she'd offer no resistance: the perfect host for a psychic parasite. We have to get to her before it can fully settle in and gather strength."

"I think you're too late."

His memory played the few seconds of film on Lisa's camera. The brief image of two figures and then Lisa's slow dislocated shuffling dance. Jim was right; they should all stay clear of this.

"Giles, listen to me, Giles, what do you mean too late?"

"Sorry, Claire, she's undergone some type of change, not that she was ever stable. The other night she tried to seduce Jim then nearly bit his ear off. I saw the marks and…"

He stopped, wondering what to say next.

"And what Giles: what else is there?"

"Well, when she was in the chamber her camera was shooting footage and there's a clip that looks like two women, Lisa and someone else, someone like you, dancing then merging. The camera was probably faulty but…"

She cut him off.

"The camera wasn't faulty and you know it. Oh God, what have you done?"

"I should have listened to you at the site."

"Yes you should, I told........."

She stopped herself and put her hand on his shoulder.

"Sorry. No, it's as much my fault: I had the warnings but I didn't want to believe them, I should have acted quicker. But now it's happened; I think I realised that as soon as I saw the look in her eyes when she left the tomb. We just have to wait and hope she's too disorientated to do anything yet."

Giles said nothing; they both sipped their wine.

"Giles, you need to come back here tomorrow and talk to this damaged ex-priest I know."

"Sounds a really attractive offer."

"No, I'm serious."

She came to a stop. Giles stayed silent. Life seemed to have lost all the rules that make it normal. He sat next to her on the sofa and noticed that her shoulders were shaking, she was silently crying. He poured the last of the Amarone into their glasses and they sat staring into the fire as they finished the wine. Then as there was nowhere to go and nothing they could do they began to kiss.

***

Giles woke early in the morning, he'd slept badly: an unfamiliar bed and two people unused to sharing it. Outside it was dark, no sound of traffic, too early to leave for work but he couldn't get back to sleep. He rolled carefully out of bed disturbing the mattress as little as possible. Even so she murmured quietly in her sleep, aware at some level of consciousness he was moving. He gathered what clothes he could find on the floor and went downstairs. In the main room he was greeted by detritus of the previous night. He made himself a cup of herbal tea, there was no coffee in the house, and sat at the kitchen table to drink it. For a few minutes he enjoyed a feeling of peace of the kind he couldn't remember for years, or even ever, and thought back to last night.

They'd stayed on the sofa kissing and fumbling until the stage of starting to remove each other's clothes, like teenagers she'd said, at which point as if by unspoken mutual consent, they moved half clad to her bedroom and into bed. Afterwards, before sleep, she made him agree to return the following night to meet her friends from Shrewsbury.

With this thought the sense of peace left him replaced by his default setting of anxiety. He left a note on the table saying he'd be back about six, hesitated a moment over whether to sign it 'love Giles' and then did. Perhaps, he thought as he put on his coat, one day they might both wake at the same time.

Outside it was deep cold. It took some minutes to scrape the ice off the windscreen by which time his fingers were numb and frozen. Driving, it seemed as if his was the only car on the roads and the pre-dawn darkness made the journey seem unreal. Then, at the turn where the road forked for Skendleby, he noticed a police car parked up in a lay-by with the silhouette of two figures inside. By the time he'd reached the inner suburbs fringing the university he'd spotted four more.

It occurred to him if this was the best response the police had to the spate of attacks then they obviously didn't have much to go on. The car heating system didn't work leaving his hands frozen to the wheel. His nervous system craved a hit of caffeine; he was cold and hungry so parked up by an all night café. The newspaper hoarding by the roadside read

'FRENZIED ATTACKS PANIC CITY.'

He bought a tabloid in a newsagent then entered the café, frequented by students and nocturnal workers, and ordered the breakfast special, which offered cholesterol and caffeine in the quantities he craved. The front page of the paper carried the headline

'TV Psychic says killer is Ripper reborn'

Having read the few words that went with the pictures, which included the police version, he decided it was a close run thing as to who between the psychic and the police had more evidence. He was brought out of his morbid reflections by a bleary eyed student in a heavy floor length hooded leather coat asking him if he minded him taking one of the seats at the table. He didn't and got up to leave.

It was still dark when he reached his house. Inside was cold and empty. To his relief the bath taps weren't running but the kitchen tap was and all the downstairs lights and the TV were on. There was a horrible stain in the middle of the floor and something near it smelt bad. He packed a bag then backed out of the front door quick as he could.

He arrived early at the Unit to find Steve and Jan already sitting at the big meeting table with some of the post grads, studying a collection of finds from the dig. To his surprise Leonie was there.

"Giles, I'm sorry."

Leonie looked intently at him through haggard sleepless eyes; she seemed to have aged years in a few days.

"I shouldn't have walked out on you but even you must understand there's something wrong with this site, something we shouldn't have messed with."

Giles felt inclined to give way to his feelings and tell her she was stating the bleeding obvious but said nothing and she continued.

"We've been working on some of the finds while they're running the data on the body in the labs."

She'd taken the seat furthest away from Steve.

"Jan and I've been examining those two slabs of rock placed over the body. I know Steve says there's evidence of bodies weighed down with stone objects in Cyprus and the near East but something's different about these slabs, something we've noticed now we've cleaned them up. None of us has dealt with anything like this."

He followed her to the table where the stones were being sketched and photographed by two post grads.

"We all agree these slabs were to prevent her rising from the dead. But look, there's more."

Giles looked. He could make out a rough triangular shape scraped into the surface of each stone. Inside each triangle were a couple of deeply incised circles. Eyes.

"Look how much more effort has gone into the eyes than the shape of the face. The design is all about the eyes. It's deliberate: must have taken them ages to finish. The stone is local so it was done on site, probably last thing before the tomb was sealed. Think about it: these people are terrified yet they take time to decorate the stones. They have a special purpose; they watch, they keep her ghost in as well as her body; that's what frightened them most."

Across the table Steve snorted derisorily.

"What, you mean, like an astral insurance policy? If the weight doesn't do the job the eyes will. Get real, we've hardly any idea what psychology drove these people. We can't get inside their minds. You can't even be sure that these are eyes or faces; they didn't do faces. They could just be patterns, or have a meaning we don't know, there's no evidence for what you're suggesting."

"Exactly."

She spat the word back with real venom.

"Exactly, Steve, something we don't know – that's what I've been trying to tell you since we opened the mound. There is no evidence of anything like this is there? This horror stuck out on its own where there's nothing, not under, not round, not for bloody miles. What does that tell you? The place isn't meant for people: it's there because the place frightens people."

She stopped, on the brink of tears, but recovered some form of control.

"It should never have been found. Wake up to what's happening Steve. Look at the site history, the warnings, that foul rotting bird crucified in the desk, what happened during the excavation. Or is this normal practice on all your digs, Steve?"

She glared at him for a moment then shouted,

"And stop stalking me, stop hanging around outside the house after dark, stick to whatever little groupie you're currently screwing."

Steve started to say something but Giles got in first.

"OK, calm down both of you, there's too much personal feeling creeping into this. What else have you got for me?"

"It's in the lab, come on we'll show you."

Steve snapped.

"Well, you'll have to excuse me. You know you're really sick, but listen carefully: if there is any poor bastard desperate enough to stalk you it's not me. Now if you've finished I'm going to do some non-supernatural work on the site report. We've got to write this up to justify our funding or perhaps on this dig even these rules don't apply."

He walked off muttering and lighting a cigarette then stopped to talk to the Unit's administrative secretary, Sophie.

Giles followed Leonie and Jan through the passageways under the university's Victorian administrative building to the labs they shared with two other departments. They moved through the storage area to their own section and entered a windowless room like a mortuary with the three skeletal remains on slabs. It smelt of mouldering earth and some type of sickly disinfectant. Giles felt claustrophobic and the longer he was in the lab the sensation grew he was being watched. He sensed the women felt the same; Leonie said.

"Look at the woman's body – crushed by the stones and disarticulated over the years. The two men died violently. The Neolithic one has a crushed skull consistent with the blow of a stone axe and his shin bones had been shattered. The other we're not sure about but there's evidence from the neck and top of the spine to suggest he was garrotted like the Lindow body. Both of them were sacrifices; there's a good two thousand years separating their deaths yet they both end up in the same pit. The pit is linked directly to the tomb, so we've got two sacrifices linked with one unique burial and a corpse that had been dead for millennia before the second one was killed. Try explaining that."

Giles had no answer; she was right, there was something frightening about this. Leonie returned to the female skeleton.

"Look at what's really strange: some of the small bones are missing, finger, toe, bones from arms and legs. Cut out so the body wouldn't work when it came back from the dead.

But get this: the tests indicate the bones from the middle finger were removed quite recently, probably no more than five hundred years ago. Which means that since our Iron Age villagers hurriedly resealed the tomb and we opened it, someone else had been in?"

"What! You've got to be wrong on that; why would anyone open it up in the late Middle Ages. You'll have some occult code, Da Vinci and the Knight Templar's mixed up in it next."

"I know how weird it sounds but we're pretty sure."

"Come on: it makes no sense; you're saying people are so scared of this place that they won't go near it in one breath; then you say they pop in from time to time to open it up and choose a bone. That means knowledge of the Neolithic ritual survived and we know that's not possible"

"Yeah, disturbing isn't it?"

Giles didn't have an answer and didn't want to think of one and particularly not there amongst the ancient dead. They completed the inspection of the bodies and left, locking the door behind them, relieved to be out of the room. Leonie left the unit without saying anything else and Giles returned to his desk and forced himself to address the pile of paperwork accumulating there. By lunchtime the Unit had emptied leaving only him and Steve.

"What's got into you, Steve? You need to keep your private life to yourself. You could have been easier on Leonie; she's right on the edge."

"You heard what she accused me of but, yeah, OK, I know, I'm sorry but all this horror movie stuff is bugging me. We excavated too quickly so there's evidence we missed and probably destroyed. Now we're just jumping to conclusions. Our interpretation's more Julian Cope than Julian Thomas."

It was a rubbish joke that only an archaeologist could get, but it broke the tension and Giles was vaguely reassured by Steve's attempt to rationalise his fears; he managed a weak laugh.

"OK, point taken, anyway I've got a planning meeting at the Town Hall this afternoon about the Borough constraints map, it'll go on forever so I'll probably go home from there. I'll see you tomorrow, and go easy on Leonie."

"Yeah, OK, have fun; oh hang on, Gi, I meant to tell you Jan suggested we contact that pompous vicar who came to exorcise the site. You know the one I took the piss out of; you should have seen his face as he left, hilarious."

"Yes, I'm sure it was, Steve, I wish I'd seen it. Anyway I'd better get off, never does to keep council officers waiting."

Giles hadn't found it hilarious and wondered why the vicar wanted to bless the site and why Jan agreed with him. What were they messing with? He thought about this all the way to the Victorian Gothic Town Hall and throughout most of the meeting, which dragged on seemingly unending for three hours. It was after five and dark when he got out.

The square outside the Town Hall was blazing with the glow of the stalls and Christmas lights. The streets were crowded and the European market packed and noisy, even the street cobbles glittering with hoar frost seemed to give off cheerful vibes. Pushing his way through the crowds Giles thought Skendleby might as well exist in a different world. He decided not to pick up his car but do some Christmas shopping, perhaps have a drink, and then take the train.

He imagined spending Christmas with Claire as he walked the brightly lit streets looking in windows and dreaming of a happy future. Sitting in a bar with coffee and grappa watching the people he tried to think of a gift for Claire and came up with red roses. He enjoyed buying them, talking to the shop assistant, beginning to feel that he was starting to re-engage with life. After listening to the Salvation Army silver band outside the theatre for five minutes, he helped an elderly woman loaded down with shopping onto a bus and then, feeling sentimental, he rushed off through the crowded streets and gathering fog to try to catch the packed six fifteen to Wilmslow.

He decided to walk from the station to Lindow and the first ten minutes, strolling past the shops with their Christmas window dressings sustained his unusually cheerful mood.

By the time he reached the fringe of Lindow, fog was hovering and the cold palpable. To save time he decided to take a short cut and follow the footpath across the Moss. He reckoned if he cut through the trees he should hit the path on the other side in a couple of minutes. He climbed the low ranch style fencing and picked his way through birch, alder and scrub oak. Fog flowed after him.

In the dark of the trees it was cold and silent, fog muffled any noise; this was disorientating. Where was the path? He should be on it now: he paused trying to get his bearings; if he crossed the open ground ahead he must eventually find it.

This had been a mistake: he considered heading back to the road but couldn't trust his sense of direction to get him through the trees; anyway the open seemed less threatening. As he hesitated the fog thickened. He made himself set out across the shrouded space in what he guessed must be the right direction. It was an open patch of ground he knew well and yet tonight in the cold with poor visibility it seemed bigger. He began to feel afraid.

Perhaps it was this that made him think of the warning one of the council officers, a guy he quite liked, gave him as he left the meeting a couple of hours earlier. He'd taken Giles into a quiet corner saying,

"Listen, don't say this came from me, Giles, but you need to take seriously what Richardson threatened you with the other day. He's the type of vicious bastard who means what he says."

He looked round to see if anyone was listening then went on in a quieter voice,

"He's too deep in this Skendleby scam to get out. Once Carver gets his hooks into you, you're stuck. Richardson's trapped; if the deal goes down Carver will make sure he does too. You need to watch out, Giles: you're on Carver's radar, he doesn't stop at threats, if you cause him too much grief he's got psychos on his payroll who'll break your legs or worse; he's done it before. I've got to go; not good being seen talking to you. Take care."

He tried to push this out of his mind but only succeeded in replacing it with the memory of his last visit to the Moss. Of the woman who saw the figure walking behind him: 'He had his hand on your shoulder and did seem to be moving in a most peculiar way.'

The fog was thicker now, he could hardly see. He quickened his pace; even if he'd missed the path he must be almost halfway across the Moss

But the idea something was shadowing him fixed in his mind. He found himself repeating 'moving in a most peculiar way' over and over to himself. He tried to rationalise, given his experiences of the last few days, it was no wonder his imagination was playing tricks. But the phrase 'moving in a most peculiar way' had lodged in his brain and he couldn't shift it. What was it moving in a peculiar way and how could it have had a hand on his shoulder?

He thought about the peculiarities of fog, the way there was always something just on the edge of vision. He remembered the attacks stretching from his house to the dig. They only started after Rose surveyed Devil's Mound. Then he thought of Carver's hired thugs. He broke into a jog.

But he was lost in a darkly opaque world, cold and silent. Lost but not alone; there was something behind him. Something just out of sight. Just out of sight moving in a peculiar way, he could hear it moving with him.

He increased his pace but it didn't help; the fog distorted any sense of speed or direction. Something brushed against his cheek, like the light touch of a wet glove. There was an exhalation of breath close by as he pushed his way through stunted thorn trees.

This brought him to a halt. What was he doing in the trees? This should be open ground leading to the road, the trees shouldn't be here. He shouted out in panic,

"Is anyone there? I'm lost."

His voice sounded puny and muffled but the ensuing silence was worse. But listen: it wasn't complete silence: there was sound: rustling like something moving with purpose through thick forest undergrowth. He heard the crack as a branch close by snapped.

"Oh Jesus, this can't be real please, what's happening?"

He tried to run but the trees were too thick, they seemed alive. He had to force himself through their clawing, scratching branches. Unspeakable things, dead things, were grabbing him, pulling him towards them, reeling him in. The rank undergrowth was winding itself round his ankles dragging him down. Next to him there was an exhalation of foul breath; he could smell it, almost taste it, feel it on his cheek. Something sharp was jabbing him in the back, he heard a horrible sucking sound like some deformed chuckle. He could feel liquid oozing beneath his shirt.

"Oh Christ, I'm going to die out here, please, please make it stop."

He screamed for help, a tiny gasp like the snivel of a petrified child. He stood rooted to the spot screaming and swinging his arms to beat it off. He jerked a foot free and managed to move forwards: open ground, he was out of the trees.

Then he was running, terrified, breathless, heart pumping, panicked, arms flailing, roses discarded. Glancing back he saw a patch of shadow tracking him. He swerved to the right. Surely he must be close to the road. He turned his head. Something hit him with a crash. He hit the ground. Darkness.

CHAPTER 19
THIS WAY COMES

Sophie was putting on her coat before locking up for the night. The phone rang. She debated whether to answer it. Not much point, no one here to answer any questions, but habit overrode logic in its atavistic way.

"Hello, Archaeology Unit, Sophie speaking."

"Hello, I wonder would it be possible to speak to Dr Steve Watkins?"

"Sorry, he left about half an hour ago, can I take a message?"

"No, it's really important I speak to him, it's about the pictures for tomorrow's feature."

"You mean about the Skendleby dig, I thought that had been cancelled."

"No, it's back on. Dr Glover and my editor agreed a general feature on the site would be possible for tomorrow but I need to check more details with Dr Watkins before it can go to press."

"Well, as I've said, you've missed him."

Sophie was keen to end the conversation, she was due to meet a lawyer she'd met through an internet dating site, but the voice on the end of the line was insistent.

"Could you put me in touch with him or give me his mobile number?"

"Sorry, we can't give out phone numbers."

"This is really important; the feature only works if it includes his evidence."

Sophie wanted to shut the conversation down and be off.

"Look, I'm sorry, but as I said we don't give out people's numbers."

Then as an afterthought to prevent further dialogue,

"He usually goes to the Royal Oak after work. Your only chance is to find him there."

The line went down without any recognition or thanks at the other end. Sophie arranged her hair over her coat collar, touched up her lipstick in the small mirror hanging behind her desk, switched off the lights, and hurriedly closed up. It was only as she was crossing the quad heading for the downtown bus stop that it occurred to her that she hadn't asked who it was on the other end of the line.

***

Steve hadn't had a good day. Anna hadn't put it quite this way but she'd dumped him, giving some reason about too many complications. So, after a brief word with some of the early evening regulars at the bar he had taken his pint, bag of salted nuts and free copy of the *Journal* to a corner table. The paper's lead story was the death in hospital of the last attack victim and it had a special feature on how to stay safe at night in the south of the city. To his relief there was no speculation connecting the attacks with the dig but all the same it was the last thing he wanted to read so he discarded the paper and sat nursing his pint wondering what to do that night.

He didn't want to go home, in fact he didn't really have a home; he'd never moved on from student flats and the state of his current one made most student accommodation look distinctly up-market. He didn't have any close friends, just drifted from one girlfriend to another, but as he aged the girls stayed more or less the same and he wondered if he was getting too old for this lifestyle. His work life wasn't much better; short term contracts alternating between England and Southern Europe offered no future in terms of either pay or prospects. So he drifted downhill through life incapable of growing up; uncaring and, in the main, uncared for.

He'd been deeply hurt by Leonie accusing him of stalking her: why would he do that? Perhaps she just imagined it or maybe it was wishful thinking but neither explanation seemed convincing. He finished the first pint too quickly, bought another and sat gloomily trying to listen in to an argument between two couples at the next table. Despite their advanced middle age and beige blandness he envied them their stability.

He was watching them so closely that he didn't notice the attractive, heavily made up girl enter the pub obviously looking for someone, nor did he notice the look of anticipation cross her eyes as they locked onto him.

It was only when she was a few yards from the table that he sensed a presence and looked up. Approaching him he saw a striking blonde in a long black coat and boots and wearing bright red lipstick.

"Dr Watkins, do you mind if I join you?"

She slid, smiling at him, into the seat opposite, opening up the coat and crossing her legs. He noticed a great deal of bare leg but no apparent hemline beneath the coat.

"You obviously don't remember me. We met at the excavation. I'm Lisa Richardson and I was wondering if you could do me an enormous favour."

She rolled her eyes flirtatiously and it took Steve some time to connect this woman with the mousy photographer from the *Journal* but by the time it clicked he was on his way to the bar to buy her a drink. He found it difficult to believe that Lisa could look so different. On the site she'd been anonymous, almost not there, whereas here in the crowded pub she was the focus of attention. Perhaps his luck was changing.

"Here, Lisa, house white wine, a large one, I hope that's OK. I'm sorry I didn't recognise you at first."

She laughed throatily and tossed her hair back but her eyes remained locked onto his.

"No, I look different out of work, don't I? Is that why you bought me a large one? I hope you're not trying to get me drunk, you naughty boy, I've heard about you and girls."

She held eye contact as she said this and circled her tongue round her lips.

"But seriously, Steve, would you mind if we talked about the dig for a bit, I'd be ever so grateful and I'm really sorry to be taking up your time."

She said this in a breathy girly voice and as she finished the sentence she stretched her hand across the table and gently placed it on his wrist in a way that managed to be familiar and yet also suggestive, he felt the hairs on the back of his neck prickle.

"I rang the Unit's office but you'd left. Sophie was very helpful though when she realised how urgent it was, she suggested that you might be here."

Good old Sophie, thought Steve, she has her uses.

"Still, it was lucky to find you and, I have to say, I'm surprised to find you on your own, most unusual for you I hear."

She fluttered her eyelashes and smiled at him in a manner that suggested a shared intimacy and then moved across to the seat next to him.

"It's so noisy in this pub isn't it, Steve; good atmosphere but it's hard to make conversation. We've come up with a new idea for the focus of the piece on the mound."

"What do you mean new idea? Giles told me that your editor abandoned the idea. Giles seemed to think he was frightened of the place; Giles certainly is."

Lisa laughed softly and brushed aside the sweep of blonde hair partially covering her face.

"Is he now, Steve? Well actually that's the whole point. Now Jim thinks it would be a good spooky story for Christmas; people love Christmas ghost stories don't they? You know the haunted tomb type of stuff – a mix of archaeology and local legend. He thinks we can run the story and then sell it on as an idea for *Cheshire Life* and some of the nationals. We need a picture of it in a night setting for atmosphere and Jim suggested you as the centrepiece of the story."

She re-crossed her legs and began smoothing her stockings, watching his eyes follow her every movement.

"It's a great idea, you're much better looking than Giles, long hair, stubble, a bit like Johnny Depp or that Scandinavian actor in those old *Lord of the Rings* films. You know the one, moody and quite dishy. The idea is: a picture of you by the tomb at night with a piece about the weird happenings when you opened it. A kind of male tomb raider."

Under normal circumstances Steve would have rejected this out of hand for the crap it clearly was. But after three pints the idea that the *Journal* recognised he, not Giles, was the main man on the excavation seemed no more than fair. But really, it was the aphrodisiac effect of Lisa's seduction that did it, the flattery and flirting persuaded him to suspend common sense. Anyway no one else had any time for him and the thought of his lonely dirty flat drowned him in self pity.

"I know that it's a lot to ask you to drive out to the site with me on such a cold night Steve and I'm sure you've got something far more interesting laid on, but I would be very grateful. Tell you what; if you like I could get us some supper and a glass of wine at my place later as a way of saying thank you."

As she finished speaking she placed her arm lightly around the back of his neck and moved her face close to his.

"I think you'd like that, wouldn't you, Stevie?"

Steve, tongue thick in his mouth, agreed, like she knew he would. As she led him out of the pub he was aware of many envious pairs of eyes following them. Outside she took his hand as they walked to the car.

She seemed unused to the car yet drove fast and, Steve felt, dangerously, particularly when they reached the country lanes near the site. She talked for most of the journey and seemed even more hyper than she had been in the pub. From time to time, as if to explain a point, she placed a hand on his thigh. They parked in the lane by the site gate; it was dark and silent. As she twisted to unbutton her seat belt she brushed his lips with hers but as he tried to hold her she quickly opened the door and got out.

"No need to be so impatient, Stevie, there's plenty of time for that later."

Out in the cold night air and the dark of the field, the wrongness of what they were doing hit him. It was cold and silent, the site was locked up. The skeletal trees and the estate wall looked dark and threatening. What the hell was he doing here with a girl he hardly knew and particularly one behaving the way she was? His mind flashed back to the day of the excavation and Lisa the photographer.

This woman, Lisa the seductress, was nothing like her; slight physical resemblance maybe but this was a different person, behaviour, body language, eye contact, everything. The photographer had been non-existent, this incarnation was predatory. She sensed his uncertainty.

"Come on, Steve, the sooner we finish here the sooner we can get away. I don't suppose you've got the padlock keys. You'll have to help me climb over the gate. If you are a gentleman you'll look away as I swing my leg over, I've not much on under this coat. But from what I've heard you're not a gentleman are you?"

They climbed the gate with Lisa laughing suggestively and set off down the path to the mound. It was rough underfoot and in the dark they had difficulty negotiating the hazards of the archaeological site. She led the way, moving quickly. Steve thought she was becoming agitated, casting rapid glances towards the trees as if she suspected someone watching. He remembered Leonie's stalker in the trees obsession.

The track leading through the village boundary was particularly difficult and frost cracking underfoot produced sharp jagged sounds which pierced the silence. Lisa moved quickly looking from side to side but Steve, feeling rushed, slipped twice. On regaining his feet the second time and pausing to brush the dirt and frost from his knees he thought he saw movement at the fringe of the woods. He thought of the ride back from the Windmill pub with Jan and how normal and comforting she was. Then he saw the shape move again.

"Lisa, there's someone over there. Have you told anyone else about this? Because if not, then I think we need to get out of here."

Now he wanted to be away, the effects of the alcohol were evaporating and the sexual allure of his companion diminished. He'd made a mistake, had he been set up for something?

"Don't be silly, it'll be just someone up to what we're doing, it could be the local dogging site; come on only a few more minutes."

Her voice was urgent. She took his hand and hurried him through the gap in the village boundary and then they were at the tomb. Devil's Mound looked desolate with the scars of the excavation fresh upon it and Steve couldn't think of a place he less wanted to be. From the distant woods there were sounds: twigs snapping, perhaps some animal breaking cover followed by the mournful hooting of an owl.

Lisa froze and looked towards the woods while Steve, whose mind was not working clearly, found himself wondering if owls were meant to be out and about in winter or whether they should be at home hibernating like other woodland creatures. He was sure he'd been taught something like that at primary school. Then a sensible thought entered his brain for the first time that evening.

"Lisa, where's the camera? You haven't got a camera."

She turned to look at him.

"What was that, Steve?"

"You haven't bought a camera, we're meant to be taking some important film but you haven't bought a camera."

"Doesn't matter, I'll use the phone, we can download the images, it's no problem, come on."

"For the excavation you had all the gear, tripod, light meter, lenses. Tonight, for a more difficult shot, only a mobile. I don't think so."

"Well maybe I like a bit of adventure, Steve, and from everything I've heard so do you. Perhaps I fancy it on the mound and we can take a couple of shots later; don't tell me that you don't want to, there's no strings so loosen up, it's your type of scene, come on."

She took his hand and led him to the mound but stopped as if looking for something particular then said quickly,

"We'll do it here."

She positioned herself at the edge of the ritual pit where the bodies of the sacrificed men had lain for millennia as eternal sentinels.

He heard hooting again as the moon broke through the thin blanket of fog. Silver light flooded the mound dappling Lisa's body and causing weird shadows to dance. She'd undone the coat and flung back her hair whilst opening her arms in a gesture both inviting and symbolic. Bathed in moonlight she stood like a mythical queen dazzling all around her.

"Well, come on, you won't get a better offer than this."

Mesmerised by the light and her presence he moved towards her, a supplicant to some pagan goddess. For that was what she seemed like to him; a promiscuously charged version of the goddess Diana, sexual and terrifying.

For Steve everything lost any sense of reality. He was physically aroused but mentally dislocated. He watched as a dark shape detached itself from the distant tree line. But now, within touching distance, inhaling the scent of her perfume he'd gone too far to stop. He felt her breath on his face and slid his hands beneath her coat. She undulated against him and he felt her breath on his neck. Felt the soft flick of her tongue moving up towards his ear as her left hand pulling at his long hair forced his head back. He noticed that the shadow from the tree line was closer now, capering in a way no human bone structure could possibly accommodate, like it was here and there at the same time.

But that was just part of the wonderful hyper-reality of the moment. His hands were under the skirt, on the back of her thighs, gliding upwards over her stocking tops, her perfumed breath wreathed his face, her mouth was over his ear whispering softly, sensuous but in no language he'd ever heard. Everything felt liquid; swooning, suspended, he felt himself dissolving into the moonlight.

Then sharp, terrible pain: tearing and cold. His ear was being shredded, bitten right through, and ripped away. The voice changed, the words the same but now harsh and high, the same phrase repeating. His head was jerked back. He felt hot liquid flooding down his neck soaking his shirt collar. He couldn't move, felt, more than saw, her right hand stretch up and then come down with terrible force as something sharp and thin pierced his leather coat and glanced off his shoulder blade. He recognised the thing in her hand as a flint knife; she stabbed down at him again and again. There was sharp, jagged pain near his neck, the warm gush of blood. He tried to hold her off but she was too strong, the knife cut into his flesh and his strength leaked away as his blood spurted in spasmodic gouts onto the frozen ground. The voice, chanting, triumphant and vindictive increased in volume. She was shrieking, screaming in ecstasy and he was unable to move; now there was only pain, cold and terror. Something black and ragged was near, approaching like something fast forwarded. Now he recognised it: his death.

He was down on the cold hard ground slippy with his warm blood pumping out onto the mound. He felt her begin to cut at his left forefinger, he watched his death coming for him, he heard the voice, hers, change to something like anger, perhaps terror. Then nothing.

CHAPTER 20
A VERY ANCIENT EVIL

"Can yer move, can yer 'ear me?"

The words sounded muffled as if strained through cotton wool, his head ached and there was orange light slipping in and out of focus. Something soft and wet snuffled his face, there a dog standing over him. Two arms helped him to sit up.

"I were worried there for a moment, thought you was a goner."

A man's face swam into vision and the orange light settled down into a streetlamp seen through freezing fog.

"Give us quite a shock when you come running out of the Moss screaming and shouting, must have been a shock for that feller behind you. Mind, he made off sharpish like."

Giles flexed his arms and legs, realised the shock had made him wet himself. He was sufficiently recovered however to be relieved that he was wearing black jeans and it probably wouldn't show. He felt the man's hands on his back.

"That's strange and you didn't get these when you made that bloody great jump, it looked like you'd been thrown. Your coat's all tore down the back, it's got bits hanging off like streamers."

He stopped talking and Giles realised he was very frightened by what he'd found walking the dog. The man helped him to his feet; Giles didn't physically feel too bad.

"Will you be all right? It's just that me and the dog, need to be getting off like."

"Yeah, I think I'll be OK; thanks very much."

The man started to go but turned back.

"You need to go to the police you know, with all them attacks and stuff. If it hadn't been for me and the dog coming along who knows what might have happened?"

"Yeah, I'll do that, thanks again."

But he was pretty sure that whatever had been after him only wanted him scared and he was way beyond scared. His only consolation was that it must have only wanted to warn him: if it had wanted to do more it would have. He stood taking deep breaths to steady his heart while he got his bearings. Then dusted himself down and set off for Claire's house.

An hour later, after a bath, he sat wrapped in a blanket in Claire's lounge relaxed by several glasses of wine, apparently brought by the damaged ex-priest from his Shrewsbury cellar: Aloxe-Corton burgundy, and a good year according to him. Towards the end of the second bottle Giles understood some of the history connecting this strange trio.

Marcus and Gwen, contemporaries at Oxford, had not fitted the mould and had drifted into alternative lifestyles ending up as outsiders. Even after his scare Giles was sufficiently composed to recognise the fragile nature of Marcus' character and his problem drinking. Before his Skendleby experiences he'd have laughed at them but not now. Besides, his fledgling relationship with Claire was the most important and satisfying element in his life and they were her friends.

So he lounged back on the sofa next to her waiting for the conversation to wend its way towards the elephant in the room. He didn't have long to wait. Marcus offered refills from the remaining half bottle, studied the dark colour of the wine in the light reflected from the fire for a moment and then turned to Giles.

"I've listened to your disc more times than I cared to. You have been very unlucky to get mixed up in it all but not as unlucky, I fear, as the one who opened up the tomb. I can tell you are one of life's sceptics, feckless even, and the only reason you're listening to me is that you're scared. Your rational background denies all the things you've have seen and heard, yet still you are scared.

"I sensed it as soon as you appeared at the door. We live in a world we don't understand, we utilise only a part of our brains, we can't conceive of infinity. Despite the fact that quantum mechanics demonstrate that things can be in two places at the same time and that time itself is a human construct and therefore relative, we refuse to countenance the presence in the world of things that transcend the a priori."

This was exactly the type of statement that Giles hated, typifying everything that he considered snobbish and patronising and which he bitterly resented so he reacted accordingly.

"Drop the lecture and get to the point, it's been a long day."

Giles may have been scared but he was also irked, after all he'd found the disc, and he didn't like being talked down to in front of Claire.

"I'm sorry, young man, it was unintentional. I just wanted to establish there are many things we do not understand that future research might explain. Because what I am going to tell will not seem logical but you need to believe it. I often feel with academics it's best to proceed from the established position of a cogently argued and reasoned base."

Gwen leant forward and gave Marcus a shove, which coming from one as strongly built as she was, effectively stopped him in his tracks.

"Like he said, get to the point. I'm afraid Marcus doesn't get out much these days, Giles, so now he makes the most of any audience he gets, not that he was much different in Oxford."

"Well if you want brevity then here it is. That tomb should never have been touched. Whoever was put in it was meant to stay in it forever. They used procedures to keep her in place, things the credulous would describe as magic and the sceptical as superstition, things of which there are examples in deviant burials all over the world and which still happen in Eastern Europe as we speak. These procedures proved effective for several thousand years. People over hundreds of generations recognised the place for what it was and kept away.

"Then a bunch of meddlers turned up and became infected. Your disc is a tangible manifestation of this infection but I'm sure if you cast your mind back over the duration of the excavation you will remember people having mood swings, behaving strangely, imagining they see things no one else does."

Giles irritation was replaced by a sense of sickening familiarity with the incidents Marcus was listing.

"And why is this? It's because these things are actually happening. If the people who built the tomb were concerned to keep the spirit inside it you can bet they didn't leave much to chance. The tomb and the stone weights are only part of the equation, they will have left other things to watch and contain. Those bodies you found in the pit opposite the tomb's entrance for instance. Whoever went into those pits was special in life and special in death. They had to be, their role was to guard the tomb through eternity. However, the fact that this tomb was placed so far from any human occupation and they were prepared to travel to it, suggests the place already had an evil reputation stretching far back in the folk memory of the tribe. Doesn't that fill you with a sense of awe as an archaeologist, Giles? A place associated with evil for so long that it pre-dates any records. Understand; we are dealing with a very ancient evil."

He paused, stared at his wine glass, then stood up and moved to the fire as if struck by a sudden chill despite the warmth of the softly lit room.

"Anyway, it's out now, thanks to you and your bungling friends. It's moved into your photographer. When you listen to the voice on the disc, Giles, think of the photographer because that's her now and she's acquired millennia of accumulated malice. The first recipient of that malice will be whoever opened the tomb. So contact that individual and tell him to be careful and not spend too much time alone."

"Steve. No need to worry about him. He's sceptical as they come and probably never spends a night alone. If there's one person you don't need to worry about, it's Steve."

He paused and added as an afterthought,

"Strange about his hair though."

If Marcus heard this he showed no sign, just continued.

"I've researched the area, there are legends attached to the local landed family and also a strange tale concerning one of the eighteenth century incumbents of the parish church. We need to contact the family and the present vicar."

"The vicar, well that's a coincidence because before he left tonight, Steve reminded me that the local vicar turned up on site and asked if he could carry out a blessing. Steve found it hilarious, called it an exorcism."

"That's what it should have been! I think I'll pay him a visit, his name's Edmund Joyce and, fittingly enough, he attended the same college as I did but about thirty years later. He's lived a troubled life: I've already read his curriculum vitae and asked a few old acquaintances about him. It seems he suffered some sort of breakdown during his ministry in Birmingham and consequently left the parish to take some time out.

"Since then he's continued very much as a moderniser, tends to shy away from any spiritual interpretations, sees the Bible as a social work manual rather than divine text. Makes one wonder why he joined the church, but I digress. Now he's in the wrong place at the wrong time again. All the same we'll start with him, see if he's noticed anything strange in the parish. I've got the Rectory number so I'll give him a call and arrange to cut across tomorrow."

He got up and moved into the hall to phone leaving Giles and the others finishing the wine.

"You really believe Lisa's inhabited by some ancient demon? Mind you, she scared the life out of Jim. I suppose I'd better just ring Steve and warn him. He'll wet himself laughing at me over this for years; he already thinks I'm incompetent, now he'll think I'm mad."

He searched in his pocket for the mobile and keyed in Steve's number. Neither of their calls was successful. The Rectory was engaged and Giles got the answering service on Steve's phone, and unable to think of a reasonably sane message to leave opted to leave none. Marcus returned to the room.

"I'll try the Rectory number again later. I think it advisable to talk to Joyce sooner rather than later. Because once the photographer's finished with Giles's colleague, it's him she'll turn to – the man of God; spiritual descendant of whatever shaman incarcerated her in the first place. Given Joyce's mental state, it's unlikely his spiritual defences will serve him particularly well. I take it you're staying here tonight, Giles? Yes, I think that's best. In that case we'll have another bottle."

***

The reason that the Rectory phone had been engaged was because just before Marcus left his chair to phone the Reverend Joyce the phone rang and Ed picked up the handset.

"Listen, Joyce, this is Si Carver. I told you to sort out the goings on in your churchyard, get rid of the dossers. Well you didn't, so you'd better get over there right now or I'll come across and bloody well sort it out and I'll sort you out whilst I'm at it; you get where I'm coming from?"

"I'm sorry, Mr Carver, again you have me at a disadvantage, I've no idea what you are talking about. Perhaps you be kind enough to explain a bit more clearly."

"Save that poncy talk for your church tossers, there's been someone in the grounds again, near the old chapel."

Si Carver paused for a moment as if uncertain, which surprised Ed, then he continued,

"They've been trying to get in there and I've seen lights and heard sounds over by the mound. I've already warned you about those tramps I've seen hanging around the churchyard. If you want to support work-shy dossers that's your business but I've told you; keep them off my land, and listen, when I tell someone to do something they do it; understand Vicar? Now shift your arse over here and get them out otherwise I'll be having a word with my friend the Bishop, do you want that?"

Having delivered this most unsubtle of threats he put the phone down leaving Ed to consider a course of action. He decided to ring Davenport and ask him to go with him into the estate hoping that, following their last conversation, Davenport would feel some sense of obligation perhaps mixed with a desire to revisit his old family home. Also he needed to tell Davenport about the phone call from Lisa. He had to tell someone as the voice had stayed clear and ominous in his memory and, although a pitifully weak man lacking courage and faith, he was aware of his own moral responsibility.

Davenport, to his surprise, agreed without hesitation and Ed met him at the Rectory door. He arrived carrying a torch and thick oak cudgel. There was heavy lying frost and the iron hard ground crackled under their boots as they set out together for the gate in the estate wall linking the church land with the old house. Their present circumstances reminded Ed of the passage in Heatly Smythe's journal where the Squire on a similar night delivered his warning to leave well alone.

Now here he was, one of Heatly Smythe's spiritual successors, accompanied by the Squire's ancestor, making his own entrance into the story. He felt comforted not only by Davenport's presence, but because it was evident that the normally unflappable village leader was almost as agitated as he was. For the first time Ed felt that he wasn't alone in this nightmare.

"I'm only doing this because I feel you need looking after, Vicar, and I suppose I'm curious to see what that creature Carver has done to the estate."

Despite his normal bluff delivery Ed knew this was not the complete truth but all the same was childishly touched that Davenport should feel a sense of responsibility for him. By the light of the torch the ill matched couple picked their way through the trees to the estate wall then followed it until they came upon the long disused and overgrown entrance. Davenport ran his fingers almost lovingly across the rusty, frost covered gate.

"It's hard to let go of the old place, Vicar. Some of my earliest memories are of playing out near the estate wall and trying to squeeze through this gate when I was a little boy, before I got packed off to school. Not much chance of squeezing through now I'm afraid, so it's lucky I decided to hang on to the key, save us having to go round to the front."

He fiddled with the key in the lock for a moment and then with a push and a creaking sound the gate opened and they were inside. It seemed darker this side, and the trees pressed more closely together. Ed thought it best to put this down to imagination; but it was clear that Davenport felt the same.

"Something's changed, the place feels wrong and it's more than just the estate grieving the passing of the Davenports. The sooner we deal with Carver and get back home the better as far as I'm concerned. When you rang I felt a pang of nostalgia to see the old place again, but not now. I'm not an imaginative man but I'm getting the strongest feeling that I'm not wanted here and that it's the ground itself that wants me to leave."

Ed felt Davenport's description of himself as unimaginative was an understatement but he was impressed by the depth of feeling he could sense in the older man. So together they stumbled and blundered along the winding track through the dark wood towards the great house, which they could now discern, gaudily lit, in the distance. During the walk through the woods Ed felt a sense of companionship and calm infuse him, which made him feel part of something, however odd, for the first time in years. It was like he'd imagined it would be to share an adventure when he was a friendless boy at school. They reached the tree line and gazed across the lawns at the back of the hall. Davenport noticed trees had been cut back to provide Carver with a golf driving range and a few holes. The scene, lit sporadically by the moon penetrating the fog, looked almost like a Christmas card with the moon bathed frosted lawns sweeping up to the brightly lit house.

However, the peace was broken by the arrival of a figure rapidly striding across the garden towards them and in a moment the red angry face and polished head of Si Carver confronted them.

"Hey how did you bloody get here? I was waiting for you at the front, that's where you was meant to have come. Anyway you're too late, they've gone, it's quiet now, but I warn you, Joyce, don't think you've heard the last of this."

He addressed himself to Ed but couldn't help pointing out to Davenport the recent improvements.

"See you noticed the golf, do you play? I do, like a pro. I'll invite you over for a game; you can see some other changes I've made. You won't recognise the old place once I've finished with it."

Davenport ignored him; he was staring intently at the woods separating them from the estate wall with beyond it the mound. Carver turned back to Ed.

"Now, I'll be making a complaint to your boss unless you get your churchyard cleaned up by Christmas Eve. I've already had to call the police twice. I want it done by Christmas Eve because that's when we're having a house warming in style; know what I mean; quality, celebs, footballers and wags, only the best."

He put his face intimidatingly close up to Ed, glaring through small eyes, his mouth forming a threatening smile.

"You do understand what I'm telling you don't you Joyce? I don't want no disturbance from your church at

Christmas. You should have enough to keep you busy without sheltering tramps, there's places for them paid for out of my taxes. Should be the busiest time, in your job. So just stick to your bleeding church and your own fucking business. I won't tell you again, you've had your last warning."

Normally a mild man Ed responded.

"You never even visit the church, so how can you be so sure they are members of the mendicant community?"

"Oh Christ!"

The shout was Davenport's. Ed and Carver, startled, turned to stare in the same direction. First they heard the sound of a distorted screeching voice, and then, across the lawns, running towards them saw a wild figure, long coat billowing behind, moving at a speed no runner could match. And certainly no human voice could make that sound. The manic high pitched and unintelligible chant bordering on the pitch of hysteria held them rooted to the spot.

About twenty yards away the figure stopped and for an instance it looked straight at them, eyes wide in a rictus of fear and hate. Its mouth and jaws were masked with blood dripping down to cover the neck and shoulders. Fixing them with a glare it made a sound pitched somewhere between a hiss and a snarl in no language they understood. Then it changed direction, passing them at an angle, and headed towards the woods and the church gate. As it disappeared into the trees Carver's jaw dropped open in shock.

"Jesus, what the fuck was that?"

The other two ignored him as Ed, who thought he knew what it was, gasped in horror to Davenport,

"Oh God, Lisa, I think that was Lisa, quick follow, we must catch her."

Ed and a shaken Davenport turned and chased after the apparition with Carver's voice ringing behind them.

"There, see, that's the type of thing I deal with here. That and the shadowy one, he's worse. It's your fault, your fucking fault. Clean it up, deal with it, get rid of them; now! Do it now because I know people who'll make your life hell if you don't. I know people, I know people."

Then as no one was listening and he was alone, he turned and moved back towards the Hall, after a few steps breaking into a run and not looking back.

This was fortunate for him; because if he had dared to look back he'd have seen a shadow moving among the trees. Was it moving? Certainly it seemed to arrive in different places but its movement was hard to track, peculiar and jerky, yet swift. The manner of its perambulation suited its stature, which was long, tattered and dislocated, dark as if a collection of raggedly blackish shrouds had achieved life independent of any occupant. It paused at the tree nearest the house and from there it watched the owner rush rapidly in through the rear entrance, slamming and bolting the door behind him.

CHAPTER 21
IN THE WEE SMALL HOURS OF THE MORNING

The phone rang again as Ed replaced the handset and the noise in the silent kitchen made him jump. It was after eleven, far too late for a normal call. Phone calls at this hour meant trouble or at least nuisance, and on a night like this it was unlikely that anyone was ringing up with Christmas greetings. He and Davenport hadn't found Lisa. They'd followed the course of the estate wall, searched the church and churchyard then followed the silent deserted lanes that fringed the site. On their despondent trudge back to the Rectory Davenport suddenly stopped.

"We forgot Devil's Mound."

"Yes, but that's where she came from. You saw the state she was in – that's the last place she'd have gone."

"But the blood, what if the blood wasn't hers? Listen, go back home, phone the police and her father in that order. I'll cut across to the mound and see if anyone's there."

"Is that wise? After what we've seen tonight? You've no idea what else might be out there."

But Davenport had already gone, heading for Devil's Mound. Ed set off home to carry out his instructions. He'd rung the police, who'd promised to send round a car when one was available, and left a message for the Richardsons asking them to call when they got back in from whatever function or party they were attending. Then the phone rang. He lifted the handset.

"St George's Rectory, Reverend Ed Joyce speaking."

"Joyce, we've not met but my name is Wolf; we attended the same college and have a few common acquaintances in Oxford and Litchfield. I don't want to alarm you but I think you are in danger and we need to talk."

A few weeks ago Ed would have regarded this as the type of crank call all clergy get. Now in his present state of mind it came almost as a relief and he agreed without hesitation to meet the next day. Mary entered the kitchen in her dressing gown, unable to sleep, and made a hot chocolate drink for them both. They sat in the warmth at the kitchen table for a while in companionable silence. She was unwilling to question Ed too closely for fear she'd find he was descending into the depressive state that was the first step on his path to mental breakdown.

To her surprise he seemed calmer and more content than he'd been for days. She knew beneath his pompous exterior he was essentially a kind man, willing to take on other people's problems beyond his capacity to cope with them, and that he was frustrated by his faith and career. But most of all he never seemed to belong anywhere or fit in. He'd no self confidence and the unctuous manner was his way of protecting himself from an uncertain and frightening world. But what she didn't know was that he recognised this only too well and was bitterly ashamed of himself and the pathetic figure he cut.

Ed Joyce despised himself for his uncertainty and lack of moral courage. He suspected the world took him for a caricature of all that was most risible and derided in popular perception of the clergy. At his core he was still the lonely and frightened child he'd been at boarding school, friendless and the natural target for bullies. Tonight however he felt he might finally have arrived in the right place, he and Davenport acted as a team. He felt closeness; and then the call from Marcus Wolf like a *deus ex machina*. So someone else knew there was something wrong in the parish. Unlike Heatly Smythe he wasn't alone, perhaps this time God would include him. He finished the hot chocolate, left his chair to stand behind Mary, massaging her shoulders as she finished her drink. Then, hand in hand, they went to bed.

***

PC Wilson and WPC Dixon pulled into a lay-by on the Silk Road to drink the coffee they'd bought at the all night garage and take a break on the long night shift. They were waiting for a serial attacker that no one in the force had any idea how to catch. The first couple of nights had been edgy, even though they were issued with a tazer for use in extremity, but now it was just boring. They kept the engine on so the heater would continue to run. The night was cold and steam from the Styrofoam cups filled the car's interior. Outside it was quiet, the road empty. Another four boring hours to fill, with banter and bickering, unless they got a call. That would be worse than doing nothing; bringing more paperwork to no real purpose other than help the division make its targets, all of which were manipulated and pointless anyway. So they settled to pick at the point of contention between them.

"You'll never get anywhere singing with that band, George. Face it, you'll be stuck filling in forms and sitting in stinking squad cars until you marry some randy sergeant from CID."

George, whose real name was Gemma, settled happily to the routine.

"Piss off, Ges, you've no idea, even if we don't get a recording deal we're getting plenty of bookings. Soon I'll earn more from the band in a month than from the force in a year and then I'll be off. The next time you see me it'll be on the pages of *Hello*, and I won't be in this poxy uniform."

"What about seeing you without the poxy uniform now? I'll tell you what I'd like......"

But he never did. A heavy container lorry approaching the squad car sounded its klaxon loud and abrasive in the still night air. They looked up startled causing Ges to spill coffee over his groin. Gemma saw the lorry swerve to avoid a wild figure zigzagging across the carriageway. She would never be quite sure what happened next but the front of the lorry clipped the figure throwing it in a heap into the dark at the side of the road. The lorry corrected its swerve and sped off into the night, maybe the driver never felt any contact.

Gemma, followed by a spluttering Ges, ran towards the prone figure, nerving herself for the horrific injury she expected to find; sweating despite the cold night. She was just a few feet away when suddenly it jumped up like a Jack in a Box and stood for a moment facing her, an image from hell.

For an instant it seemed to hover unsupported in the freezing air as its legs unbuckled and straightened to support it. Then, slowly, it turned its face towards them and they saw the rictus of its blood stained mouth grinning horribly in the sickening parody of a smile. After a few seconds, which seemed an age to Gemma, its eyes focused and it hurled itself forward. Gemma took the brunt of its velocity and was knocked off her feet landing badly several yards away, the breath crushed out of her. From the ground she could see Ges struggling with the wild figure, being forced back towards the squad car. He was gasping and squealing for help in a voice raised in pitch by fear and the hand clasping at his throat.

She radioed for assistance then got shakily to her feet. With one hand round his neck the figure lifted Ges and bent him backwards over the bonnet of the car like a torn rag doll. She could see Ges trying to free his throat from the force of the grip squeezing it closed. Gemma was dizzy and frightened, too frightened to disturb the figure that was killing her colleague in case it should turn on her. Her one contact had been sufficient for her to understand this was no normal thing. It could survive the impact with the lorry and hit her with such force. Every instinct in her body urged her to turn and run. She'd stumbled a few steps when a repeated strangulated cry stopped her. She looked round and saw Ges, now screaming her name, his voice strangely high pitched like a girl, he'd given up struggling. Then he started to cry.

She watched as he lay prone across the bonnet with the creature over him tearing at his face with its teeth, its mouth covered in blood. Ges managed to sob out,

"Gemma, pleeease, pleeease."

She could never understand what made her to do what she did next, perhaps it was training, maybe love. Taking deep breaths she checked the tazer then advanced towards the creature and standing behind it deployed full force. The creature let out a hiss, like a geyser erupting, and turned its head to face her. What Gemma faced, the blood, the eyes, the sharp teeth, would inhabit her nightmares until she died, but the red-tinged eyes lost focus and it staggered unsteadily on its beautiful legs. Gemma used the moment's grace to snap open her baton and hit it as hard, quickly and often as she could until, to her relief, it released Ges and stumbled to the ground. She quickly cuffed it then dragged Ges into the car, which she reversed away from the prone, but still struggling, handcuffed body. Close enough for it to be just inside the main beam of the headlights, but far enough for her to accelerate away if it showed signs of getting to its feet. There, sobbing, bloody and badly bruised, they waited until the blue lights of relief appeared in the distance.

***

At the same time, on the same road, Davenport sat in the ambulance with the mutilated man who, though no longer babbling had continued to grip his hand. In the gloom of the ambulance interior it was like the road to Hell. But he could see that the long blood-soaked hair of the man that he'd taken for fairish was in fact dead white. Yet the man was, at least from his perspective, young. Despite the night's unnerving sequence of events he felt calm, almost disorientated, as if he'd entered someone else's dream, yet he knew that if it was anyone's dream it was his by ancestral right.

He felt more concern for the vicar than for himself; he should have kept him out of all this. There was a bond between his family, the land whether for good or evil. This was a local problem that a series of strangers had come and disturbed: they could take the consequences; they'd brought it on themselves. But the vicar, he was different. The local clergy had always been the responsibility of the Davenports and he should never have involved Joyce in any of this. The ambulance pulled to a stop and the doors opened revealing the well lit entrance to the A and E unit of the general hospital.

The victim was stretchered out of the ambulance and into hospital accompanied by Davenport. A police officer standing by the reception crossed the floor towards them, recognised Davenport and took him to one side as he watched the stretcher recede down a long ill-lit corridor.

"I thought I recognised you, Sir Nigel, back on your old lands tonight then. I'm afraid I'm going to have to ask you for a statement."

Davenport realised how tired he felt and how difficult all this would be to explain. The look of weariness at least communicated itself to the policeman who in an unexpectedly kindly way led him across to a waiting area furnished with some of the types of chairs that all hospital waiting rooms contain.

"Perhaps you remember me, Sir Nigel: Wayne Barford. I lived on the estate near the church, my uncle Eddie used to work for you. I'm a policeman now."

He added, as an unnecessary afterthought,

"You sit down there, Sir, and I'll get us a drink."

He moved across the hallway to the drinks dispenser and while he manipulated the controls for two coffees, Davenport was left to try to make enough sense of the night's events for a coherent statement. He remembered Wayne Barford as a large and violent youth whose parents had moved off the estate before Wayne had the opportunity to cause any major trouble. Barford returned with the drinks.

"I've put extra sugar in your cup Sir; good after you've had a shock like."

Davenport took the cup of hot coffee thinking perhaps the boy hadn't grown up too bad after all. Over the next few minutes he gave his statement, which, although deliberately low on motive or content, was factually correct. He'd been alerted by the Reverend Edmund Joyce of a disturbance occurring on the fields at the back of the Hall. In the Hall grounds they'd encountered a blood spattered and deranged young woman who'd disappeared into the night. He made no mention of the unnatural speed at which she moved or the unnerving noise she made, which still echoed inside his head. Then he sent the Reverend Joyce to phone the police while he had searched the fields from which the young woman had emerged, and there he'd found the victim lying semi conscious on the feature known locally as Devil's Mound. He didn't mention the horror he felt at the discovery or the fear which almost stopped him functioning.

Davenport was a brave man, he'd faced death as a young subaltern; he'd been wounded and decorated for his part in the pointless fiasco in Aden. He'd checked the man's injuries; the left ear was almost completely severed at the lobe, and the fleshy flap left dangling by a couple of skeins of muscle that had not been quite cut through. There was a great deal of blood at the base of the neck and across shoulders and chest. He was in a state of shock, too terrified to speak, only emitting a continuous whimpering sound. He was also bitterly cold and near death.

Davenport removed his own coat and covered him having checked the bleeding was not too rapid. He called the ambulance and, when he heard its approach, made his way down the rough track to the lane to guide its path. On his return to the mound with the paramedics the man had gripped his hand and held onto it until they arrived at the hospital.

He answered Barford's questions as quickly as he could and was offered a lift home. He accepted gratefully but felt obliged to find out how the victim was and who he was. So Barford accompanied him to the room in which he was being treated and left him at the door. A nurse told him the victim had lost the lower section of his right ear but that the piercing to the left shoulder and lower neck had done less damage than they'd feared and no major arteries were severed. However, she said, with a trained look of professional empathy, the main danger could be psychological. He was in a disturbed state and had been sedated but Davenport could see him if he wished. He didn't wish. He'd carried out his responsibilities. As he trailed back down the long corridor towards reception he thought it was no wonder the mind might be disturbed. But what the hell was he doing on the mound on a freezing cold night with such a murderous fiend?

The reception area was a bustle of activity as groups of nurses and orderlies standing round the desk watched a group of paramedics escorted by four police officers hurry a stretcher down a corridor leading to the isolation wing. Davenport noticed the figure on the stretcher was struggling but heavily strapped down. Barford was talking to a young, good-looking but unnaturally pale, WPC, but on noticing Davenport, walked over to him.

"There's a coincidence, looks like you've seen both sides of this incident, Sir Nigel, seems like that's the thing what tried to kill your friend. She's just attacked two of our officers, like something out of a horror film it were. It's been knocked down by a lorry, stunned by a tazer, hacked down with a baton but it still took several of them to tie her down to the stretcher. Still I suppose it could be that we've solved all these attacks now: by accident as usual. There's something creepy about that, I hope I never meet her on a dark night. Anyway, I've finished here for the day so I'll drive you home; I'm sorry but I'll have to speak to you again tomorrow, Sir."

On the drive home Davenport gazed from his rear seat as the moonlit countryside flashed past. Once off the main road the car took the country lanes near his home more slowly so he had time to look at the back of the Hall as it came into view and then recede. The site of the family heritage struck him, as always, with a mixture of nostalgic sadness and anxiety. He noticed that despite the lateness of the hour, it was 1.45am, there were still lights on in the Hall.

The Rectory, by contrast, was in darkness, so at least the vicar was able to sleep. Wayne Barford talked throughout the journey but by the time he'd been dropped off and said goodbye Davenport couldn't recall a single thing he'd said. Some lights had been left on for him, with a note telling him Debo had gone to bed and for him not to make any noise. He felt weary but not ready for sleep so he poured a half tumbler of brandy and sank into his armchair and tried to switch off his mind and float downstream but, after a few moments, the thing submerged in his subconscious surfaced.

Finally it had struck: just when they'd fled the Hall and escaped, the meddling archaeologists had released the evil they'd contained over the centuries. The curse had come upon them and the modern world of science and rational thought was as powerless as they were.

The family motto since the fifteenth century had been 'Guarding the Watcher'. But he hadn't noticed that all the elements of the family misfortunes had converged again. An attempt to open the mound, sightings of the Watcher, a disturbed cleric and now, tonight, a violently-possessed young woman. The past was re-woken, it had been on his watch but he hadn't been watching.

CHAPTER 22
THE ANATOMY OF A GHOST

Marcus Wolf put down the phone mildly surprised. He'd expected the Reverend Joyce would, at the very least, have asked a series of questions and suspected would prove very difficult to persuade. In fact Joyce sounded like he was expecting the call and was relieved when it came. He walked back into the lounge. Gwen was slouched, drowsy, in the armchair by the fire, legs stretched out towards the flames, thick grey woollen socks on her feet, boots discarded by the hearth, sipping a glass of wine. Giles was sitting in his blanket at the edge of the sofa with one arm around Claire, who was lying back against him holding his other hand in both of hers.

Strange, Marcus thought: we create moments of peace even in the middle of disaster. His re-entry into the room broke the spell. He was used to this, his ravaged countenance wasn't comforting. He sat in the chair across the fire from Gwen and poured himself half a glass of wine.

"This is purely to soothe the vocal chords. I've arranged for us to meet Joyce tomorrow. Before that I need to explain what we're facing. Giles, I don't know how much Gwen has told you but some years ago I had a very unfortunate brush with the occult; I was prevailed upon to undertake a blessing to rid a building of something that was making a large number of highly sceptical people too frightened to work in it. A haunting I suppose you would call it. Initially I was sceptical; afterwards I was just very afraid.

"I don't know what was actually in there, but a memory of it still existed, an impression like the rather more apparent one Gwen will leave in that chair when she gets up. The things we do generate energy which does not immediately dissipate. Particularly evil things generate high concentrations of energy and these energies cling on and grow, like mould; thus a type of possession takes place.

"Some places, for reasons we don't know, seem far more susceptible to this and there are people whose minds are sufficiently attuned to pick up messages the trapped energy transmits. Animals are affected far more than us; we appear to have lost our antennae.

"This is the basis of haunting. You, Giles, employ such a device to measure the age of artefacts because radio carbon dating operates on similar principles. Put like that it doesn't seem too bad does it?

"However, with concentrated evil the negative emotions are strong enough to take possession of any unfortunate who is sensitive enough to be tuned in. So the original evil is passed on spread through a living agent. Psychologically disturbed individuals are particularly prone to such infection and I wonder if what we diagnose as mental illness is often the manifestation of a haunting.

"In the case I attempted to mediate, a random group of individuals claimed to have witnessed inanimate objects move independently. They heard voices and footfalls in empty rooms and witnessed a rocking chair gradually begin to move, at first slowly then with the full swing, as if someone was in it. All these individuals were frightened enough to refuse to work in the building until it was cleansed."

He paused for a moment and glanced at Gwen who nodded sympathetically and refilled his wine glass. He took a long swallow and continued more haltingly, the didactic and logical manner of his address now vanished.

"I saw these things."

He paused again, blinking.

"I spent the twilight of a winter's day in the most affected room with two of the least affected workers, confirmed atheists, hard men. At dusk, as the light faded, we heard a faint voice and then footsteps crossing the room. Our eyes followed the sounds across the floor towards the rocking chair, there was a faint creaking of wood, then, almost imperceptibly, the chair began to move. My blood froze. Then, creaking and banging the floor, it was rocking violently and we were down the stairs and out of the front door.

"The papers reported a blessing of the building I carried out the next Sunday, and that as far as the press was concerned was the end of the matter. But of course it wasn't, the work continued but only in daylight and the workers refused to enter that room.

"There was a child who lived in the building prior to the work being carried out. She was confined in a sanatorium with a severe personality disorder. The mother read the coverage in the papers and requested I visit the child to carry out a similar blessing. The girl claimed there were people inside her. She spoke in different voices, often saying things she couldn't possibly have known. The mother persuaded me to see the child and the remembrance of the Tuesday afternoon that I spent with her in the sanatorium never leaves me. Foolishly I attempted to interfere with something for which I was unprepared. I lost my mind and, for a time, my faith."

He faltered and there was silence; time dragged, he rubbed his eyes then blurted out, voice quavering,

"There was talk of abuse."

Again silence before he croaked almost in a whisper,

"The Diocese managed to keep the matter hushed up. It was easier in those days. I lost my parish. I had nowhere to go and then I remembered Gwen."

They sat in silence listening to the crackle and splutter of the wood fire knowing he hadn't finished. After some moments Gwen said gently,

"But you've put yourself back together haven't you, dear, you've had time to reflect and seek help."

"Yes. I travelled for a bit, joined the Orthodox Church and tried to come to terms with the experience. Since then I've hidden myself away in Shrewsbury and on the Welsh borders and tried to help out whenever I can. I've not got the strength to take a front line role in this type of thing anymore but I can advise you."

He sat back in his chair and sipped his wine, staring at the fire while he tugged at a fringe of wispy beard beneath his chin. None of the others spoke, partially mesmerised by the play of light and shadow across his face knowing that there was more to come.

"The site of your dig is cursed; interesting that the last sacrifice is contemporary with those on Lindow Moss. Perhaps they are linked: strange also, Claire, that Lindow is the place you chose to live. There's something about the spirit of a place and this place has been calling out to you: it wants you here but whether for good or evil I don't know.

"There are more things to be found deep under Devil's Mound, it welcomes evil. If the police want to look for the cause of the attacks it's your site they should investigate. I suppose that as an archaeologist you find all this far-fetched?"

"As an archaeologist, yeah. But after the last few weeks I just don't know any more and it scares the shit out of me to think there may be worse things deep under the mound. You're right about place: loads of features are built on earlier sites, some dating as far back as the Mesolithic, but I'm not sure where that gets us."

Giles ran his hand through Claire's hair as he spoke feeling comforted by the warmth of her body leaning against his.

"It gets us further than you think. Whatever ritual they performed worked: it kept the thing in there. Whatever it was, the demon is still part of that culture. It doesn't think like us, it's not modern; it's rooted in its own past and observes ancient laws and conventions, not ours. So we are dealing with something that still believes in those things and will continue to be conditioned by them."

Gwen turned to Giles,

"Marcus is suggesting that if we can get this entity back into the tomb and recreate the ancient burial there's a good chance it will obey the ritual laws and stay put. Your Iron Age villagers broke into the tomb. It scared them away from the place but they successfully resealed it. If they could do it so can we."

"You mean like we conduct a human sacrifice. Get real, who do you think we can convince to volunteer for that?"

"No need to be sarcastic, Giles, obviously no one is suggesting that. But you could re-bury the original two sacrifices."

"Hang on, let me get this straight; you're suggesting that having excavated this site we now need to go and put it all back. Like re-packing Pandora's box, right?"

"Precisely."

Marcus, having regained self control, reached across and gently squeezed his arm.

"You took it out; you put it back, although not you alone. Your friend who opened it will have to close it up again. You'll have to use the same stones because I think those stones with the eyes must represent some ancestors with undying power."

Giles was getting angry, finding it difficult to control himself. He spat out,

"And that's it yeah? That's what you've come up with?...... That's it; a de-excavation? A new one for archaeology text books that; magic."

Marcus didn't react; he recognised stress when he saw it and he pressed on in the same gentle manner.

"No there's more to it than that, but we've not worked all of it out yet. If the residual is in your photographer, Lisa, then we need to find a way of getting it out of her. The church does have a manual on how to do that, fortunately."

Giles snorted with dismissive laughter and Marcus paused for a moment smiling coldly before saying quietly,

"It has been known to work on occasions."

"Oh yeah and you can name check someone who's managed it can you?"

"Well, I think that Christ would be the best example; someone even you might have heard of, Giles."

The acid reply was a barometer of the way the conversation was souring and Marcus recognising this took a deep breath and tried to smile an apology, saying,

"No, I'm sorry for that, it was a cheap retort but please hear me out. If we drive it out of Lisa it will have to return to the site it haunts, that's one of the rules it's governed by. Once it's there we can reseal it. We just need to work out the necessary ritual so you can leave it as you found it. We must pray that it hasn't been in the girl long enough to permanently affect her. Or, worse that it doesn't switch to another, stronger, host. If it manages that, it gathers power and we lose it."

Giles saw Claire flinch as Marcus said this and, sorry to have lost his temper with her friends, said,

"OK, OK, but even if I bought all of this stuff I'd never convince Steve. He's angry enough about the way we excavated the site, he'd never allow us to put it all back and there's no sane archaeologist who would disagree with him. When he stops being angry he'll just laugh."

"Have you got a better idea, Giles? Have you forgotten how frightened you've been over the last few days? Forgotten the state you were in when you arrived tonight? No I thought not, don't say any more now. I'll work on the detail, you and Claire go to bed; we've a busy day tomorrow."

Giles hadn't a better idea and didn't want to argue any more, he was tired and the idea of going to bed with Claire sounded good. As they were leaving the room he heard Marcus say softly to Gwen,

"And of course we will need a holy man, a shaman, to conduct the ritual; normally a difficult one that, but I think I've got the ideal candidate."

CHAPTER 23
THE CALM BEFORE

The morning sunlight streamed in like butterscotch, bathing the table and bowl of oranges in warmth. Claire stood at a work surface making tea, toast and honey for her and Marcus. Through the window, at the back of the garden, Lindow Moss, dusted with frost, basked benign and welcoming under a clear blue winter sky. At the table Marcus felt as close to peace of mind as his disposition allowed.

"You know, Claire, this is about the closest I've been to family life since I was a boy."

He took a bite of toast failing to notice the thin viscous stream of honey gently sliding off its edge and onto his black sweater.

"Admittedly a strange type of family, and I know this is the calm before the storm, but we seem to fit together, a family of the failed and broken."

"Speak for yourself, I don't feel either failed or broken, just a mixture of content and horror. I don't know where one ends and the other starts."

Gwen had gone for a walk to buy the morning paper, Giles was still in bed. In an hour they would set off to meet the vicar of Skendleby and Woodford.

***

In Skendleby Ed was sitting in the rectory kitchen waiting for Davenport. He'd called earlier asking him to come over. Ed was stuck between epiphany and malediction. He was involved in something too frightening to think about and last week he'd been on the brink of mental breakdown. Yet last night he and Mary had made love for the first time in as far back as he could remember, and now here he was awaiting the arrival of Davenport and Marcus Wolf with a sense of almost pleasurable anticipation. He wasn't alone anymore; he was part of a team.

Even more significant: he was convinced of the evil he faced; he'd seen it with his own eyes. He believed it existed and, if it existed, against all rational sense and empiricism, then God existed, so all this was happening for a purpose. It was meant to be and he was meant to be part of it and not just a smarmy and irritating presence at the periphery of other people's lives.

He was also enjoying another emotion for the first time, a strong, angry, dislike bordering on hatred, for Si Carver. Most unchristian yet strangely fortifying. Carver had threatened him twice in a contemptuous manner. But last night on Carver's land he realised the link with the mound was not with the Rectory, not with him. Heatly Smythe's problems had arisen from his trying to excavate the mound, his meddling in things that were none of his business. The parish priest was not the target of any animus, never had been, in fact the lurking thing that terrified him had tried to warn him off; perhaps even to protect him.

No, the link was with the Hall and its owner. The one who had most to fear was Carver. Cheered by this he experienced a delicious, if guilty, frisson and settled to his breakfast with a hearty appetite.

***

Later, at eleven by the chime of the clock, high in the bell tower, a strange assortment of pilgrims sat round the large rectangular Rectory table. At the head a smooth-faced, bespectacled cleric sat opposite a slender, beautiful, dark haired woman. At one side of the table sat two men who could not have looked more different. A youngish tousle haired man wearing old jeans and Parka over a T shirt baring a mildly offensive message, and next to him an elderly, strongly built man with the stamp of landed gentry like the writing through a stick of seaside rock. He was engaged in conversation about mutual acquaintances with a heavily built woman with short cropped grey hair wearing a second hand man's suit.

"Yes, that would be Richard Davenport, a cousin of mine from the Devonshire branch of the family, a bit odd, some type of academic in Cambridge now, a sensitive sort of chap from what I remember."

The others weren't part of this exchange. They sat with eyes fixed on the sixth member of the group, an oldish man with a deeply lined face wearing a shabby wool sweater streaked with honey stains. He was fiddling with some notes preparing to make a speech but never had the opportunity because the shrill ring tone of a mobile phone diverted all attention. The youngish man fumbled in the pockets of his Parka and eventually located it.

"Hi, Giles here. Jan, what's up? Steve? What's he done now? You're joking. Attacked? Jesus. Listen, calm down, no don't worry, I'll come and get you, we'll go together, about forty minutes maybe an hour. OK, stay calm, yeah. See you."

He turned to explain but before he could, Davenport spoke to Ed.

"Unless there's been an extraordinary coincidence I think we now know who my friend in the ambulance from last night is. I'm sorry about this, Mr Wolf, I know you have important matters you want to discuss with us but I think we'd better tell you what we know first and I'll be surprised if the two aren't related. Do you want to do it or shall I, Vicar? Sorry, Edmund, I mean Ed."

The question was rhetorical, Davenport's tone and body language made it clear he was going to tell the story. He outlined the events of last night culminating in the destinations of Lisa and Steve, mildly satisfied to see the effect of his narrative on the others. On concluding he turned to Giles,

"It's too late now to talk about blame but it would have been far better if you'd left that place alone, young man. I warned you about excavating in that field and now look what's happened."

But Giles wasn't listening he was heading for the door.

***

The day was still crisply invigorating with deep blue sky and pale lemon sun but, for Giles, Davenport's account of the previous night had drained any warmth from it. The image of Steve sacrificed at the site brought back his own terror. This wasn't just some weird type of haunting he'd blundered into, that would have been bad enough, but Steve could have died and Lisa was possessed; a killer. Now the pattern of attacks, desecrations and disturbance made bizarre sense. His excavation had unlocked the gate which, over the millennia, kept them in check. This attack had happened whilst he spent the night with Claire almost enjoying the spookiness of it. He even felt a sense of responsibility, not something he normally associated with himself.

Jan was waiting outside the front door of her terrace, teary eyed and smoking. They drove to the hospital in silence. The police found her telephone number in Steve's wallet at the hospital and had phoned her in lieu of next of kin. She spoke only once more as they approached the hospital gates.

"Why did he go there with that woman? He could have been with me, he knew that. The bastard, I don't know what upset me more, that he nearly died or that he went off with some casual pickup. Oh God, makes me sound like Rose, what a bitch I am."

She began to cry again. The tension of the drive made arriving at the hospital almost a relief. From reception they were directed to a side ward at the end of which was a small room with a police woman sitting outside.

The room contained one bed, one chair and a haggard, elderly man with long white hair propped up on some pillows. The right side of his face and ear were smothered in a bandage; other dressings covered his shoulders beneath the loose hospital gown. He greeted them without emotion, just a grunt of recognition. Giles sat on the chair, Jan on the bed, holding Steve's hand, her face wet with tears.

"Oh, Steve, oh love, look what they've done to you. Your beautiful hair's all white, even on your arms and chest."

Giles looked and saw she was right, the hair on his arms and at his neck was as dead white as that on his head and his face seemed to have aged thirty years overnight. As Jan fussed and petted him Steve turned his gaze and attention to Giles.

"She bit my ear off, Gi, tried to kill me. I thought I was dying; it was like something out of a horror movie. And the voice, I'll never forget that. But there's something worse, frightened even her. I saw it. It makes no sense. But it's real and I'm so scared, even in here."

He faltered then started to cry, the tears soaking the thin material of the gown, Giles watched in silence as Jan cradled his head. Then through his sobs he blurted,

"It left me to die out there. So cold, alone and frightened. I could feel my blood pumping out but I couldn't move. Someone found me, I felt him take my hand in the ambulance. I thought I'd died and that it was Dad come back for me."

He stopped. Jan tried to brush back his hair.

"Steve, you're safe now, love. I'll stay here till they say when they'll let you out. Why did you do it? What happened? Who was she?"

Giles decided he'd leave them together even though he hadn't said a single word.

"Steve, you take care, all right man. You're safe in here, but listen, I'll come and see you tomorrow, OK? We need to talk. Jan, I'll wait for you in reception."

He walked to the door, noticing there were no flowers, no cards or chocolates in this room. No family, no ties, nothing. Steve called after him,

"Giles, it's you that needs to take care, none of us are safe, maybe that witch woman was right."

He decided to call in on Rose while he waited. It was the last thing he wanted but he felt morally obliged. He found her at the other end of the hospital grounds in a single room off the psychiatric wards. He needn't have worried about the length of the visit, it was brutally short.

He thought he was in the wrong room at first. The wild looking creature in the badly stained hospital gown with part of its scalp shaved looked unfamiliar. It sat in bed rapidly turning its head from side to side snapping its jaws. Rose recognised him though.

"I see you Giles. You woke the dead, now you pay the price. Worse for the bitch, that witch you're with, worse for her."

She fixed him with her bloodshot eyes as she opened her mouth and cackled, he saw that there were teeth missing and her tongue was palsy white.

"It tricked me, it was never meant for me, it was for her and now there's nowhere to run."

She threw back her head and began to make a high pitched yipping cry. Giles backed out of the room.

***

It took several minutes out in the cold air to compose himself sufficiently to return to the main building and wait for Jan. Giles hated hospitals, everything about them, but most of all the smell and the lack of independence of action that outside of them, or prison, we take for granted. He wanted to be out in the clear, crisp air, not breathing the infected atmosphere of the wards. He saw two men approaching and Jim Gibson took him by his arm.

"Giles, what are you doing here? We've just been to see Lisa; this is her father, you know Councillor Richardson?"

It was only then Giles recognised the man who'd threatened him at the planning meeting: he was almost as badly changed as Steve, dishevelled, papery skinned, grey and old. Giles felt an impulse of sympathy and offered his hand. Instead of taking it Richardson shouted,

"What we've seen in there is not my daughter, not my Lisa. It's something broken, not right any more. Do you know what this is going to do for my reputation; it's my turn to be mayor next year. You were meant to give her an interest, build up her bloody confidence. Well you've done that all right, turned her into a mad thing, dressed up like a tart and murderous, now she's strapped down to a bed, drugged and raving."

His jaw quivered and a tear ran down his sunken cheek. When he spoke again it was like a different man.

"What have you done to her, what have I done to her? To my little princess, my little girl."

Richardson paused, choked back a sob then managed to refocus on Giles.

"But I'll have you, or my lawyers will. When they've finished with you, you'll wish you were under the bloody ground, not digging it up."

His face was so close that Giles could feel the bubbles of spittle splashing his cheeks. Jim put an arm round him and steered him to the door.

"Come on, Derek, this won't help Lisa. You've had a nasty shock. Let's get some fresh air and then I'll drive you home."

He turned back briefly.

"Jesus, Giles, I'm not surprised he's like that. He's right, the thing in there's not his daughter; it's like something out of '*The Exorcist*'. I don't know what we've done, the world's gone mad, but something happened that day, you let out something unspeakable now it wants vengeance."

His face was red and he took Giles by the arm as if trying to anchor himself.

"It could have been me, she sat in my car, bit my ear, I could be the one in that hospital room, not Steve. Thank God they've got her sedated. Look, I'm going to take Derek home. Don't feel too bad about what he said, he's pretty broken up, he's really not as bad as he appears. He thinks what's happened to Lisa is his fault, some type of retribution for his Skendleby scam. Listen, you need to watch out, don't spend time on your own. See you."

He walked off towards the automatic door but half way there he halted.

"I hope you've got some idea how to put all this back together again Giles, because I don't think it's going to stop; this is just the beginning."

The doors soundlessly opened and closed and Giles was left alone in the hospital reception with all its stark associations. The next fifty-five minutes waiting for Jan dragged and dragged. He drank two plastic cups of foul coffee, paced the car park, watched the inane daytime television with the sound turned down and read the various targets of customer care that were proudly pinned up on the hospital notice board. From time to time a stretcher was pushed down one of the corridors. Eventually Jan appeared, red faced and weepy eyed, but under control.

"Amazingly, apart from his left ear the other injuries aren't too bad. She tried to kill him with some type of stone blade, there were fragments left in the wounds. If it had been steel he'd be dead.

"He's sleeping now but he wants you to come back and talk to him later. He wants to warn you again. He's not so bothered about the girl who stabbed him now she's been caught; it's the other thing that's really scaring him. He thinks it's what attacked Rose and what Leonie tried to warn us about. He's terrified it'll come back to finish him off but he told me to tell you to watch out because it wants you too."

They walked to the car and as they set off for her house she said,

"His hair started to go white the day we opened the tomb, there's something toxic in there, and it's poisoning everything it touches. That night on the mound only accelerated it. We've started something that we can't stop and I'm too frightened to stick around. I've got some leave due, Giles, and I'd like to go and spend some time with my Dad. I'll leave you his number in Glasgow in case you need to talk to me. When we get home I'm going to pack a bag and catch the first train I can."

They lapsed into silence until they reached her terrace. She leant across and pecked Giles on the cheek, handing him a folded piece of paper.

"It's Dad's address in Glasgow. When they discharge Steve tell him he can come up to join me. But tell him to come only if it's me he wants to be with, I want to help him but I don't think I can stand being messed around any more. Bye Giles, take care."

Giles drove to his own cold empty house. It felt different as if whatever haunted him here had moved on. Considerately, it had turned off the lights and taps. The house felt like an empty grave and he wanted out. He threw some things into a rucksack, constantly glancing over his shoulder. He was relieved when he'd locked the front door behind him and was out on the street.

Rose, broken up and raving, Steve, damaged in hospital, now Jan escaping to Scotland. There was only him and Leonie left of the core team. He tried to warn her to be careful but got no answer from either her mobile or her home phone.

Driving to Lindow he passed attack sites littered with floral tributes and thought about the thing that attacked Steve on the mound and chased him on the Moss. Marcus might have a plan for purging Lisa and re-sealing the tomb but what was he going to do about this other thing? He found himself muttering "it moves in a most peculiar way". Despite the brightness of the sun and the warmth of the car heater he felt cold and very afraid.

CHAPTER 24
NO ESCAPE

Claire greeted him at the door; immediately he felt better.

"Gwen and Marcus stayed in Skendleby. Davenport's going to take them to the mound and walk them round the estate boundary. They'll have dinner in the Rectory and stay overnight; I'll pick them up tomorrow. So we have the place to ourselves."

They spent the late winter afternoon in bed watching as the onset of night exsanguinated the sky and the red sunset turned black. A wispy covering of fog began to drift in over Lindow Moss. Lying side by side and silent in the gloom they were thinking of the same thing: Lisa.

"You know I'm the one who has to do it, Giles."

"Do what?"

"Do what Marcus said to drive out whatever's inside her."

"No way; you know what she did to Steve, what she's become. Believe me, you don't want to go anywhere near her."

"Giles, it's her on the disc, that's what she's become. I have to try, while she's in hospital sedated, tied down, whatever. We decided how to do it when you were visiting Steve."

"And how do you think that you're going to manage that then? For a start you won't be allowed to see her. I saw her dad today, Richardson; he's as callous as they come, but even he couldn't stand to be with her, his own daughter, she frightened him; he was crying, a man like that crying. You should have seen Steve; he's like an old man, white haired and terrified. You can't, it's too dangerous."

He'd already decided not to tell Claire about Rose and the image of Steve and Richardson stifled any desire for further conversation. So they lay slumped and silent in the twilight of the bedroom, until Giles couldn't resist the urge to ask the question.

"What does Marcus want you to do?"

He was about to say 'I won't let you' when he realised that he had no control over her, in fact he hardly knew her but he didn't want to lose her, so again they lapsed into silence as the room darkened. But the question hovered over them so after about five minutes:

"Giles, it's what I do or what I used to do, I have a type of gift. Under certain circumstances I can make contact with people's inner consciousness and I can see things, things other people can't, things most people think don't exist. I've tried to run away from it but this is meant for me. The old sensations have all come back; it started with the dream of the dig. This thing, whatever it is, found me, I'm meant to be here. I know you don't understand any of this but you have to trust me because this isn't going to be without danger for you either."

After his recent experiences he couldn't find a convincing argument. He felt her slip from the bed and begin to shuffle into her clothes.

"Come on, get up, it's grown too gloomy in here. I'll take you out to dinner and tell you what Marcus has lined up for you."

They ate in a bistro by the fire station that had changed hands and identity several times. It wasn't particularly good but was just within walking distance. The place was noisy and decorated for Christmas. A large works-night-out dominated one end of the room, shouting and cackling, so they and some other couples were shoved over to the back by the side window, an area only infrequently visited by the waiters.

Giles picked at his food thinking about his meal in the Trattoria with Jim. It seemed a lifetime ago but was only a matter of weeks; he began to consider how much longer he could stay with Claire and was wondering if she minded he'd brought some of his stuff over when he realised she was waiting for an answer to a question he hadn't heard.

"So will you be able to do it, Giles?"

"Sorry, I was miles away."

"Will you be able to seal the tomb and put enough of the bones back to make it work?"

"Oh God, I didn't think that was serious, I can understand some attempt to get this thing out of Lisa, you know, deal with the psychology of it and all that; but the rest, that's just…"

He was going to say bollocks but he didn't believe that either so he trailed off limply, fixed by her intent gaze, and scooped up a forkful of the glutinous and rapidly congealing gnocchi on his plate.

"Giles!"

She talked quietly but in a tone of voice he now recognised as her assertive mode; he'd learned enough about her to understand there was no point arguing. She spoke to him like a teacher instructing a slow and reluctant pupil.

"We have to put things back the way they were before. I know it's not easy for you to understand, but you need to find a way to do it and you need Steve and, of course, Ed."

"Ed, you mean that vicar?"

"Yes, the mound was closed with a ceremony. You opened it and you've seen the consequences. Now you need to close it. Believe me, it is very necessary."

Her angular face was sharper, her mouth a fixed line. Giles blurted,

"Well there's no chance of ever getting Steve near that place, you should have seen him, Claire."

The teacher in her was getting angry.

"You will get him there whatever Giles. These entities are guided by the rules they're used to. We are dealing with something that still exists in its own long dead time, we have to contain it using things it will recognise and obey. Once it leaves Lisa it has nowhere to go but the mound. Once it's there we make sure it can't move out again. Understand?"

"It just doesn't make sense."

Her face chiselled like a diamond, the line of the mouth more fixed; now he was almost frightened of her.

"Whether it does or it doesn't, Giles, you are still going to do it."

She must have realised she was being too heavy so tried to soften her face with a smile and said more gently,

"Giles, don't you understand the danger we're in, what you've done? There's no alternative. I've gone over this enough times for one evening, I'm going to the loo, you ask for the bill."

She left him gazing out of the window at the fog. It was crazy but he had no alternative ideas; here he was, an atheist cynic pursued by an ancient curse, and in love. So he had no choice and although it made no sense, he would do it.

The opaque shifting light brought something else to mind: the stalker on the Moss. The same Moss they'd cross on the way home. It must have been there since the tomb was built, maybe even before. Steve was obviously off his head yet he was clear about seeing something which scared him more than Lisa had. What was it, what did it want? Would it just stand and watch as they carried out their ritual of de-resurrection? Claire and her crazy friends hadn't thought about this or how to deal with it; he felt Steve's terror beginning to infect him.

Outside the night had one more shock for them. They walked through the freezing dark to Claire's house arms round each other aware of strange sounds reaching them through the distorting blanketing fog. Tonight he saw no police cars and couldn't decide if this was a good thing and was relieved to reach her driveway. But something had spooked her.

"Look, Giles, the outside lights are on. I know I turned them off and what's that on......oh, God."

Incised into the white rendering of the cottage wall, in letters a metre tall right across the house front, was a message. The lines of the letters had been made clearer for having been traced over in blood and the eviscerated body of what looked to have been a cat was spread across the doorstep. Giles cradled Claire's head into his shoulder as he read the words,

"B U R N I N H E L L F O R E V E R W I T CH"

CHAPTER 25
THE DARK CHURCH

In Skendleby, after dinner at the Rectory, Marcus asked Ed to show him round the church. Whilst Gwen stayed behind with Mary to finish the wine, the two clerics put on coats against the cold and walked across the churchyard to St George's. Ice crackled underfoot as they picked their way between gravestones cobwebbed by frost to the vestry door. The familiar old dry smell of an ancient church brought Marcus a pang of nostalgia. Inside it was decked for Christmas with a large tree, traditional crib scene and oranges with little candles stuck in left over from the Christingle.

Standing before the altar in the dimly lit thirteenth century body of the ancient church Marcus paused to pray. He insisted Ed kneel with him then raised his hands and called out in a surprisingly loud voice that echoed round the empty church and disturbed something high above in the rafters,

"O Lord, lead your servant Edmund Joyce towards the faith he so badly wants and which will sustain him in the coming time of spiritual and mortal danger."

Then they sat side by side on the front pew.

"I know you wanted to come here for reasons other than just to see the church, Marcus, so come on, out with it."

"I think you know what I am going to ask of you. This is happening in your parish. You are as much a part of it as Davenport and his family. We're only here because of Claire, or at least Gwen's here because of Claire and I'm here because of Gwen."

He paused for a moment aware of how small and insignificant they seemed under the high roof of the nave, the only section of the church illuminated, and how quickly the light faded to shadow then dark before it reached the aisles. The medieval stone of the walls radiated a cold that seemed to force back the light dimming its power. There seemed little cheer or sense of salvation here, just the dry cold odour of sanctity and centuries of fear. Ed thought about the bones of the dead slowly shifting in the crypt below their feet.

"I think that you lost your faith in the same way you lost yourself, Ed. This is your chance of personal redemption, because your belief in what's happening to us is stronger than your belief in God. There's nothing more disgraced or pitiful than an agnostic priest, but now you can find self respect and regain your faith. Whatever we worship is far older than the rules of our faith and far older than whatever faith or ritual governed the people who built that burial mound. But they believed the ritual handed down to them would imprison for eternity the evil that terrified them."

He gripped Ed by his shoulders staring into his eyes with an almost messianic fervour.

"You must understand this. Everything comes down to belief: if you believe then the rituals work! These rituals worked for thousands of years; they still have power. But you have to believe. To put all this back together, to remake the world as it should be, we have to retrace those rituals and restore that power."

There was a strange skittering noise high in the dark above them somewhere in the roof; an unnerving sound: dry and brittle. It stopped but its presence seemed worse in the silence that followed and both men sat gripped, waiting for it to start again. After some moments of heavy silence Marcus started to speak again aware of his faint distorted words echoing off the walls and dispersing through the columns and arches.

"We have to put everything back the way it was. Giles needs to find a way of re-sealing the tomb and restoring the ritual pit immediately after we manage to dislodge the entity from inside Lisa. If we manage to accomplish this it will be lost and have nowhere to go but the tomb and, with luck, Giles and his friend can imprison it forever."

In the silence that followed this frightening if weirdly logical plan of action, Ed began, not for the first time in recent months, to doubt his own sanity. Even this church, his place of work, seemed strange, as if its dimensions had spread and he was trapped in a pool of light in a limitless stone cavern. Somewhere above he could hear a faint grating or rasping sound which he hoped must be occasioned by the effect of the extreme cold on the workings of the bell tower. Whatever it was he was pretty sure it wasn't a metaphor.

"But what has this got to do with me?"

He immediately regretted the question.

"You are the shaman. You will conduct the ritual. You are the holy man of this place, Ed, the spiritual descendant of shamans, Magi, cunning men and wise women going back to the beginnings of history, older even perhaps than those who left their marks on cave walls in the Upper Palaeolithic. All of them, like you, bound by ritual."

"But look at me, I've no faith, you must be able to see that; look at me, I've nothing, I'm empty, pitiful, not a real priest. I don't believe in prayer, never mind ritual, to me it's little more than…"

He was going to say mumbo-jumbo; but managed to stop himself, merely letting the thought hang in the cold air as he shuffled in anxiety on the hard wooden pew.

"Yes of course, I see all that, Ed: I can spot it a mile off and so can your parishioners. Probably, for them, no priest is better than you: but you, weak and lost as you have made yourself, are the only one we have."

He watched as Ed sat with his shoulders slumped then spoke again, hard and authoritative.

"So it's got to be you, hasn't it? There's no one else, no better option. Only you."

Then he smiled grimly.

"But there is some good news because there is one thing close to faith that fills every moment of your life, Ed, and that's fear. You're terrified and you believe in the thing that's frightening you and out of that faith may grow. So listen very carefully. Once you have conducted the ritual of the sealing of the tomb you will conduct another ritual where you will bury one of the bones under this church."

"Under St George's? Whatever for?"

"This is holy ground and was probably holy ground long before the church was even thought of. It's why the church was built here: this is ground with the power to keep and hide the bone! Come on, think about it, Ed. You got into this business because you offered to conduct a ritual at the site, and that's all you're going to do."

"Don't you patronise me in my own church; that's not true and you know it; I may be weak but I'm not an idiot. Anyway, if you're so clever, then why don't you do it yourself, you're obviously far more accustomed to these things."

"Because what we're dealing with is not reaching out to me, Ed. This isn't my story, it's yours and besides, I don't have the strength or courage, I'd be found wanting, but I'll help all I can."

Deep inside Ed knew this was true but even so asked with a touch of petulance,

"And when do you suggest I conduct this act of necromancy?"

Marcus ignored the sarcasm.

"On the twenty-first of course, the winter solstice when the power of the sun is at its weakest and the dark fully risen. The most ancient festival and the most appropriate. I do have one message of comfort for you, Ed. When things are at their worst and you feel about to break you will find help if you have the faith to look for it."

"What help? What do you mean? I've tried prayer before; it doesn't work: no one listens or answers."

"No, that's not what I meant. All I can say is that many before have trod the path you're about to. What you are, Ed, stretches far back in time, you are part of something much bigger, one of many. You are just the last in the line, that's all, and after you there will be others; so when things are at their blackest reach out to them, they'll be there if you know how to see them. Perhaps even Heatly Smythe."

They sat in the cold silence listening to the noises in the empty church thinking of the restless dead. Then

Marcus placed a hand on Ed's arm and spoke to him like the father he always wanted but never had.

"All your life you've wanted to be part of something but never made it, you want to believe in something. All you need is courage: God never went away: he's there waiting, all you need for commitment is to take the first step and when you're tested, as you soon will be, then love, don't envy, be angry not scared. That's all I can offer, the rest is up to you."

The great iron bell in the tower boomed out the hour of eleven, the reverberations rolling round the vast stone nave broke the spell. They felt the cold of the church stone penetrating their bones and heard the noise high above them start up again. Rising to leave, their breath steamed before them in the sepulchral light. They exited hurriedly through the vestry door which Ed locked behind them with a rusty iron key. As they retraced their steps towards the Rectory, Ed realised that the awful noise he heard intermittently in the church was now louder, harsher and nearer. They were met at the Rectory door by Gwen and Mary standing on the front steps looking over across the estate wall towards the Hall.

"Ed, dear, this is most peculiar, look there."

He followed the direction she indicated. There was a monstrous dark mass like a groaning and shrieking thunder cloud. A dense swarm of large black shapes was slowly circling the Hall swaying between the trees and swooping down to peck and claw at the brightly lit windows in the roof.

"What are they, Mary?"

"Corvids: the ones that have gathered and swarmed round here these last weeks, the ones on the cricket club roof and by the dig. Except they're all together now."

Marcus looked at the black swarm: crows, ravens, rooks,

"This is their time. It has started and they sense it. They've been called."

"But they shouldn't be out now, this time of year and at night, surely?" Mary asked, pulling Ed towards the open door, light and warmth.

"Normal birds, no, but I don't think these are normal birds. They bring retribution and there's death on the wind."

Gwen took Marcus by the arm and walked him towards the Rectory saying to Mary as she passed,

"Whatever they are that's the most horrible noise I've ever heard, thank God we're not over there in the Hall."

And the noise was horrible; the leathery flapping of the great black wings underscoring the grating carking and cawing of their savage calls.

Well, better visiting Carver than us, Ed thought as he shepherded Marcus and the two women in through the front door. He glanced back over his shoulder at the dense raucous mass of ill omen above the Hall. He felt a shiver run through him as he closed and locked the front door.

CHAPTER 27
TERM'S END

Giles was in the Unit early next day to clear his desk before he took the staff out for a Christmas lunch. Although not entitled to the generous University academic holidays, the Unit would shut down today and not open again until the second week in January. There wasn't much festive spirit evident in the offices except for a miniature fibre optic Christmas tree on Sophie's desk.

This year's Christmas lunch was a smaller event than usual with Rose sedated, Jan in Glasgow, Leonie missing and Steve in hospital. So the six survivors ate their travesty of a Christmas dinner in a dismal student pub. The news of Steve's attack depressed spirits, and Sophie, feeling guilty, was tearful throughout the meal. The admin staff left as soon as was polite, to do some shopping in town before going home for the holidays, glad to be away. They left Giles and Tim Thompson finishing their drinks.

"Let me buy you another, Giles."

"No, I've got to go back and finish a few things off before I close the place up."

"OK, well I'm not going back. I'll finish here if you don't mind. I think I've been overdoing it a bit. I never saw myself as the imaginative type but the site research on Skendleby was strangely unsettling and I'm glad it's finished. I've left you a note about my last efforts at the office.

"Apparently there are some Davenport family papers archived in Ryland's library and the earliest date from the fifteenth century, you need special permission to see them; which could mean there's some stuff in them not considered suitable for public consumption. Also there's a collection of papers belonging to one of the Oxford colleges you might be interested in. One is written by Gilbert White. It makes reference to the Reverend Heatly Smythe. It suggests some quite odd behaviour on his part after he left Skendleby, and that the circumstances of his last days were somewhat unusual to say the least. It's macabre reading.

"He cites a college don who had dinner with Heatly Smythe after he fled Skendleby, telling him that he felt the man was terrified out of his wits. Apparently during the meal he drank heavily but just fiddled with his food and kept looking round the room as if searching for someone. Then, to his host's surprise, before the college servant had even brought the port, Heatly Smythe jumped up from his chair, sending it crashing to the floor and shouted, 'There you must have seen it. Again, look it's there, yes over there, clear as day. Oh dear Christ, even here: it has pursued me; even here.'

With that he ran out of the room and out of the college never to return. Straight out of a horror movie don't you think, Giles?"

Tim Thompson stopped and looked over Giles's shoulder at the door.

"Don't look now."

He removed his glasses blinking his eyes as if trying to focus on something.

"Sorry, I thought I saw someone staring at us from behind that screen. Lately I've had the most peculiar feeling that someone's watching me from the shadows, even at home. It started when I was in Rylands looking at the Davenport papers. You know how strange the light can be in there particularly when you're on your own."

Thompson stopped for a moment as if confused; Giles was certainly confused as he'd never noticed anything strange about the light and was about to say so when Thompson started again.

"Yesterday as I entered the long gallery I thought I saw something tall and bent in a long black wrapping like a cloak flit across the staircase. It must have been some eccentric academic."

Thompson looked round again.

"You see that's why I was so sure one of the archivists was working in the next bay. I mean he must have been because I could hear him moving about muttering and whispering. I felt sure he was whispering something to me. Yet every time I looked there was no one there. I've been working too hard I suppose. As an historian you live with the dead and then there's all this business with Steve.

"Anyway I need a holiday so I'm flying out to Venice tonight for ten days. Oddly enough there's a Davenport connection there too; some papers in a private collection I'd never heard of before. And listen, Giles, because this really is strange; this morning someone left an unsigned note about it on my desk in the faculty; kind of them, if slightly disturbing. Because how would they know I was off to Venice? I've told no one but you just now. How would anyone know about my research for that matter? Anyway the collection's housed in an old palace off the Canale Della Giudecca just behind the Redentore so I might as well take a look at it while I'm there; I've already written to the curator."

He paused again as if struck by something he'd rather not remember; then got to his feet.

"The truth is I need to get away from here for a bit. I feel, not haunted obviously, this is the twenty-first century, more like someone's after me. I need a change of scene. Have a good Christmas, Giles, and watch out for yourself."

He stood up, looked behind once more and scurried for the exit; Giles settled the bill and walked back to the Unit. The occasional light shining amongst dark windows in the silent Neo-Gothic quad made the place appear all the more deserted, emphasising the number of empty rooms. The Unit's offices felt unnaturally sepulchral and the small sounds Giles made as he finished his work seemed to resonate with a volume they didn't deserve. He left Sophie's fibre optic tree turned on in an attempt to make the atmosphere more cheerful but the small light it shed in such a large space only increased the melancholy.

He hurriedly finished and decided Tim Thompson's note could wait until after Christmas. He'd had enough of the macabre so began to shut down the computers and turn off the lights. It was as he was about to turn off the Christmas tree that he heard the footsteps. They were echoing along the outside corridor but stopped at the door. He watched in horror as the latch began to rise and door opened.

His heart nearly stopped with fright when he saw what came through the door. The macabre figure could have been the long dead Jacob Marley: it was no less disturbing.

Steve, backlit by the fluorescent lights of the corridor looked like something fresh out of Hell. His long hair was cropped to stubble, his face attenuated and angular. The mutilated ear was bandaged and the pale papery skin sat well with the grotesque white stubble on his head. His face was a ghastly sight: lined and anxious. Giles couldn't suppress the thought that Steve would no longer be so attractive to women.

"Steve, for Christ's sake, you almost gave me a heart attack, what are you doing here, you should be in hospital?"

"Got nowhere else. I hoped I'd find you here, Gi, I couldn't hack it any longer in hospital, waiting for that horror to find me like I know it would; I'm unfinished business. I should be dead and I'm not sure that wouldn't have been better. Rose and Leonie were right, and the witch and the vicar. Even you, Gi, even you got it eventually. Oh Christ what's happening?"

He moved to the nearest chair, Sophie's, and slumped on the desk, his nightmare face incongruously lit by the soft twinkling lights of the tree.

Giles, moved by a sympathetic impulse, went and stood behind the chair and gently placed his hands on Steve's shoulders, which, to Giles's embarrassment, but not surprise, began to shake. The sobs seemed to start at his shoulders and for a few moments they remained stuck in the pose. Giles gently massaging his shoulders and Steve quietly weeping.

"I've seen things, sensed things, that no one's meant to and there's no way back now; I'm broken: I feel broken and nothing's ever going to put me back together. Every time I close my eyes I'm back on the tomb and it's cold, so cold I can't feel my fingers. My teeth and bones shake and there's something unspeakably foul in there and it's about to reach out and touch me and I know that if it does I'm lost; lost and damned."

He paused wracked by a spasm, coughing and sobbing. Giles continued to stroke his back, the way he would a frightened puppy. Slowly Steve regained sufficient control to blow his nose and wipe his eyes with a filthy handkerchief and after a pause that seemed an age, he started to speak again.

"I can't stand the idea of going back in there but all I can think is that having caused all this by opening the tomb we have to find a way of closing it. So I discharged myself and came to look for you because if anyone is more to blame for this than me, it's you."

"Thanks, Steve; might not be as much a forlorn hope as you think. Listen, you look like shit. I'll make you a drink; your clothes are filthy and you stink. When did you last eat?"

"I don't remember, I don't want to eat, I don't think I can."

Giles made him drink some coffee and tried to patch him into what was happening. They sat close together at the desk illuminated by the fibre optic tree until after six by which time Steve was calmer.

"Come on, I'll drive you to your place to pick up some clothes and then you can stay with us while we work out what to do."

"Us?"

"Yeah, I forgot to tell you, I've temporarily moved in with the witch, even the vicar doesn't seem too bad now and there's weirder ones hanging about; should make you feel at home. But you'll be surprised to know you've another option."

He handed him Jan's address in Glasgow and passed on her message.

"I think maybe later on I'd like that, but first I have to come with you because there can be no peace until this is finished."

Giles ushered him out of the office and turned to lock the door, casting a final glance at the large cavernous space dark except for the twinkling blue, green and red lights of the Christmas tree on Sophie's desk.

CHAPTER 28
THE VIEW FROM ROOM ONE7B

Hospital manager Jenny Dawlish had a problem she didn't know how to solve. None of the ward staff would attend the patient in room One7B.The room was the most remote from all other wards in the hospital. It had to be; the complaints from the wards, staff and patients, even visitors, had been bad enough but once a number of patients began to experience inexplicable rapid deterioration in their medical condition something needed to be done.

Morale in hospital wards, although never particularly high, has an effect on recovery times. The decline in morale and deterioration of patients was most marked in wards closest to where Lisa Richardson was confined.

At first it had been a series of complaints about rapid changes in temperature on the wards, and of things patients claimed to see that shouldn't be there. The heating system in the hospital had always been erratic and imaginings, morbid fears and shifts of perspective are common enough among the unwell, particularly those in hospital. An elderly woman recovering from a minor operation in the women's ward at the end of the corridor leading to Lisa's room claimed a nurse she didn't know had tried to pull out her stitches in the night.

The stitches had been disturbed and there was fresh bleeding. The doctor on his ward round said it was merely the consequence of a disturbed night and prescribed a mild sedative. When her son visited in the evening she pleaded with him to discharge her and take her home. The ward nurse spoke to the duty doctor who persuaded the son to make his mother stay. After the son left for home she became disturbed and began to tell the other patients about the weird nurse who visited her in the night. Fear began to spread. Ward staff moved her into a separate side room nearest to the corridor.

But the noises she made were still audible and they weren't pleasant. That night she was given a much stronger sedative. But the cries and screams continued into the early hours and none of the night staff enjoyed their rounds. In the morning she was pale, weak and wouldn't wake up. That evening, when her son arrived to visit he found his mother sitting bolt upright in bed, eyes distended in an intense stare at the wall as if something on it terrified her.

She was also quite dead. The body was quickly and discreetly removed but the rumour spread outwards like a miasma from ward to ward and from relative to in-law and, as a consequence, an unusual number of quite sick people asked to be discharged. The official response was to diagnose a ward outbreak of paranoia and prescribe counselling and sedation.

However, it was only when these fears, or in hospital parlance, psychoses, spread to doctors, nurses and even managers that it was decided a change had to be made. The decision was taken when a consultant on neurology, with an interest in psychology, observed in a dry and analytical statement that, rather like the tremors in an earthquake, the further the wards from the Richardson room, the lesser the number and severity of complaints. This, with its connotations of a spreading infection supplied by one of their own and most respected, prompted the authorities to action.

So Lisa Richardson had been moved with some difficulty. She had to be strapped to a reinforced trolley by a group of burly orderlies and police officers and escorted from her austere but increasingly chaotic room to the more remote and larger, cell-like room One7B. This lay at the end of a long corridor, the rooms off which were largely used for storage in a decaying area of the hospital scheduled for demolition. This move had immediate benefits for the patients and staff on their wards but an inverse proportion of effects on the few staff whose duties included the care and maintenance of One7B. Seen in daylight from a rational perspective, the room, although sparse and unappealing, was in every other way similar to regulation hospital accommodation.

But now it was always damp; the windows and walls spotted with condensation. Sometimes it was warm and damp, sometimes freezing and damp, and at times it seemed to be both. It could manage to go from hot and muggy to icy in a matter of seconds and the light, to say the least, was inconsistent.

However, the most alarming aspect of One7B was that the unfortunate nurses who serviced the room were never entirely sure where Lisa was. They knew that in reality she was heavily sedated and strapped to the bed, despite this contravening hospital regulations, but then they would see her crawling across the ceiling or lying in the corner of the room halfway up the wall. What's more, and this they could objectively verify, the position of the bed in the room was never the same on any two visits. The bedclothes placed securely round the patient each time the bed was made, found their way to the furthest fringes of the room. On one occasion they were found placed neatly folded in the sink by the door with the tap turned on. The nurses had become used to the tap, which turned itself on and off at will.

But it wasn't just the room. To the staff, including Jenny, the length of the corridor leading to One7B never seemed the same and as a consequence it was difficult to estimate how long the walk to minister to Lisa would take. The lighting was only predictable in that it never worked as expected. The whole block was bitterly cold although Lisa herself seemed unconcerned by this. She never moved or spoke, just lay on her bed, face turned towards the door, eyes wide open and her mouth making the shape of what, on anyone else's face, would have been a smile. But on her it was like the grimace of the hideously corrupt clown from your worst nightmares. In fact it was this last detail more than anything, which, over the few short days that Lisa was in the room, caused the staff either to refuse the duty or go off sick.

Jenny had just finished speaking to the hospital chief executive about the problem when two men, who were the only visitors to room One7B, knocked on the door of her office. Councillor Richardson looking haggard, stooped and increasingly frail was accompanied as usual by the man she now knew was the editor of the *Journal*. She rose from her desk and shook hands.

"There's been no change in her condition and I'm sorry but you'll find the room even more of a mess this time."

The men followed her through the over lit corridors of the main hospital with the antiseptic artwork on the walls and the infectious hospital smell, to the corridor leading to One7B. Here the lighting, although of hospital standard, seemed to flicker and dwindle and there was a very different type of smell which, although it defied description, was worse than sickly and felt strangely threatening. All three of them had learnt from a harrowing previous experience that it was better not to look at the walls. They finished the short walk in an altered and far less secure state of mind than they began it. Jenny Dawlish unlocked the door and let them in.

"I'll wait outside if you don't mind."

Since the disturbing encounter with the smeary substance, that on inspection had proved to be a half eaten human liver, she'd not been able to make herself enter the room.

Jim hated these visits, but as Lisa's mother refused to go, felt he had to support Derek. It was only four days since Lisa was admitted to the hospital yet in that time her father seemed to age twenty years. Jim, after visiting, found himself constantly looking back over his shoulder. The experience left him feeling contaminated and on returning from hospital he'd drink a large whisky whilst drawing a bath and then take another large whisky with him into the bathroom. He needed cleansing to rid him of the contagion he feared would otherwise become a permanent part of his life. Gradually during the long soak and vigorous scrubbing he would lose the sensations of taint, impurity and deep rooted unease that the visits imparted. It was only after the drink and bath that he felt sufficiently decontaminated to mix with his family.

Jim and Derek entered room One7B reluctantly; these visits never lasted more than five minutes but they were a very long five minutes. Jim hovered by the door as Derek advanced halfway towards the bed, never nearer, from where he tried to think of something to say to his daughter. He no longer brought flowers, not after that first visit; what had happened to them had caused the nurse too much work. Not that they'd seen any nurses in this part of the hospital recently.

Jim, keeping his eyes away from the bed and whatever was making the noise in the corner by the window, looked at his watch again. There were still two minutes to go. He sensed a movement and looked up. Derek had moved to the bed. He was standing with his hands on the raised sides leaning forwards as if listening. To his relief he couldn't see Lisa's face but suddenly he heard a voice, soft but harsh, not Derek's and certainly not a young woman's. Just one sentence, quietly spoken yet clear.

"They know what you've done and it's time you paid."

Richardson began to back away but then the voice, this time different: a much lower register,

"You know the place, the binding place, go there."

Then a mocking travesty of Lisa's voice; girly and cruel.

"You can join me there, Daddy, but it won't be the way you used to like it."

There was a burst of deeply unpleasant giggling that seemed to come from every corner of the room. Then a voice screeched

"They watch and wait."

Derek shuffled quickly and shakily back across the room to Jim, who opened the door and backed out as fast as possible.

***

Jenny Dawlish locked the door and shepherded them down the corridor with Jim anxiously turning to look over his shoulder and Derek stumbling like a zombie saying nothing. She walked with them to Reception, the Councillor appeared to be in shock, and the *Journal*'s editor hurried him out of the hospital turning only to say,

"I don't think we'll be coming back."

"Yes, that would be best."

Jim helped Derek into the car. He scraped the accumulation of frost from the windscreen with bare hands without noticing the cold. On the drive back to Richardson's house the councillor sat hunched in the front seat rocking back and forwards. Jim could think of nothing to say to comfort him. The car pulled up at Richardson's well lit house and before Jim could ask if he wanted any help, Richardson turned towards him and said calmly in a resigned tone with his eyes focused somewhere behind Jim's shoulder,

"That's where she is, I'll join her, they're watching."

He opened the door, got out, and walked up the driveway towards the light. Jim drove home quickly trying to concentrate on whisky and hot water.

***

For Jenny Dawlish, however, the night had one more trip to One7B in store. A local policeman who'd attended the night Lisa was admitted turned up. Barford she thought his name was. His last duty of the day was to check if the patient was sufficiently well to make a statement. On being told no he insisted on checking himself. Jenny was irritated by the man's manner and patronising attitude; she knew she shouldn't let him but she was on edge and frayed. It would serve him right to get a taste of what they had to deal with; see if he felt so sure of himself then.

So she agreed but was almost disappointed; this time the walk to the room seemed quite normal. Jenny unlocked the door and waited outside, but not for long, within moments the door burst open and the policeman hurtled out screaming, hands scrabbling at his neck and ran off down the corridor. She locked the door and followed but he'd disappeared from view. A nurse told her later he checked into A and E complaining that his throat had been damaged from the inside. So Jenny picked up the phone and made the call leading to Lisa being moved to a secure unit within eight hours.

CHAPTER 29
A MURDER OF CROWS

Next morning Davenport was mopping up the last of his breakfast egg yolk with a piece of buttered toast when he saw a police squad car pull up in front of the bungalow. He rose stiffly, brushed crumbs from his sweater, downed the remains of his tea, straightened his tie and slowly marched to the front door. He unlocked and opened it just as one of the police officers was about to ring the doorbell.

"Morning Sir Nigel, sorry to disturb you but we'd like to ask you a few questions if that's all right."

"Yes I suppose it will have to be. I thought they'd have sent the local chap who gave me the lift, what's his name, Barford?"

"You won't be seeing him for a bit, Sir, he's signed off sick, had some type of nervous problem, you know, gone in the head like."

"Funny, he didn't strike me as the sensitive type. Anyway you're wasting your time, I told you all I could about that attack over on the dig."

The police shuffled about uncomfortably for a moment then one of them said apologetically,

"No it's not about that, it's something else is this, Sir. The thing is like, we've had a complaint, several complaints in fact, but we've got to follow this one up because the Chief Constable seems to have taken an interest in it. Seems he's an acquaintance, through golf and the Lodge, of Mr Carver who lives up in your old place."

"What's that creature raving about now?"

"Well it seems like, that he sort of thinks that you and the Reverend Joyce are involved in some type of conspiracy to drive him out of the Hall, in fact when we've spoken to you we have to go across to the Rectory."

"Rubbish, that's what comes of chiselling little spivs like him moving out here and expecting life to be just the same. I'll come with you to the Rectory and we can get this ridiculous business dealt with at one go."

He called a brief goodbye to Debo and the three of them followed the path to the Rectory gate. Ed was far less agitated at seeing them than he would have been the previous week. He ushered them into the kitchen where Mary, who was baking cakes for the church Christmas Fayre, made a pot of tea. The homely smells of the Rectory kitchen, combined with the impeccable solidity of Davenport and the earnest features of the vicar, made the police officers visibly uncomfortable. However, after a couple of false starts the older of the two began.

"Well, it seems that Mr Carver believes that the two of you are hiring vagrants or perhaps local youths to try and frighten him away."

"And how precisely have we been doing that, Officer, and why would we want to frighten him away?"

"Well, Reverend, he says that there's some type of, er, ragged figure as watches the house from the trees and, er, sort of well, he sort of you know, er, moves about a bit like."

"Sort of moves about a bit?"

"Well it's because of like how he, you know, moves about and that, as is why Mr Carver is bothered. He thinks it must be more than one person. Then there's the noises in the house and two of the domestics, young girls from somewhere in Eastern Europe, have seen things that shouldn't be there."

"Shouldn't be there?"

"Yes, like they go into an empty room and it's as if someone's just been there. You know the feeling, like there's someone in there when there isn't. Look I know it sounds bloody daft but it's frightened them enough to persuade them to give up their jobs. I've spoken to them, Sir Nigel, they are genuinely scared, believe me."

"Would you want to work for Carver?"

"Course not but…"

"And we're meant to be responsible for this are we? How precisely do we manage to arrange it?"

"Then there's them birds, Sir, they're round the house all day and at night they tap on the windows and make that bloody croaking noise, see you can still just hear them in here."

"And we're supposed to have trained the birds too, have we? Well you'd better arrest us and throw away the key."

"Yes, rather like Elijah and the ravens but in reverse. I suppose that as the cleric that one would be down to me,"

Ed chipped in; the police tried not to laugh.

"I know how it sounds, gentlemen, and we wouldn't have followed it up unless we'd been instructed, like."

"Well it's nonsense isn't it? Now you've seen us and we've discussed it, if you're not going to arrest us then you can consider you've done your duty, unless you would like some more of Mrs Joyce's tea and cake."

"No I think we've taken enough of your time, gentlemen."

And with mutual thanks to Mary they left the Rectory, shown out by Ed. When he returned to the kitchen both men burst out laughing.

"There is something frightening going on over there though. Whatever's happening here is obviously affecting him and they're right about those birds. I'd hate to have even one of them near me. I've been afraid of them ever since I was a little boy, the thought of one of those black wings touching me still makes me shiver."

Davenport had no such sensitivities.

"Well he can expect no sympathy from me. The fool, thinking we'd waste time playing tricks on that little fraudster."

Davenport got his coat, said goodbye, and left the house thinking how glad he was he no longer had responsibility for the Hall and its legacy. At the Rectory gate he caught up with the police officers, who were watching the dense cloud of huge black corvids circling the roof of Skendleby Hall.

***

Derek Richardson had sat since early morning in the large chandelier-festooned entertaining room of the new detached home which sat swollen and opulent in a row of similar houses in this most desirable of locations. Now even more to be desired as it was also the exclusive estate chosen by a number of footballers whose gated mansions shone with bling and glitter each evening. These latest arrivals had bestowed the highest accolade the estate could have wished for: celebrity. To live here you had to be a winner. None of this, which normally gave Derek a tingle of pleasure, now seemed to matter. He'd sat in the chair despondently since before dawn and now it was dark, had long been dark and he knew what he had to do; it seemed so clear just like she'd told him it would be. He glanced at the note on his knee that he'd written in the early hours of the morning.

'Carver, they've called me in, it's over, almost a relief, we've brought this down on ourselves. What have we done? I don't think you've got long. I hope it'll be worse for you. You deserve it.

See you in Hell,
Richardson'

He pushed it into the addressed envelope with the festive Christmas stamp then got up and walked through the state-of-the-art exclusive kitchen, gleaming with granite, steel and minimalism, into the utility room. He ignored, and was ignored by, his wife, who was sitting drinking gin on a raised bar stool at the island in the middle of the marble floor, staring at a huge wall mounted flat screen TV, its volume turned down. He picked up a torch from the shelf and unlocked the door that led to the integral garage big enough to house a large family of cars. From a hook on the wall he took a coil of rope then, without bothering to either turn off lights or close doors, he retraced his steps. As he was leaving the kitchen something, perhaps the ghost of some lost emotion, impelled him to make some final contact,

"I'm going out, don't bother to wait up."

There was no answer just the clink of the neck of a gin bottle against the rim of a glass.

The Jag was on the drive, front door open, and after throwing the rope and torch onto the passenger seat he climbed in and started the ignition. The sleek purr of the engine starting almost touched him, he had always loved these cars but the moment passed.

He left the estate and drove towards the village, past the primary school he'd attended when he'd not been rich or important, past the lane of cottages where he'd been born, past the bus stop where he'd waited each day to travel as a poor, scholarship boy, the pride of his family, to the grammar school in Macclesfield. Then the journey was over, he turned into the lane at the side of the estate leading to the archaeological dig where he would leave the car, perhaps the closest thing to a friend he had. He took the flashlight and rope and walked into the woods until he could see Devil's Mound and beyond it there was the tree, just like she'd said. He threw the coiled end of the rope over the thick low hanging bough and tied it on; for a moment he thought of the cottage he'd driven past and then he thought of his mother but it was too late.

The gnarled black raven paused from pecking at the skylight window on the Hall's roof to watch for a moment. It heard the quiet noise stop, saw a man walk rapidly from the source of the noise leaving it open and blazing with light. Saw the man walk among the trees until he saw one he liked, saw him climb then swing, jerking at first, then still. It sensed the feast he and his brothers were offered but couldn't take. So with a croak of anger and malice it returned to its pecking of the glass with renewed vigour

CHAPTER 30
A CURTAIN ON THE DARK

Safe inside; the dining room of St George's Rectory was cosy and softly lit. Ed wondered if the room had ever hosted such a curious gathering. For the meal he'd heated up large quantities of the bouef bourguignon Mary had prepared earlier in the week and then frozen. Usually, when she went to visit her mother in Wales at this time of the year, Ed felt bereft, but this time he was glad. She would be safe in the valleys and by the time she returned on the 23rd, mother in tow to spend Christmas with them, this business should be finished.

Despite the macabre reasons for the gathering Ed enjoyed the meal, the company and the sense of being part of the gang for the first time in his life. This was enhanced by the half case of St Emilion that the heavy drinking Marcus had brought, the last of which they were now finishing. They were now seven, a number he always associated with cowboys or samurai, the seventh being a gaunt man with close-cropped white hair whose age Ed felt it hard to judge. He was quite transformed from the long dark haired archaeologist who mocked him on the site when he'd offered the blessing.

Well, he was in no state to mock anyone now with his sagging skin, lined face and torn apart ear: ironic he thought that this was the man who most needed his ritual expertise. Marcus had told them that it must be Steve and Ed responsible for the ritual closing and sealing of the tomb. They had to reverse all the harm they'd caused and shut the door finally on all that was meant to stay buried. But he wasn't sure if Steve was capable of this, he looked too damaged and broken. However, the thought there was someone weaker cheered him up.

The prelude to the meal had been less convivial. Ed made a pastoral visit to Councillor Richardson's wife but the house was dark and empty. The police were treating the matter as suspicious and it was unlikely that Richardson's body would be released until the New Year. The shadow of Derek Richardson hung over them as they sat in the Rectory lounge for a drink before the meal. A shadow that darkened as Giles recounted the association of the site with suicides since written records had begun with the medieval suicide of John de Balnea.

Despite the range of philosophies in the room they'd all felt enough of the site to understand it was the malign nature of the land itself that led those sensitive or unstable enough, to take their own lives. They'd arranged to eat together to plan for the next day when they would split into two groups. Claire, Gwen and Marcus would drive up into the Dark Peak to the secure sanatorium where Lisa was incarcerated. Giles, Steve and Ed would later that day re-seal the tomb and the ritual pit having first stolen the bones from the Unit's lab. Davenport would accompany them on the site, not to perform any particular role, but because it was his legacy. He would watch. This they would do once Marcus had phoned them from the sanatorium to tell them that the time was right. It would be tomorrow because tomorrow was the day the dark was fully risen: the winter solstice.

***

Next day a small car twisted and turned through the narrow lanes that traverse the Dark Peak. The abrasive, grit stone walling on either side restricted the view but at any break in the walls the bleak moors could be seen stretching morosely away to the horizon. The day started dark grey and cold and as the car climbed the grey deepened and the cold intensified. The slate sky was heavy with snow as they turned down the narrow drive leading to the sanatorium. The wind rose and the first snowflakes were whipped horizontally across the windscreen.

High Edge sanatorium had been built by a nineteenth century mill owner turned philanthropist to house the tubercular children of the indigent poor. The idea being that the fresh hill air would revive them after the damage done to their lungs by the smoke and soot of industrial towns. Claire found herself wondering as she ran from the car to the door, lashed by the stinging snow, that maybe it had been a move better designed to reduce the surplus population, so bleak and desolate was the place. There were two doors, alarmed and electrically controlled, that visitors had to pass to gain entrance to the sanatorium. They'd been in too much of a hurry to get out of the weather to spend any time looking up at the windows set deep in the damp and blackened millstone grit walls, but had they done so they would have noticed that they had been made equally secure with iron gratings. The sanatorium no longer housed dying and malnourished children from the mill towns, unless perhaps their ghosts. It now had a small number of violently disturbed patients kept in a state of high security. The architecture of the building seemed to match its bleak and rugged surroundings; there was no sense of healing here.

Inside it was warm but utilitarian; none of them had ever been in a prison, but the building had as much prison about it as it had hospital. To their surprise, rather than a scarred and brutal looking attendant, they were greeted by a genial red haired young woman in a black business suit.

"Hello, I'm Helen Moores, I've already had your clearance, but I don't know what you think you're going to find in there. She has no rational connection with reality and won't understand anything you tell her about her father's death and as for the religious service you intend to conduct, I'm afraid it will be a complete waste of time."

She led them down a long internal corridor to a sparsely furnished and rarely visited visitor's room. Somewhere down the corridor someone was howling.

"I can arrange a cup of tea whilst they prepare her for the visit."

No one wanted a drink. They wanted to get this done as quickly as possible. The room was very warm, a large old iron radiator against the far wall throwing out prodigious heat. Claire noticed Marcus was sweating and Gwen was talking quietly to calm him down. After what seemed an age Helen Moores returned and led them down a long funereal corridor, where the howling was louder, to a heavy door at its end. The door had a hatch with a grille like a police cell. A doctor in white medical fatigues awaited them at the door. He had a shiny scrubbed red face and was wearing small steel rimmed glasses; like Helen he also smiled and shook hands.

"This is Dr Simon Masters; he's just checked the patient and he'll wait outside the door."

"Hi, you need to prepare yourself for a shock in there. The mind is a powerful thing and there are levels of disturbance that manifest themselves in a physical way. We can't quite understand the scientific reasons but, in a sense, normal rules don't apply here. Still, she's sedated and secured so you won't be in any physical danger. There's a bell push by the door and another by the bed, when you want to come out ring and I'll open up immediately. Believe me I don't think you'll enjoy it much."

He continued to smile as he made this speech but only with his mouth, his eyes remained curiously neutral. He unlocked the door and ushered them into the room. Claire was wondering why a doctor would want to work in a place like this when the door shut behind her with the sound of the electronic locking system engaging.

The room was large and bare. Small, barred windows high up in the thick walls, a huge iron radiator by the door with two wooden chairs either side. Over by the far wall a bed, nothing else, no table, no vase, no pictures. The cold in here was intense; Claire felt the radiator and quickly moved her hand. It was burning to the touch. Suddenly the room was hot. She shouldn't be here, she couldn't do this.

The figure in the bed turned its head slowly towards them and smiled. It was like the smile of a ghastly deranged circus clown; the lips fatly spread and the corners of the mouth turned up towards each ear. The type of smile no normal mouth could manage. The eyes weren't smiling though; they were tiny, old and hate filled, set in the cold white pallor of the recently dead. Marcus slumped into one of the chairs. Horror undiluted.

"O God, it's worse than I imagined, I'm sorry, I don't think I can cope with this, we shouldn't be here, I was wrong; we have to go."

He was sweating heavily and his legs were shaking.

"It's like before, Gwen, help me out. Claire, this is a mistake, it's too powerful, too evil, there's nothing you can do."

He was breathing with difficulty. Alarmed, Gwen pushed the bell and helped him up, she heard Masters' chuckle through the intercom.

"I said you wouldn't last long, hang on I'll open up."

The door opened and Gwen managed to push Marcus through when almost immediately it swung closed with a metallic crash leaving Claire on the wrong side locked in the room. She screamed with shock then tried to turn the handle shouting to Masters to let her out. But her voice couldn't cut through the thick security door and there was no reply.

Then the truth hit her: oh God, she'd been lured here: this hadn't been their plan, it was the entity's. It wasn't Lisa it wanted, it was her, it needed her. In panic she pulled and scrabbled at the handle until her nails were broken and bleeding but the door wouldn't shift. So, out of breath and on the edge of hysteria she stood with her face pressed against the grille in the door praying for it to unlock, unwilling to look over her shoulder at the ghastly thing, now gibbering, on the bed behind her. There was a scraping sound next to her.

She watched in horror as one of the chairs left its place by the radiator and, at first slowly, then gathering pace, slid across the room to the bedside coming to rest by the nightmarish head of its occupant. And then a sibilant voice bloodless and inhuman issued out of the unmoving lips of the thing lying there.

"I've been waiting for you little pretty one, beyond the universe and all through the ages; much longer than you could ever imagine, far outside time."

She struggled desperately to cling to the grille of the door but, against her every instinct, felt herself begin the walk across the room to the bed. The wall by the door had become suffocatingly hot, but with each step the temperature fell. By the bed it was so cold she could see her breath streaming out before her. This side of the room was deep cold, permafrost cold, the walls flecked with frozen damp. Against her will she found herself sitting down on the chair next to the terrible thing in some awful travesty of a hospital visit.

Claire knew the thing in the bed wasn't the girl photographer. There seemed so little of the skeletal figure beneath the heavy bedclothes for it to be a grown woman. But the head with its face turned towards her was large, disproportionately so, and everything bad in the room emanated from within it. Its eyes were now blank voids but she knew that something deep inside it watched her with malicious hunger. The thing spoke again and up close the sound was even worse grating in her head.

"It's started already; the first one's gone now, hanging from the tree, swinging in the wind for the crows to peck at, it can watch for us from there, poor deluded fool, doomed to dance among the branches forever."

Claire looked towards the door but it was so far away now; it had receded to such a distant speck that it may as well have been on a distant star. She was gripped by the mental numbness that used to precede her attacks. The mouth in front of her exhaled a plume of steaming breath that hung rotten in the cold air whilst from under the bedclothes a claw-like hand that should have been restrained reached towards her; fingers open expecting to be held.

"Take it; you know that this is what you came for."

And she knew it was, even though she'd been tricked. She had no choice, no freedom of will, so she took the hand in hers. A cackle, then the voice again, this time softer but more frightening.

"Now come inside."

There was a brief sensation of cold, roughened and very ancient lizard skin and then fusion.

She was inside; Claire knew she was deep inside the ruined mind. This was how it used to happen but this time she'd not willed it. It was unclear, occluded, somewhere there seemed to be the sound of a bell ringing faintly on a sea shore. Then she was seeing through Lisa's eyes, seeing the tomb as it had looked when she first entered it. Then Lisa's mind was gone replaced in rapid succession by the minds of hundreds perhaps thousands of others, millennia of corruption and bitter hate. Claire's final thought as an independent rational individual was that it was like getting random glimpses of the memories of different people, at first jumbled like the shuffle on iPod without meaning, but then as a sequence.

Starting with Lisa looking through the camera lens it changed and became Skendleby Hall, through the eyes of a girl running towards it, turning from time to time to look back at something black and insubstantial that came bounding out of the fringe of trees behind her. The door of the Hall was opened by a man dressed as a liveried servant from a bygone age and she ran through the door, but the fear of the thing outside remained. The image dissolved to be replaced by that of the girl in some type of ancient cellar watching as a man with blood streaming from a deep cut in his face, scraped a hole in the earthen floor to bury a small bundle wrapped in cloth. The man's hands shook as he dug by the light of a guttering lantern set down on the floor next to a cloak and a bloodied sword. Then the vision that Claire had dreamt, the girl screaming and cursing, being dragged towards the opening of the low mound. Her voice, clearly the voice on the disc, terrifying yet desolate.

But this was not the end, rather the beginning. A group of people in rough dirty wool robes were holding down a naked man in a ring of high standing stones under the direction of a tall, red haired woman. Chanting ceremoniously one of the group opened the man's throat with a flint knife. The memories now came thick and fast. A small boat on a storm-tossed sea; a child tied and carried through thick woodland, the smell of the place earthy and fungal. Then, heat and blue sky; dry arid terrain, a woman watching with shy pleasure while another was tied and placed in a narrow, hastily dug pit under the floor of a stone hut. Trying to struggle as a heavy grinding stone was broken then laid across her chest and the earth replaced. The chuckling of the woman faded and there was darkness, the smell of cold dry earth. By the flickering light of some stone bowls of burning animal fat a group of people danced, while a shaman in trance state daubed images of bison and mammoth onto the cave walls. He was watched by someone who envied his shamanistic power and would soon get it. Now some things that might have been people but might have been something else squatting by the side of a large body of liquid, making squealing noises as lightning flashed and rain tore down out of a pitch black sky. Then there was nothing, only darkness.

For a moment Claire felt relief, the journey was done. But it wasn't total blackness. Cosmic microwave background radiation, the faint light of the newly formed universe. An empty landscape like a lunar surface, far away the cold light of some long dead stars, not the universe we know. But Claire knew that something waited there, waited for her. In this dead cold place where there was neither atmosphere nor sound, nor time, new life was beginning. Here was something far older than the Neolithic villages, the Palaeolithic artists or the glimpses of the earlier inhuman things she'd seen.

In quantum measurement, somewhere in the multiverse, this had been waiting for her across dimensions and beyond measurable time; unfeeling, shape unrecognisable, cold pitiless gaze, 'fear in a grain of sand'. It looked up, saw her and recognised her. In the darkness she screamed but of course in the void there's no sound.

***

Outside the secure room it was chaos. Once the door slammed behind Gwen and Marcus it proved impossible to reopen. In that sense it functioned as a good security door should; but in no other as it seemed to possess a mind of its own. Masters tried to open the door using its electronic code and then manually. He sent for technical assistance from the premises team but to no avail, the door wouldn't shift. The hatch remained closed. The CCTV of the room, which had stuck on one angle, showed only Claire sitting quietly by the bed not moving. They shouted through the door to her but got no response. From the room there was only silence and on the screen just stillness. But it was not a comforting stillness, just an absence of movement, a state of non being. Of the occupant of the bed there was no sign, just a slight bump under the bed clothes. From time to time there was interference on the CCTV screen, but when service was resumed just the same image, no more use than a screen saver. Time dragged on and after about forty-five minutes they decided to cut open the door. During most of this time Marcus knelt intoning a series of prayer while Gwen obsessively watched the intermittent footage on the screen.

The cutting equipment arrived and was being prepared when suddenly the door swung open; without a sound, apparently of its own volition. There was a blast of cold filthy air from the room freezing them in their tracks like a physical assault. Across the room in the leprous stillness and silence Claire sat hunched over the bed, only the faint vapour trail of her breathing indicating life. Masters and Gwen, followed more slowly by Marcus, crossed the room to the bed. Gwen reached out to touch Claire but before she could, she sat up and turned towards them. Gwen couldn't interpret the look in Claire's eyes although she smiled faintly and her voice when she spoke was unexpectedly calm.

"It's all right it's left her, I reached her and it's moved on."

"How, Claire, how did you reach her?"

"Across strange dimensions, not the universe we know, something older, older than life, older than you could imagine and far away beyond dead stars, not even last time around. But it's evacuated the girl, she's served her purpose. Something stronger is needed now."

Masters was taking Lisa's pulse, the girl, recognisable as such now, was lying back on the bed her hair bathed in sweat despite the sub zero temperature.

"She's breathing normally, the pulse is OK, and she's certainly different to what she was, it feels like something's gone, she feels empty."

Gwen moved to help Claire but with surprising fluidity she sprang up from the chair. Masters stepped forward and for a moment he and Claire stared into each other's eyes as if sharing something. Then, to Gwen's surprise, they performed something that was almost a hand shake. Claire released his hand and moved towards the door; pausing by Marcus she stared straight into his eyes and whispered,

"You'd better hope those were powerful prayers, holy man."

This sounded more like a veiled threat than an expression of hope. Claire moved out of the room and down the corridor towards the exit followed by Gwen. Marcus walked to the bedside, removed a small phial from his pocket and sank to his knees to pray whilst Masters continued to check the patient. Gradually some semblance of warmth returned to the room as the smell began to leave it.

This time they accepted the hot drink from Helen Moores as they waited in the visitors' room. Claire sat still and upright in her chair, Gwen stood by the window sipping her tea. Outside the snow had, for the moment at least, stopped but a thin covering lay frozen hard on the ground contrasting oddly with the outcrops of black rock, protruding like bones from thin white flesh. After twenty minutes Marcus returned and they quickly left the place. Driving rapidly through grey light the bleakness and desolation of the snow-shrouded moors stretched away on all sides.

While they'd drunk their tea Claire had said nothing and in the car Gwen, worried, tried to get her to talk but with little response. In fact she only spoke once to reply when Gwen asked her if she felt all right.

"Yeah, feels good, safe in this one."

So, sitting in the back seats Marcus talked to Gwen.

"During all the time I prayed with her I could detect no sign of what we felt before, just exhaustion and emptiness. Whatever was there has moved on."

"So Claire was right, she's left."

"If it was a she? Perhaps it was once, but there are things in God's universe much older than we are, things that we never see but occasionally glimpse at the periphery of vision. An ancient Gramarye moving through time as enduring malevolence. But whatever it is, it's not in that sanatorium any more. It's time to make the call, Gwen."

"But can they do it? Ed's no real faith in himself, let alone God. You saw what it was like in there, Marcus, you couldn't cope and you know what we're dealing with. He's such a puny excuse for a priest. If the demonic force that possessed the girl has returned to the tomb and it confronts him he'll fall apart; you can't have faith in him."

"Faith is all we have. Make the call, Gwen."

In the driver's seat, unnoticed by the other two, Claire smiled out at the bleak expanse of snow strewn moorland and began to sing quietly.

CHAPTER 31
WINTER SOLSTICE

Earlier that morning they furtively opened the door of the Unit to see the soft twinkling lights of the Christmas tree on Sophie's desk keeping its lonely vigil. It seemed out of place and cruelly inappropriate as a backdrop to their actions. They backed the Unit's minibus up to the entrance, wanting to load it and be away as quickly as possible. Both men knew their act of de-resurrection was professionally unforgivable but they'd long passed the point when such things mattered.

They'd come for the three bodies and the rough stones with terrible carved eyes. Their removal wouldn't be noticed for a considerable period, or at least until Giles published his report and the academic world showed interest. Fragile cadavers like these wouldn't be exhibited and besides there were hundreds of Neolithic and Bronze Age bones bagged and tagged in museums, university departments and units the length and breadth of the country.

But it wasn't being discovered that worried them, it was the crossing of a professional Rubicon; archaeologists didn't do this. But it wasn't for archaeological reasons that they hesitated before entering the lab's cold storage room. It was fear. In the unnatural silence of the empty Unit they felt the presence of something they couldn't see watching.

By the time they entered the mortuary in the lab it was worse and Steve, doubting his own sanity, couldn't stop his limbs twitching. So Giles had to direct and display what was, for him, an unusual amount of leadership. They moved the stone weights first, trying not to look at the crudely scratched faces but horribly aware of the cold gritty feel of the stones as they manhandled them onto a trolley. Gently transferring the bones from the sacrifices in the ritual pit without damaging them was a nightmare that took forever, leaving them covered in sweat despite the near zero temperature in the lab. But it got worse because when they came to take the crushed remains of the body from the mound they saw the bones had moved, shifted along the slab, inching towards the door.

No one had been in the Unit since Giles locked it up. A month ago they'd have laughed this off as imagination; not now. The lights began to flicker and dim but they forced themselves to concentrate on not jumbling up the bones. Then one light died and Steve scrambled up and out. Giles heard his footsteps fade away down the corridor and worked on alone in the half light and shadow. He couldn't afford a mistake, any cross contamination would provoke horrific consequences.

Finished, he carried the grisly cargo in its container back up to the Unit cradling it like a baby. Behind him, unseen, the lab lights came back on. Steve was sitting on a desk drawing frantically on a smoke, Giles caught the fragrance of cannabis: not a good sign.

Desperate to get away they hurried the bones onto the trolley and transferred the entire nightmare into the minibus. It was as Giles returned to the Unit to turn off the lights and lock up that the call from Gwen came through. He phoned Ed and arranged to meet him and

Davenport at the entrance to the site in forty-five minutes. He switched off the lights including the tree wondering if this would be his last act as the Unit's Director of Archaeology.

Outside, under the lowering city sky it was cold and grey with the threat of snow; they'd only a few hours of daylight left. The traffic was heavy. It seemed as if all the world was finishing early for the Christmas break. The queues radiated out from the city centre through the dilapidated inner suburbs then the progressively more affluent ones. Confined in the bus with the gruesome creaking cargo the journey seemed endless and when at last they hit the clearer country lanes leading to the site, they were running late.

Ed and Davenport were waiting for them by the gate, Ed wearing elaborate customised clerical robes that looked as if they belonged to an earlier age. It was bitter cold and they were stamping their feet on the iron hard ground to keep warm. By the time they'd unloaded the bus and transported the grim contents to the mound the light was fading. Unfortunately it was still good enough to see the tree at the estate boundary with the floral wreath attached and understand why it was there. The ghost of Richardson had joined all those others unfortunate enough to be tangled up with this place in order to watch their ceremony. The tree tops were packed with silent crows.

At the entrance to the mound Ed made them stand in silence as he said a prayer invoking protection. In a way that none of them had expected, particularly him, Ed had assumed control.

"Giles, take Steve, open the tomb and replace the bones as they were before the excavation, then place the stones over the skeleton in their original position: make no mistakes. Then as you close the tomb I will perform a type of blessing followed by a service for the departed. I've brought a wafer of the Host, consecrated wine and some sanctified water as a spiritual symbol to re-seal it. The transubstantiated body and blood of our Lord will prove the equal of human sacrifice."

No suggestion of metaphor flickered through his mind as he spoke; this surprised him.

"If we believe in what we're doing, our faith will replicate the ritual that successfully worked for so long. First though, we need to do the same for the two unfortunates from the ritual pit. You must hurry: the dark is rising."

To the west, the Edge was beginning to blend into the shadows and the wind was stinging them with the first small flakes of snow.

Ed turned to Davenport,

"You know what your role is, Nigel?"

"Yes, I watch."

"Then let's do this."

It was a phrase he had enjoyed in an American movie though never imagined himself using, but in a strange way it gave him a little jolt of self confidence.

While they opened and refilled the pit Ed paced in a circle round them sprinkling water and intoning a service. It was a most unusual service although as non-believers neither Giles nor Steve would have recognised much odd about it. Davenport might have, but he was halfway to the tree line, watching the birds circling the Hall, and therefore out of earshot. But an odd service it was. Ed had mixed the Anglican canon with borrowings from Greek and Antiochian orthodoxy and some suggestions from Marcus. It was a mixture never heard before, and which he hoped would never be heard again, intended as it was to quiet the restless dead whilst protecting the living. He'd even been able to borrow a censor from an Antiochian priest in Levenshulme. So, with much sprinkling of water, kissing of a large crucifix and scattering wafers of the sacred host he hoped that even the most malevolent revenant should be sufficiently cowed to remain in place. He was deeply afraid.

***

By the time they'd reburied the bones of the sacrificed carefully in two distinct levels, the east wind had picked up driving snow before it and across the fields towards Skendleby and the Edge. Giles and Steve, cold, despite their exertions, tamped down the earth over the pit and moved towards the tomb. They picked up the cardboard container, fingers frozen with cold, and carefully carried it to the mouth of Devil's Mound. Ed preceded them chanting his adapted service of burial. They crouched at the entrance, the wind and snow whipping at their faces, and then Giles followed Steve and the container into the tomb. He looked round once to see the increasingly violent wind swirling round Ed, attacking him, forcing his hair and cassock to stream out behind and carry the words of his shouted prayers away towards the birds in the wood.

***

Inside it was cold, deathly cold, the absence of the biting wind, surprisingly, didn't improve this, it seemed worse. By the light of their torches they could see the two stones waiting to be replaced over their prisoner. Curiously in the half light the faces on the stones were clearer and the eyes were watching them.

Crushed between the crude stone walls in the weird freezing silence they manoeuvered the box with its grisly contents to the stone slab. They tried to ignore the whispering sound the dry bones made as they scraped against each other. This small sound was amplified by the silence of the tomb and they had to force themselves to begin the delicate task of painstakingly replacing the skeleton just as they'd found it, save for one ankle bone. This they removed to prevent the body from rising and pursuing them later as their Neolithic predecessors had done in the original ritual. Then, struggling in the narrow space, they replaced the ancestor stones over the crushed breast bones, wincing at the sounds of grating and crumbling.

The vicious wind driving across the fields outside was making strange sounds, a curious high pitched screaming whistle that echoed within the macabre shadow ridden tomb. Steve's face, etched with suffering, reminded Giles of a representation of death in a medieval manuscript or one of the depictions of a suffering Christ found in church icons. They crouched still, side by side, looking at the body and stones; the eyes stared back at them. Outside the sound of the wind and the chanting of the priest seemed far away; a distant echo of a remote world.

"What happens to us now, Gi, what are we doing here, how can we ever get back?"

***

Outside, cold in the growing darkness of the field, Davenport watched as the black dense mass of birds rose up from the trees in one huge black flock, deliberately circled Skendleby Hall then swept across the tree tops towards him. No cawing, they remained silent, save for the noise of their heavy black wings. They flashed over his head towards the Edge. He turned to watch them and saw the priest was still chanting with his arms outstretched. He seemed changed and was performing a strange shuffling, then stepping, dance. Silhouetted against the Edge in the dying light, cassock and cloak billowing, the image seemed familiar from somewhere. Then it hit him.

"Oh dear God, he's not the shaman, he's the sacrifice."

***

Ed knew it wasn't his dance but he couldn't stop his legs performing the steps. He saw he was no longer alone: there were others here with him, human and strange inhuman shapes, insubstantial and hard to see. All dancing the steps they'd been condemned to dance through the ages. Ed understood they were dead, long dead; he knew that the oldest and grimmest had been dead for millennia. Others had never known life as we know it.

The last in the line, dressed in the robes of an 18th century priest stared at him as if he knew him and for a moment seemed to smile before the dance whirled him away. Ed understood they'd never been permitted to leave this place or any of the other places of dread like it. They recognised him as one of them, one of the lost. One of the seers, shamans, healers, wise women and priests through the ages who'd failed their people and were damned to re-live that failure through eternity.

Slowly the oldest recognisable of the human forms, the shaman leading the line, shuffled in the rhythm of the dance towards him. Ed felt mortal terror yet was rooted to the spot in his strange dance. The old shaman came close enough for their breath to mingle and Ed saw a look that might have been compassion in his eyes. Then the shaman passed into him, merged with him, became him. The rest of the dancers followed, Ed felt them enter and pass through him one by one, filling him with a strange type of pain and loss. But also recognition which grew as they merged with his spirit.

Then he was alone bearing the guilt, failure and expectation of them all. Yet not quite alone because he sensed other memories, rituals, curses and benedictions begin to mingle, disrupt and finally settle into his soul.

***

Davenport saw none of this but watched transfixed. The dense black mass of birds had almost reached the Edge when suddenly they swirled round and swooped towards the tomb. The sound of the beating wings became louder.

And then the cawing and carking, started: guttural and loud. It was as if they were joining the prayers or trying to drown them out. The voice of the priest had greatly increased in volume and become stronger as if joined by others and the pace of his dance quickened.

Some of the shouted words were clear now to Davenport.

"Thou shalt not be afraid of any terror by night, or the pestilence that walketh in darkness, God who has exalted the horn of the faithful."

A gap in the words, the terrible increasing sound of the beating wings, then the voice louder still.

"He shall defend thee under his wings and thou shalt be safe under his feathers."

Davenport watched the birds with growing horror as they swept towards the possessed priest, he understood what they were about to do but was powerless to stop them.

Then they were on him, the nightmare of his childhood, the black mass of feathers, beaks and claws covered him completely obscuring him from vision. In the place of the priest there was just a frenzied, swirling mass of feeding birds. Davenport saw the newly fashioned bird scarecrow begin to totter from side to side as the heads bobbed, beaks pecked and claws tore and gouged ferociously, like nothing he had seen even in his very worst dreams. The man who'd feared the touch of birds since boyhood had become a living bird statue.

The writhing black mass sunk almost to its knees, but managed to rise, then began to lurch and stagger towards the tomb. Ed may still have been praying but nothing could be heard above the harsh and raucous cawing of hundreds of birds fighting for purchase on the cleric's body so they could tear off their lump of meat. After a few uncertain stumbling steps the weight and feeding frenzy of the black scavengers brought him down yards short of the entrance. There as Davenport watched in horror the whole feathery black mass crashed to the earth and he heard the bird's savage ululation of delight.

Suddenly stillness, and for a moment, silence: then a rippling of wings as the scarecrow tried to rise up onto its knees. In that same moment, as it began to slump back to the ground Davenport saw a single hand push itself free of the birds, the skin palely white against the black. The bloodied hand made a gesture of supplication, towards the entrance to Devil's Mound. The birds screamed and swarmed, the hand disappeared, the cacophony was so loud Davenport had to clap his hands over his ears. But he couldn't tear his eyes from the dismemberment of the cleric although he felt bile rise from stomach to throat. The corpse was still but its black skin was writhing and threshing over it.

***

Inside the tomb the noise of the birds woke Giles from the despondent lassitude that paralysed him. He thought he saw some sliding movement beneath the stones, one of the torches flickered twice and then faded, the other abruptly went out. Only a dim light from outside penetrated the darkness, faintly lighting the exit. Yet the faces on the stones glowed as if illuminated from within by some ghostly phosphorescence. Next to him Steve was motionless and silent, slumped against the cold wall, legs stretched out almost touching the stones. His mouth hung open and a thin line of spittle drooled from his lips and down his chin.

Deep down in his dream state Steve saw a large grey mountain rising from a wine dark sea. He saw a black haired woman standing on a cliff above the sea, arms raised in strange, archaic gesture as if in tableau. He felt compelled to walk towards her, feeling the sand hot beneath his bare feet, the warm, arid smells of herbs in his nostrils. He knew this Greek mountain from pictures but had never been here The woman was close, and he had to reach her, wouldn't be free until he did. Her hair covered most of her face but he saw in her eyes there was no pity only extinction. But he couldn't stop. He picked his way haltingly along the shelf of rock where she stood; she smiled, full lips the colour of blood. Now at last he knew her and took the hand she proffered and moved his lips towards hers, which moved to slide around to his neck. He began to say her name.

Then there was pain, not in the neck, but in the leg. Giles was beating at something twisted round his ankle, cutting at it with his trowel. He felt himself being dragged along the short tunnel; something behind him was trying to pull him back, to reel him in to where the bones were waiting. The force increased and he felt the strength in Giles's hands fading, heard Giles shouting his name over and over, felt himself being drawn towards the stones and the unquiet bones, which were making a sickening hissing noise. He looked towards the woman but an unbearable pain washed everything away

***

Inside the nightmare scarecrow of birds the smell and sound of the corvids was almost as foul as their filthy touch. But no pain, Why was there no pain?

The weight of the birds brought him to his knees then crashing down onto his stomach and face. He was suffocating in the atmosphere of their fetid carcass breath and rank feathers.

But they weren't dismembering his flesh: they were sharing it with him. The shamen inside were excited, he could feel them exulting. Now he understood; the birds were giving not taking; they were shredding away his external weakness while his core strengthened. He knew they weren't doing it for him and that, left to themselves, they would have picked his bones clean and eaten his eyes. They felt nothing for him except an impersonal hate but something else was directing them, this was a role they had to play, like him they were merely an agent of something else. In the deepest recess of his mind the atoms of a cleansing prayer, or spell, began to combine.

***

Davenport watched transfixed as, with a sudden and shocking beating of wings, the birds rose from their victim as if at some sudden command. The feathered inky conglomerate disentangled itself into hundreds of individual large, night-black birds ascending into the skies. So rapidly did they go that the tumult of their wings suddenly ceased, replaced by a strange calm. He forced himself to look on the spot where they'd been.

A tattered figure rose slowly to its feet then moved unsteadily at first and then with greater surety towards the tomb's entrance. It became difficult for him to see, in the dream-like light for a moment he saw other insubstantial figures crowding round Ed. Then, momentarily, the veil of cloud parted and the last red rays of the dying winter sun shone directly on the robed figure at the entrance to the tomb. The figure moved to one side to let the rays of light shine directly down the tunnel and faintly illuminate the rocks and bones in the centre of the chamber. He saw two men, one trying to pull the other from the mound, and briefly something else that seemed to be attached to the legs of one of the men. Something beyond death, unimaginable except in the darkest and most disturbed nightmares. As the last rays of sun struck the thing seemed to recoil and then, with a soft but awful sucking sound, it slithered blackly back into the chamber with the shadows and the dark. Then the sun was gone.

***

The priest bent and helped both men out of the chamber and pressed a spade into the hands of each. Davenport started to go to assist when he realised something was waiting for him at the wood's edge, a rendezvous he'd avoided for too long.

***

Ed directed the two archaeologists to re-seal the mound as quickly as they could, the sun had sunk low behind the edge and the dark was almost fully risen. They replaced the stones and heaped over the earth as the priest chanted and intoned. Then, when the last shovelful of earth had been thrown, he created an image in the earth with the shards of wafer and sprinkled water and wine across it. He'd no idea what the pattern represented, the meaning of that lay too deep within him, too far back in the past, but he knew what its purpose was. He chanted one last verse of the prayer or spell whose words he didn't understand but whose meaning was clear, turned his face towards the darkness of the Edge and raised his arms above his head. How long he stood like this he didn't know but at last he felt them restless inside him, eager to leave. It was done: he dropped his arms and felt them depart. He watched his predecessor priests, shamans, witches and holy fools leave him and felt the blessings and laying on of hands from each. Last, the most recent, Heatly Smythe he was sure, paused and smiled a blessing. Then they were gone streaming away through dark skies towards the west and he knew, for now at least, it was finished.

High above the birds still circled and watched. Ed watched back, his face scratched red, raw with exhaustion and cold. The birds dispersed and for a moment Ed saw in the pattern they made in flight, the face of a man with long hair, a face he remembered from the books of his childhood and the images in his church. The birds flew as a black cloud towards Skendleby and the three men watched. At the Hall they split into two groups, wheeling in the sky in opposite directions then flew back towards them. One dark feathered mass either side of the field, avoiding the air space over the mound before disappearing into the western twilight beyond the Edge.

"It's time to go now. Quickly, away from this ground."

Ed took each archaeologist by the arm and directed them back to the minibus. Giles was surprised by the strength of his grip. The air was still now, only a gentle breeze carrying a few flakes of snow. Yet, as they walked, he thought he could hear the whisper of chanting carried on that breeze. They reached the gate in silence and were about to leave when Giles hesitated.

"The birds? What happened?"

"They were with us, they were sent. I don't think I can explain."

"Where's Davenport?"

"He has business of his own to attend."

***

By the estate wall Davenport waited. He'd seen the movement in the trees but couldn't follow it. It wasn't sequential, more like footage on a CCTV screen that cuts from one camera to another so that things progress without actually being seen to move. But he knew it would come from the direction of the Hall, silent now, no longer troubled by the noise of birds. He knew also that it would claim him as its own; it was, after all, his heritage.

What he finally saw he couldn't have described: insubstantial, ragged, dark, here and yet not here. Then all at once it was close in front of him, taller, much taller and more dislocated than he'd imagined, almost disarticulated, yet for all that, it seemed familiar. For an instant it stood or rather hovered, motionless as if appraising him. It seemed to Davenport that the world stopped. Slowly it extended a limb, more claw than hand, a finger, long, bone white and hairless and he felt its cold touch through the thick woollen clothing over his heart. Then nothing.

ENVOI CHRISTMAS EVE

The European market had decamped, its stallholders back in Liege, Dusseldorf or Lille enjoying Christmas with their own families and trying to forget mulled wine, spices, marzipan, scented candles and the hassle of having to speak English. But the city centre was packed; alive with people doing last minute shopping or drinking in cafes and bars.

Steve walked alone through the streets; weak but glad to be alive, he felt like a mixture of the redeemed Scrooge and Coleridge's wedding guest. He'd no plans for Christmas and no one to spend it with anyway having declined Giles and Claire's invitation, to their obvious relief. He wanted to be with other people and feeling hungry by mid-day found himself descending the steps into one of the city's nineteenth century chop houses. The place had undergone many changes of style over the years but had now reverted to a pastiche of its early Victorian self, which suited it best. It was crowded, noisy and convivial. Steve struggled through the throng and found a place at the bar near to the entrance of the restaurant section. He glanced idly at the menu. A tall, kindly looking man with a European accent Steve couldn't place enquired if he wanted to eat; there was one table left.

"You have been through hard times my friend and I think there is much that you still have to endure, so take what comfort we offer."

Steve had experienced so much that he didn't even bother to wonder what made the man say this. He hadn't considered sitting down on his own in a restaurant on Christmas Eve but the place was friendly and he didn't want to be alone so he followed the tall maitre d' to a table in the corner by a large blackboard offering special dishes of a Dickensian nature. He ordered a small woodpigeon tart in a light sauce, followed by fillet of beef with bone marrow dumplings in red wine jus and a bottle of Medoc off the list of bin ends recommended by the European-accented man, in whom, for reasons he couldn't explain, he had complete faith.

The restaurant was darkish and noisy; the service on such a busy day understandably slow. Gradually he began to unwind. The food was excellent; the wine, rich in tannin, relaxed him. He lost himself in snatches of other people's conversations and drifted into a state of comfortable nostalgia. He ordered a coffee and the waitress brought him a digestif courtesy of the maitre d', who could not be found when Steve asked to thank him in person. It was this act of unexpected consideration that undid him. He felt silent tears begin to course down his haggard, ruined face and he hid his head in his hands.

After ten minutes he regained self control and as he opened his wallet to pay the bill he noticed a piece of paper fall out. It was Jan's address and phone number in Glasgow. When he left the restaurant the light was fading, he stood outside for a minute; people were rushing past with parcels, heading for home, shouting goodbyes and Christmas greetings. The shops were closing. He set off for the bus stop to get back to his flat, and then changed direction. In the relative quiet of a side alley he made a call on his mobile. Then he walked briskly through the gentle snow to the station and bought a ticket for the last north bound train. He rushed to the platform and was swallowed up by the cheerful crowd all heading home for Christmas.

***

Ed was visiting Davenport, who'd suffered what seemed to be a stroke and was confined to the house. They sat together in Davenport's living room drinking tea with a shot of whisky which Davenport insisted was for medicinal purposes only, and eating slivers of rich fruit cake. Ed had never felt better in his life and never, previously, would have felt relaxed drinking spirits in Davenport's company. The visit, however, was not purely social.

"I'm glad and relieved you look so much better, Nigel, you gave us quite a shock vanishing into the trees the way you did. I still can't work out how you got to the Hall that quickly, lucky one of Carver's staff found you or you might have died of exposure in that cold."

He paused briefly not wishing to be questioned on his own experience, which he still couldn't explain, other than to say it was like some sort of rebirth.

"I buried the ankle bone in the crypt like Marcus said, in hallowed ground, ancient and unchanging. The church felt different; felt happier so perhaps it's now ended and we did what we had to. Anyway, I'd better get off, it's my busiest two days of the year. I'll call in after the morning service."

Davenport gestured him to stay a moment and said in a tired voice,

"It served time on me, Edmund; I've not long left here. It's preparing me for something, I think. This is unfinished business; we've just played the first match."

He slumped back in his armchair and gestured Ed to leave.

He said goodbye and left, considering it best not mention the ethereal chanting he'd heard in the dark, musty air of the crypt as he lifted an aged floor slab to place the gruesome relic in the hallowed earth beneath. Nor did he say that when he lifted the slab he found a finger bone of similar antiquity, already there. He said goodbye to Debo at the door, wished her merry Christmas and set off at a rapid pace across the frost encrusted lawn towards the brightly lit Rectory.

***

By ten thirty the party had begun to get going. To Si Carver's relief, the better known amongst the guests had arrived, including some footballers. He put the letter from Richardson that someone had left in the lodge by the front gates, unread on a table. Thinking to himself as he welcomed guests, 'Not turned out too bad, got all I needed out of him, the development will still go ahead; typical loser going soft. Still, could have been a problem later on, wanker.'

He was playing the host in a designer DJ and waistcoat, patterned to reflect his new diamond ear stud and watch. The champagne flowed although some guests took lager as well. He contentedly shepherded guests around the new improvements he'd made to the Hall; the games room, gym and golf course. Explaining that next he'd bulldoze that old chapel for a heated pool and giant hot tub as soon as his people found a way round some poncy regulations protecting old rubbish. Best of all though was the cinema which he'd demolished the old library to accommodate.

"Well, who's got the time to fuck about reading?"

No one disagreed. He was feeling good tonight; the last weeks hadn't been easy but now those bloody birds had gone, and since that old fool Davenport had been found unconscious by the old chapel near the Hall, he knew where the trouble had come from. He was confined to bed now, not dead unfortunately, but he would be taken care of later. The Chief Constable felt there was almost enough evidence to press charges. Pity the pillock from the church couldn't have been found with him. His moment of seasonal reflection was disturbed by the small group of players and wags moving through to his games room.

"Nice gaff this Si innit, cheers."

"Yeah, wait till you see what it'll look like when I finish with it. You won't fuckin' recognise it."

Happy, he wondered outside to inspect the arsenal of fireworks he'd have the staff detonate at midnight. That'll shake them up in church at their poxy midnight service, the losers. He chuckled in great good humour, give the vicar a taste of his own medicine that would.

The only other thing that slightly took the edge off his satisfaction was that the 'pleased with himself' editor of the *Journal* hadn't turned up, said as it was Christmas Eve he had family commitments or some such bollocks. Even worse he'd not sent anyone to try and cover the party, not even a photographer. Hadn't Carver told them it was strictly private, couldn't they take a hint, read between the lines?

But there was a good chance that his new wife Suzzie Jade would get that last slot on the new cooking show where celebs prepared their favourite dish naked. That'd be a result after all the surgery; cost a packet that had.

Still, the fireworks looked impressively expensive. It was cold but he'd thought of that too, the patio was liberally spaced with industrial strength outdoor heaters, that'd give the globe a bit more warming. He chuckled to himself and clapped his hands together in delight.

"That's what Christmas is all about."

Pleased and relaxed he walked back through the large glass patio doors into the Hall.

Behind him, unnoticed, there was movement at the edge of the woods. Something dark began to move disconnectedly but at unnatural speed across the brightly lit, frost covered lawns, towards the Hall. As it drew closer, had anyone been watching, they'd have seen that the decayed hood had been pulled back to reveal a hideously white face, part eaten away by time, with sharply pointed white teeth fully exposed behind the maggot depleted and rotting lips. The eyes set deep in the white bone sockets were intent on Carver and greedy with purpose.

***

They'd spent most of the last three days sleeping but on Christmas Eve, their first together, they made an effort. Giles managed to book a table at the Italian they'd eaten at before. The walk there invigorated them. The table was booked for nine, the restaurant crowded.

They talked little yet it was after eleven when they left. On an impulse they decided to go to the midnight service in the local parish church and walked through the brightly lit roads with the pubs and bars spilling people out onto the street. Some drunk, but mostly just cheerful. The church was packed but the service was surprisingly uninspiring. Had they attended St George's in Skendleby they would have participated in a much more passionate and muscular service performed by the Reverend Ed Joyce.

Afterwards they walked home, avoiding the Moss, through the back lanes; it was still cold and about ten minutes from home it started to snow. He put an arm round her shoulders; how life had changed. When they got into the warmth of the house she was tired, he took her to bed and helped her undress. They made love tenderly then she turned onto her side and was immediately asleep. Giles read for a while by the soft glow of the bedside light, and then he watched her sleep, murmuring gently in her dreams, a mass of soft dark hair on the pillow. Life was full of the unexpected: sometimes it could be so good and so undeserved. He leant across and kissed the back of her neck, turned off the light with a gentle click and settled against her to sleep. Outside the snow gently covered their footsteps.

***

Sometime later that night she began to speak softly in her sleep. Downstairs, in the dark and silent living room, there was another click as the compact disc player turned itself on. Noise started to bleed out of the speakers, first, the sounds you can hear in an empty room, then a type of whooshing, white noise and finally chanting identical to Claire's in the bedroom.

> And what rough beast, its hour come round at last,
> Slouches towards Bethlehem to be born

Christmas Eve 2012